JOHN O'BRIEN

A NEW WORLD:

DISSENSION

BOOK VI OF A NEW WORLD

This book is dedicated to all of my fellow authors and friends. You write your stories and set yourself out there. Your stories allow others to lose themselves for a while providing a pleasant escape into a world you created. Thank you for the hours of entertainment.

The New World series is a fictional work. While some of the locations in the series describe actual locations, this is intended only to lend an authentic theme. Any resemblance to actual events or persons, living or dead, is purely coincidental.

Also by John O'Brien

<u>A New World Series</u>

Acknowledgements

As usual with all of the books, I would first like to thank my mother, June O'Brien for the many hours she has spent editing. This is besides finishing the first book of her series, 'The Blue Child Series.' I encourage you to take a look at it, 'On the Mountain.' It is sincerely a great read for fans of science fiction and fantasy.

I want to give a very warm thanks to the review group. Your insights and catching the things I missed, and there were a number of them, was a huge help. Thank you for all of your wonderful ideas and chats. Alex Ranka, Alexandra Snyder, Andrew Johnson, Andy Bilton, Buz Osburn, Craig Vitter, Dan Shaw, Frank Knoles, James Jackson, Jessica Woodman, Joe Mahoney, Johnny Clark, Larry Sullivan, Laurel McMeredith Andreasen, Rachel Estok, Rick Higgins, Russell Hicks, Tiffany Clark, Vanessa McCutcheon, and Wendy Weidman. Thank you!

A big thank you to Matthew Riggenbach for putting up with me through the cover art design. I'm a pain and fully realize that. Thank you for weaving your magic. The result is truly incredible and I thank you for your time and effort.

I am truly appreciative of all of the messages and mentions. I enjoy each and every one of them and would like to thank you all for writing. I enjoy the chats and messages we pass back and forth and it makes my day to receive them. I hope this book is as enjoyable to you as the previous ones. This is a cliché but so true, I write this story for the readers. If it wasn't for you, this story wouldn't be what it is.

If you do happen to enjoy the story, feel free to leave a review. Reviews are important for two reasons. One is that's how the books get up in the listing which of course means more sales. But more importantly, it lets me look at what everyone thinks of the story. Only through looking at the reviews and messages can I become a better writer.

John O'Brien

Author's Note

Well, here we are on the sixth book of what was originally supposed to be a three book series at best. And I say "we" because it is your story just as much as mine. It's your reading it and your encouraging words that keep the story going. The story grows with each part told and I am as surprised as you are when parts of the story line unfold. This book is a little outside of how the others unfold as there are a lot of parts that come together, and others that emerge. It will be interesting to see how Jack and Michael react in the future.

There are some caveats I must throw out here. One, and not to throw a spoiler out, is that the night runners do converse in this book. Please keep in mind that I have used words outside of their vocabulary to make their dialogue and thoughts understandable. The night runners think primarily along the lines of picture images which represent various patterns, ideas, or situations. The vocabulary therefore is along these lines. If I were to write it out exactly as they say/think it, it wouldn't be very readable. Please excuse a little literary license on my part.

Speaking of literary license, I know that the sub on the cover is not that of an LA class attack submarine. I used the one on the cover for dramatic effect and I hope you will excuse me for that. Another aspect I have to mention is that religion is brought up within the group of survivors. This will be an inevitable conversation when a measure of security is obtained. The dialogue within regarding this is not meant one way or the other but merely a thought pattern within the group. I ask for your indulgence with this as no harm is meant.

I have to give my thanks to you, the reader, once again. The letters, messages, and kind reviews genuinely make my day. Thank you for them. If you happen to enjoy the story, please drop back by and leave a review.

So, enough spoilers. Let's get on with the story, shall we?

John O'Brien

Prologue

She 'hears' another message. It's one of danger from fire above. The message conveys the danger of the sound she faintly hears. *Hide. And then come,* the ending message says. She turns in the direction of the one she senses. She can only feel him from this distance because of his strength. She begins to run through the night in his direction. She will come.

* * * * * *

The chilled night air blows against her face as she jogs through the darkened streets. Her pack follows behind, the sound of their many feet echoing off the silent buildings. She still feels caution at bringing her pack to join with others, but the call is persistent. The faint rumbling from the night sky becomes louder as she heads north towards the strong one she senses. Periodic flashes of light materialize from the sky in the distance. The horizon lights up a second later…followed by a thunderous roar. She feels the earth beneath her feet shake with each explosion. She doesn't know what is causing the light and the roars from above but carries the image sent by the other one telling of the danger and the demise of packs. Whatever is in the sky is dangerous and to be avoided at all costs.

She and her pack continue through the streets. Gazing up into the night with each explosion, she senses her pack's apprehension with each flash of light and roar. If the sounds draw closer, she will scatter them into the neighboring buildings as per the images she "heard" earlier. Smells of food rise from time to time, coming from side streets as they pass, but she only hesitates for a moment and then pushes on. Her goal to reach the other one stays strong with her. She senses the other pack leaders who joined her earlier hesitate with each fresh scent and they query her. *"Push on,"* she sends back. They hesitate a moment longer and pick up their pace to catch her.

She rounds a corner and comes to a stop. A large, domed building rises in front of her. This is where she senses the other one along with many other packs. Her caution deepens as she inspects the structure and outlying area. She's wary about joining a larger pack as she doesn't know what position that would put her in. She knows she will be taken care of since she is carrying a young one, but she enjoys leading her pack and is secure in the knowledge that they can support themselves. If she joins another, it will be more difficult to hunt and find food for so many. On the other hand, she knows that with so many, they can track and trap food easier; but they will have to journey far to find enough for all of them.

The others around her sense her apprehension and mill about, scanning the heavens as the droning nears from time to time. She shakes her head dispelling these thoughts. She answered the call, so she will continue on knowing she can take her pack and leave at any time. A thunderous explosion fills the night and shakes the ground as if signaling that it's time to get inside. Sending a signal that she is arriving with her pack, she steps forward and trots to an entrance door.

She enters the building as another booming explosion from nearby vibrates the ground. Proceeding through another door, she enters the interior. The room is vast and will easily hold both packs with room for others. Pack members mill or stand still on the steps and seats surrounding a large wooden floor. With each blast outside, they stop and gaze nervously at the high ceiling. She strides across the polished wood floor, which feels cool and slick beneath her feet, toward the one she sensed. He is squatting in the middle of the floor with others around him staring at the ceiling like the others. His eyes meet hers as she draws near. Her hand drops and subconsciously rubs her stomach as if consoling the young one who resides there. With her pack fanned out behind her, she comes to a stop before him.

"Welcome. I'm Michael," he says, rising.

His introduction with a name confuses her. She has never heard of a "name" before, and his naming himself in such a manner ripples through her mind. It jars something loose in her. The remembrance of another language comes to her, one that is sound rather than images. Then, as if a dam breaks, a torrent of images and thoughts flood her brain. She recoils and feels her knees grow weak as dizziness descends. Thoughts race through in an unrelenting rush. After several moments, they steady and the dizzy feeling ebbs. She knows she can speak and understand the language of sounds. The name Michael makes sense and she knows it is a form of identification. Images swirl haphazardly, memories flicker.

"*I'm Sandra,*" she sends.

"*You and your pack are welcome here,*" Michael says.

A muffled blast from outside causes a tremor to run under their feet. Their heads turn toward the entrance door as the sound rolls over the building like thunder fading from an angry sky. The rumbling dwindles into nothing with leaving only the perception of something droning in the sky outside.

"*What is that?*" Sandra asks, sending her images to Michael.

Michael looks around as heads turn towards him waiting for his answer. He says nothing contemplating his answer. He doesn't want to have the others around him "hear" his answer. Even if he turns down his projection of images to a near whisper, those close by would still "hear" him. He switches to the vocal language, hoping she can understand.

"Can you understand this?" he asks, looking back to Sandra.

The vocal language sounds both familiar and unfamiliar to her. She has a hard time at first even understanding that words are spoken but, after an internal struggle, her mind clicks and understanding follows. It seems to her to be a more cumbersome way of communicating. The images she was accustomed to convey so much more in a shorter period of time than the sounds and words of the language that Michael is using.

"Yes, I can understand," she says tentatively.

The sounds that issue from her throat and mouth feel strange. They come out raspy and feel like an unused and rusty part of her as if they haven't been used in a long, long time. She has a hard time not converting the words to images.

"Good. I don't know what it is. It's something in the sky that flashes light and I feel packs vanish whenever the flashes occur. I think it has something to do with the two-legged ones," Michael answers, his words also raspy.

"Then we should attack and eliminate them," Sandra says.

"I've scouted their lair and didn't find a way in. Right now, we need to avoid the two-legged ones to save the packs and hunt," he says.

Sandra doesn't agree. Her thought is to attack the lair with all of the pack members and eliminate them, but she doesn't voice her opinion. She wants to look at the lair for herself first. Memories arise of the two-legged one who brushed her mind not so long ago. A flush spreads through her body with the remembrance and her hand once again unconsciously drifts to her belly. No, this is not the right time. She and her pack will attack to keep the packs safe, but she envisions having the two-legged one for herself.

"You'll keep your pack as we hunt but will take your direction from me," Michael says, switching to image communication.

Sandra compresses her lips together and nods. *Yes, later I will lead the packs against the two-legged ones.*

*   *   *   *   *   *

Surfacing In Wonderland

I am being shaken, but it's a while before I realize someone is trying to wake me. I am barely able to open one eye. I make out Lynn standing over me.

"Jack, wake up," she says.

"I had better be on fire," I say, hearing my voice as if at a distance.

"Come on, Jack, wake up," she says again.

"I don't really want to do that just now," I answer.

"Okay, Jack, you're on fire," Lynn says.

"Fine, just roll me over then," I say, but my mind has now caught up to my barely open eye. "What time is it?"

"Time for you to get up. You're going to want to hear this," she says.

"No, I'm actually not," I say, but rise to a sitting position anyway. "Okay, what is it?"

"There's someone calling on the radio. Seriously, shake yourself out of it and come downstairs," Lynn says, planting her hands on her hips.

I know this is her 'I'm being serious' move, and does more to wake me than anything else. I ignored that posture once. That will never happen again.

I make my way wearily down to the radio. Squelch breaks from the speaker and I hear a voice calling, "This is the USS Santa Fe on UHF guard. Anyone read?"

I stare at the speaker as if I have discovered an alien being, but the call does shake the last of the sleep from my head. All eyes go from the radio to me and back again. I don't know why the call sends a jolt of electricity through me or causes stress to permeate my body. I am thinking that an actual military unit showing up could throw our leadership into disarray. Not that I don't welcome them, it just could mean changes. And the fact that it is a naval vessel could upset things even more. Navy ships operate in a closed environment and are usually run very tightly by their captains. They don't like sharing authority.

"I'm no sailor but aren't only the older fast attack subs named after cities?" I ask the group standing around.

I am met with blank stares and a few shoulder shrugs. I didn't even really think of subs escaping this disaster. I wonder how many actually did. I know we didn't have a lot out at any one time because we weren't facing the threat of the Soviet Navy anymore. I think most of them we deployed in recent times were to provide a vanguard for the fleets. However, the brass didn't see fit to brief me on sub deployments, so I haven't the foggiest idea. The fact is that at least one did and is broadcasting from nearby. At least I assume so unless the UHF is skipping.

"This is the *USS Santa Fe* on UHF guard. Anyone read?" the radio squawks again.

I reach for the microphone that is being held out to me by Kathy. I don't even really know how to answer the call. Should I answer with my name or throw my previous rank in to establish dialogue. There's no doubt that a sub will be handy to have, and I would welcome its members and the expertise…but how to handle the situation. I haven't really thought about coming across a regular, intact group of the military. Sure, there was Kuwait, but that seems a little different here and now.

"*USS Santa Fe*, read you loud and clear, go ahead," I answer, deciding not to give my name or previous rank.

"This is the *USS Santa Fe*, stand by," I hear.

*   *   *   *   *   *

Captain Raymond Leonard glances through the periscope seemingly for the hundredth time. Nothing has changed onshore. He doesn't witness any movement of personnel or vehicles that would normally be associated with an active base. Turning the scope slowly, the waters remain clear of any surface craft. Not that any craft normally transit through the water so close to the sub pens, but there are usually some that patrol the waters. Everything remains still as if the world is holding its breath. Gulls wheel about, but that's the only movement he sees. Turning back to shore, he increases the magnification. Captain Leonard sees only an occasional bit of paper swirl pushed along by the afternoon breeze.

He is uncomfortable with his fast attack sub lying in the shallow waters barely submerged. The observation satellites overhead can easily pick out his position with their MAD (Magnetic Anomaly Detection) detectors. What makes him even more nervous is the absolute lack of communication. He should have heard something by now given that he was scheduled for this arrival. The fact that no one was at the rendezvous, along with the absolute silence of the world, around only increases his anxiety.

He removes his eye from the scope and glances at the communications gear. It has been silent for weeks. Even if it was a fleet-wide communication, it should have picked up something by now. His only assumption is that there has been some sort of act against the United States which must have happened quickly. The sub's radiation detectors indicate normal levels and he is at a loss as to how so many people could have vanished in so short a period of time. The absence of any traffic on the normally busy routes into Seattle, the silent airwaves, and the lack of people dockside, cause the crow's feet at the corner of his eyes to become more pronounced with worry.

A corner of his mind is busy with long-range plans. Raymond isn't sure what he will do if he can't contact anyone. *Restock, that's number one*, he thinks, placing his eye once again on the scope. He zooms in on the warehouse buildings close to the submarine pens. It's from there that he will draw supplies. He stares at the structures as if he can see inside of them and they'll give up answers as to what happened. They stand blankly gazing back. Leonard wants to surface the sub, dock, and send a party out to see if they can ascertain what is going on, but having spent his whole career in the submarine fleet and in fast attack boats, he is reluctant to surface just yet. His whole life has been focused on concealment and stealth and surfacing, even in friendly waters, goes against his very nature. No, he will wait for a while longer to see if he can gain radio contact.

"Captain?" a voice says from behind.

Captain Leonard backs away from the periscope and lowers it. It's been up too long, but it hasn't drawn any attention. Turning, he sees the communications officer and nods.

"Sir, we've raised someone on the UHF guard frequency," the communications officer says.

"Who is it?" Leonard asks.

"They haven't identified themselves. We told them to standby as I thought you would want to be present."

"Very well. Lead on and let's see what they have to say. Clear out the comm room," Leonard says.

"Yes, sir," the comms officer says, and turns toward the cramped radio room.

*   *   *   *   *   *

Holding the microphone in my hand, I wait seemingly forever. I'm not sure how this conversation is going to go...or what they know. I guess I'll just wait and see. I'm assuming the delay is to notify the captain. I stare at the mic as if it will give me a glimpse of what they are thinking on the other end. The squelch breaks.

"This is the *USS Santa Fe*. Who am I speaking to?" a different voice calls over the speaker.

"This is Captain Jack Walker. And to whom am I speaking?" I ask, choosing to provide my previous rank, thinking it will be easier to establish a rapport with another military person.

"Captain Walker, what unit are you with?" I hear. I notice the other person doesn't answer my question as to who they are. I suppose I would be very hesitant as well were I in the commander's shoes.

"I'm not with any particular unit. We have a few soldiers from various Army and Air Force units in addition to civilians," I answer. "Again, I ask, to whom am I speaking with and what is your location?"

"Captain Walker, I'm not willing to divulge that information over the open airwaves," the answer comes.

It's quite apparent they don't know what has happened or is going on. It's possible they were submerged – providing they are indeed in a sub – when everything happened and don't have a clue as to the new world they now live in. I think of how confusing that must be. As remote as I was when it happened, at least I had some news. For them, this must be like living a *Twilight Zone* episode.

"I'm pretty sure there's no such thing as national secrets anymore, nor much of anyone who is going to hear what is said. I'm gathering you haven't been briefed and don't know what happened, right?" I say.

"Perhaps you'd like to fill me in then?"

"I'm not sure I could do that in a week, but I'll give you the cliff notes version. About five months ago, a flu pandemic swept over the world. Four months ago, a vaccine was developed that subsequently wiped out over seventy percent of the world's population. A major portion, and I mean a major portion, were genetically altered. They are now a different species that are ferocious and attack on sight. We've dubbed them night runners because they can only be out at night. A miniscule one percent of humans proved to be immune, although that has been whittled down substantially due to starvation, illnesses, and from the night runners," I say. There is so much more to say, but this will give them some information about the new world in which they surfaced. A silence ensues. I'm guessing whoever I am talking to is in a semi state of shock.

* * * * * *

Captain Leonard stares at the radio. He can't believe what he just heard and imagines he is on the receiving end of some hoax. Perhaps some kid has tapped into the UHF emergency frequency and is playing a game with him. Although, the situation onshore and on the usually busy waterways lend credence to what he just heard.

"Captain Walker, stand by one," he says, trying to keep any disbelief from his voice.

He wills himself to hold the microphone steady. Although there is only the communications officer in the radio room with him, it wouldn't do to show any nervousness.

"Go fetch the Blue Team leader and bring him here," Leonard directs the communications officer.

"Yes, sir," the officer says and leaves quickly.

Captain Leonard mulls over what he has heard and compares it with what he has seen. The two seem to mesh into a consistent story, but the story it presents is a far-fetched one. It's as far-fetched as the one the Blue Team leader told him upon his return from the Philippines. It's still too far from the reality Leonard left for his mind to wrap itself around. He has been trained to think outside of the box for many years…but to return to this? There must be a different plausible explanation, but he decides to keep his mind open to any possibility. He wouldn't have made it through the Cold War intact if he wasn't able to do so.

"Chief Petty Officer Krandle reporting as ordered, sir," Leonard hears the Blue Team leader report at the door to the radio room.

"Come in, Chief. I want you to hear this," Leonard says. CPO Krandle steps into the room making the tight compartment even more cramped with his bulk.

"Captain Walker, would you please repeat what you just said?" Leonard says into the radio. The words come back just as before.

"Would you please describe these night runners as you call them?" Leonard says.

"They can only operate at night or in darkness, as I mentioned, and they hide out in darkened buildings during the day. They have a paler skin than normal with darker blotches haphazardly spread. They have great night vision, can seemingly hear better than us, are faster, more agile, and stronger. And there's one other thing you might want to be seated for, we are a source of their food."

*   *   *   *   *   *

Chief Petty Officer Vance Krandle listens to the words transmitted over the tinny speaker by his head. The words coming out send shivers down his back. He thinks back to his previous mission, the images of Gold Team being overrun and going down under a horde of pale-skinned people without weapons. The remembered images flash through his mind like a movie on fast forward. The recalled screeches and screams from the buildings and jungle cause goose bumps to sprout on his arms and the hair on his neck to rise. The memory of their chase through the jungle with the hordes on their tail. He remembers the look of disdain Captain Leonard had given him when he debriefed, but he knows what he saw and he heard.

Every night since, he lay in his bunk searching for a different answer, for a more plausible one, but the images were too real. Hearing words that validate his memories is both comforting and shocking. There is a degree of comfort knowing he hasn't lost it, but the shock that what he saw is happening – or happened – on a worldwide basis is almost too much. They lost a good team and his leader to this. His jaw hangs open with the realization that there may be less than one percent of the population left and these things he encountered are roaming across the world he once knew. The fact that they could no longer be at the top of the food chain leaves him shaken.

"Chief Krandle," he hears, shaking himself out of the reverie the news created.

"Aye, sir," he responds automatically.

"Do these... things... sound like what you encountered?" Captain Leonard asks him.

"Aye, sir, they could be the same. At least the description matches."

"Did you see these things actually start eating Gold Team?" Leonard asks, looking him in the eye with deadly earnest.

"Sir, it happened so quick that I can't be sure…but it did appear that way."

"Very well, Chief, you're dismissed."

"Aye, sir," Krandle responds and turns to go.

"Chief," Leonard says as he is at the door. Krandle turns. "This is not to be discussed with anyone."

"Aye, sir."

"Oh, and Chief…thank you," Leonard says.

"For what, sir?"

"For bringing your team back safely," Leonard says.

"Thank you, sir."

Chief Krandle heads back to the crew's mess where he was downing some of the worst coffee he has ever had with the rest of his team. Ducking through hatches which always seemed too small for his size, he thinks about the ramifications of what he just heard. *Most of humankind gone? Less than one percent remaining? Most everyone he ever knew gone? What does this mean for him and his team? For any of them? And who was Leonard talking to? He heard the name Captain Walker; but was this another Navy captain, or someone else in a different branch? How much of the military is left?* These questions swarm through his stunned mind.

There is little consolation that he was correct in what he saw. He wishes that he was wrong. No answers come to him as he ponders the questions one after the other. Except one. He wants off this sub as soon as possible. He never liked being on them. They are too claustrophobic for him. If there is another operating military unit, he and his team will join them. His falling under Captain Leonard's command ends the moment his boots touch the shore.

"What was that all about?" his assistant team leader asks as he steps through the hatch to the crew mess.

"Nothing. The captain had a question," Krandle answers.

"When are we getting out of this steel coffin?" his point man asks.

"I don't know. This isn't the week the captain sees fit to brief me on his decisions," Krandle replies. "But if I had my say on the matter, we'd have left fifteen minutes ago."

* * * * * *

Captain Leonard stands in the cramped radio room, although it's not as bad as it was when CPO Krandle practically filled the room on his own. The possibility of the radio communication being a practical joke left his mind the moment Krandle verified what was said by what he'd witnessed. To Leonard's mind, that leaves very little else to explain what has happened. Either he accepts what he has heard from two different sources – trusted or not – or he has to give into a large conspiracy. And that seems even more far-fetched than anything else.

He stares at the mic in his hand and, for one of the first times in his life, feels at a loss for words. With his communications officer standing by his shoulder, indecision grips him. Should he brief his officers and come up with a solution or trust this Captain Walker. He feels like surfacing the boat and standing on the deck looking over the shoreline, waiting for an answer to float across the gentle waves. He can always turn around, take his boat back out, and lose himself under the sea. But if this is some elaborate ruse, he could lose command of his vessel and his career will swirl down the drain. He makes his decision.

"Captain Walker, this is Captain Raymond Leonard, commander of the *Santa Fe*. What exactly did you mean when you said we are their food source?"

* * * * * *

"Captain Walker, would you please repeat what you just said?" I hear and repeat what I told them. I'm assuming that whoever I was talking to had someone else listen in.

"Would you please describe these night runners as you call them?" the voice says after giving them the cliff notes version again.

"They can only operate at night or in darkness as I mentioned, and they hide out in darkened buildings. They have paler skin than normal with darker blotches spread haphazardly. They have great night vision, can seemingly hear better, are faster, more agile, and stronger. And there's one other thing you might want to be seated for, we are a source of their food," I tell them.

There is a significant pause on the other end. I can only imagine how startled they must be feeling. Well, startled is an understatement. I'm not even sure I would believe what I was hearing if I were them. The squelch breaks again.

"Captain Walker, this is Captain Raymond Leonard, commander of the *Santa Fe*. What exactly did you mean when you said we are their food source?"

"Yeah, Captain Leonard, you're really going to want to be sitting for this one. Like I mentioned, we are one of their food sources. They will attack on sight and eat anyone they can. They infest darkened buildings during the day and come out at night. I would avoid going into any building at any time," I answer. "Where are you located, captain?"

"Captain Walker, I'll determine to what extent I send my men and women into buildings," I hear Leonard reply. Another pause ensues. "We are submerged in the strait just outside of Bangor. Where are you located, Captain?"

"We should meet then, Captain. We are based down in Olympia, approximately seventy miles south," I answer. "We can drive up in the morning and meet you at the docks."

"That's a little over an hour. What about driving up and meeting us now?" Leonard asks.

"Captain, we aren't about to leave and chance being caught out after dark. We'll leave in the morning. I would advise keeping buttoned up during the night," I answer.

"Very well, Captain Walker, we'll meet you at 0900," Leonard says.

"See you then, Walker, out," I say.

The afternoon passes. The sound of semis and vehicles fill the lot as the sun settles toward the western horizon. The yellow light of the sunny day filtering in through the open front doors slowly becomes an orange hue and the crews filter in after completing their tasks for the day. I still feel exhausted from the night prior and, with the coming meeting with Captain Leonard in the morning, we won't be heading out in the AC-130 tonight. I am still intent on clearing out the area to deny night runners any sanctuary in our vicinity, but it seems like something always comes up to delay any plans we make. We still have a lot of area to search for survivors, and every day we delay means the possibility of there being fewer left. There is also still the search for the soldiers' families. I feel on edge and stretched thin. It's almost too much to handle and think about. Once again I long for the relaxing days in the country when each day was bliss and relatively stress free.

As everyone heads to the dining facility in shifts, chatter and the sound of meals being eaten drift through the interior. Small peals of laughter rise above the din from time to time. It's nice to hear and brings with it a semblance of normalcy. I make my way to the evening group meeting feeling tense about our meeting tomorrow as I don't know how it will go or even how I want it to go. To catch everyone up, I start the meeting by outlining the conversation with Captain Leonard.

"So, any thoughts on how to handle tomorrow?" I ask, looking at each one.

"Well, I for one think it's great they showed up and it makes me wonder how many more are out there in similar circumstances," Frank answers. "However, with that said, I will throw in that ship captains are used to ultimate rule over their domain. Rightly so, considering their position, but this is especially true with sub captains. He'll be thinking the military is still viable and want to be in charge. And, he'll be the ranking member present depending on how our date of rank works out. We'll have to contend with that."

"Hey, that's more than fine with me. He can be in charge and I'll be responsible for making sure the vehicle tires are rotated on a regular basis," I say, feeling very weary.

"Yeah, well, hmmmm... you know we still need

functional leadership. Maybe you can go kick tires to your delight later. Right now we need to maintain the leadership we have. At least in my opinion," Greg replies.

"So, we're back to the original question. How do we want to handle tomorrow?" I ask.

"I think we take several teams up and present ourselves as a military unit and just see how it goes from there. We welcome them in if they want to join us, but they have to understand that they will have to fit within *our* current way of doing things," Lynn responds.

"What are the chances of them joining us with those stipulations? I mean, they have a vessel that, depending on how much fuel they still have, can function for years. They may choose to stay onboard and use their sub as a sanctuary. I know I would consider it," I say.

"I would give it about a fifty-fifty chance. They're still new to the idea that the world is a much different place, so they'll come with the old world mentality," Frank answers.

"Okay, so we go up presenting ourselves as a military unit and see where the conversation takes us. Lynn, how many teams do you think we should take?" I ask.

"I'm thinking five teams. I'd like to take more but that would put us pretty thin on escorts tomorrow. Assuming we are continuing on with our daily tasks."

"I think we need to keep doing what we are doing. Every day we go out there is another day ahead we get," I say.

"Okay, then I think five teams. That will provide a good front leaving us three full teams here," Lynn says.

"We really need more teams," I say.

"We're almost finished with this current training group. We can look at expanding when they finish," Lynn says.

"How many more will we have available?" Greg asks.

"We have a good group, and we may be able to field another team out of the mix from those in the secondary training. Perhaps another one when those going through the primary training finish their secondary training," she answers.

I would have expected Bannerman to chime in by this

point and look over. Instead, he is looking up at the ceiling with his head tilted to the side in contemplation.

"Any thoughts? What are you thinking?" I ask, directing the question to Bannerman. He startles and gives his head a diminutive shake as he comes out of whatever reverie he was in.

"Sorry, the idea of the sub and having fuel for years took me down a sidetrack. You know…if we could bring a sub down into the Olympia port and hook it up – or any sub for that matter – into a power supply station, that could generate power for several years. There's a lot of logistics that would need to be worked out, but we could save wear and tear on the generators. Yes, we will have the solar and wind power, but I was just thinking," Bannerman answers.

We sit in silence contemplating Bannerman's idea and the ramifications. Yes, it would save on the wear and tear for the wind turbine and generators, but there is also the danger it poses if something goes wrong. If we didn't have the sailors around to help monitor and maintain it, I know none of us would know anything about it. And if something did go wrong, we'd have to evacuate in a hurry. Plus, the rods will wear out after a time and, other than drive the sub out and sink it far offshore, we wouldn't know what to do at that point in time. As good as the idea sounds, the idea of something going wrong doesn't sit well with me. The silence continues as the gears churn in each of our heads.

"What about if something goes wrong or when the fuel rods need replaced?" I ask, interrupting the silence.

"Yeah, I was thinking the same thing," Bannerman says. "Never mind, I was just thinking. So, where were we?"

"Taking five teams up," Greg says.

"Alright, which teams?" I say.

"Black, Blue, Red, Charlie, and Echo," Lynn answers. "We can head up in the buses and pick up troop transports on base on the way up."

"Okay. It will take us over an hour to get up there, so we should leave around 0700," I say.

"We'll form up in that order when we arrive. Do we know exactly where we are going?" Lynn asks.

"I'm guessing it won't be too hard to find. I know where the base is and we'll just drive toward the inlet once we arrive," I answer. "What else do we have?"

"The mines have been laid around the perimeter out to a distance of twenty meters and claymores positioned outside of the entrances," Drescoll says. "We've marked the mines and everyone knows not to step within that distance of the walls. The entrance into the compound has been left free."

"In addition to the skylights, the walls around the maintenance areas were finished around noon and the vehicles were moved in to the buildings. We also moved vehicles into the hangars at both McChord and Lewis. The hangars have windows around the upper levels and are fairly bright during the day, so we should be good there. We have progress on the inner compound wall. If we use the wall crews from up north, we can complete that in a couple of days. We also won't need the escorts as we're working inside, so we'll only need an escort team for the trucks driving supplies back from the distribution center. We're slowly getting the water tower up. That will take the most time, but I think we have a way to link the wind turbine to the water pump. We'll be testing that soon," Bannerman says.

"What about the guard towers?" Greg asks.

"I think we have a design that will work with an overhang and using fire escape ladders. The night runners made it up the ones in Kuwait, so we'll have to increase the height off the ground and lengthen the ladders. I still don't have a design for the base but am thinking something along the lines of a control tower. That means we'll have to pour concrete," Bannerman answers.

"What about tilting storage containers up on end and filling them with concrete for the base? I know we built temporary control towers that way," I say.

"Hmmmm…yeah, that will work. We'll need to get more storage containers which will mean another escort team,"

Bannerman says.

"That will only leave us one on standby and that means we'll have no one for the night shift," Lynn says.

"Then we either do a distribution center run or a storage container run. How are we on supplies?" I ask.

"We're okay for now," Bannerman says.

"Then let's go for the storage containers. I'd feel better shoring up our defenses here," I say.

"I second that," Drescoll says.

"We're also shoring up the animal shelters and locking the storage containers at night," Bannerman says.

"I'd like to add that we need to look at quarters for everyone soon. Bannerman mentioned this, and I think it's important before winter sets in with the shorter days. That will mean more time spent indoors. We've already seen some tempers flare. There was one argument this afternoon. Apparently one guy was caught with someone else's supposed girlfriend. This will only get more frequent if we don't do something soon," Frank says. "People are getting more comfortable and feeling safe, so they'll start focusing on other things once their basic needs are being met."

"Ugh! Okay, let's get our inner compound complete and work on the design when we get a chance. I'm thinking it should be along the lines of apartments built off the ground with retractable stairs. Maybe built on top of storage containers high enough so that night runners can't scale or leap to them. And all interconnected with retractable ramps to each other and this building. We should also think about building each with hoists so we can haul equipment, food, furniture, and the like up," I say.

"When things simmer down here, Bannerman and I will look into getting with others possessing the right expertise and come up with a design," Franks says.

"What about our continued search for survivors in the area?" Drescoll asks.

"As much as I hate to say this, we're going to have to do that on an 'as we find time' basis. We also have the search for the families of the soldiers that we'll have to take care of in short order," I answer.

"If you taught others how to fly the helicopter, we could do both and not have to wait for you to be available. Or when we have teams available, we could conduct the search on the ground, or a combination of the two," Drescoll says.

I feel a weight descend on me. There's just too much to do. I thought the burden would vanish, or at least dissipate when finished our little sanctuary, but that's just not the case. If anything, it seems to have grown. There is always more to do and not enough people or time to do it. And then there are the night runners prowling the streets, as soon as darkness falls, just on the other side of the wall. The smallest mistake or the moment we are not one step ahead of them could quickly bring about our downfall. It's this heaviness that is settling in. I wonder if the others feel it as well. I don't know if we can keep up with this frantic pace. We'll have to keep it up but on the other hand, we won't be able to much longer. If we wear ourselves out, we're going to start making mistakes or miss something.

"When we have the teams available, let's send them out for searches without stretching ourselves thin. Coordinate with Frank for the locations, and I'll take others to teach them when I get back from the search for families. I'd like to take the AC-130 up tomorrow to clear more of the area. We'll have to coordinate for clearing the rubble from the buildings we've taken down and cutting the trees back from around the compound," I say.

"We have some available for that now if we don't have to provide an escort. We can use the standby team as both parties will be relatively close," Bannerman says.

"I think that's secondary right now. The meeting tomorrow and setting up our inner defenses come first. We'll start ground searches for additional survivors when time and resources permit. Tomorrow, I'll start planning for the trip for the soldiers' families and head up in the Spooky at night. When we finish the inner defenses and have a plan for the quarters, we'll start on those. We keep the other projects moving along as planned, but I want us to start thinking about a Bio-fuel option," I say.

"We're saving the oil we use in the kitchen and I'll start my research on that soon," Bannerman replies.

"Okay, is there anything else?" I ask.

"You know, I was thinking of when we talked about the sub supplying power and the problems with that. Do all of the subs run on nuclear power?" Robert asks.

"I think so," Frank answers.

"Well, are there other subs and do they replace those rods up at the sub base?" Robert asks. "What I mean is, won't there be the same problems if those subs lose their fuel rods or if they refuel there. Won't those go bad?"

Stunned silence takes the group. I had thought about the Hanford storage facility in Eastern Washington, but I totally didn't take the sub base into account. The rods, if they are there, will evaporate their cooling water source and contaminate the area. They could possibly taint the waters of the Puget Sound if the tides and currents are right. If the radiation leaks into the air, we are near enough for it to affect us and contaminate our own water supplies.

"Fuck...piss...shit...! We're going to have to ask Captain Leonard about that and a possible solution if it is a problem," I say. The weight grows heavier.

We break up for the evening and head down to the nightly training session. Lynn briefs everyone on the day's events. After the training, I trudge slowly up to the cramped space I share with Lynn. Plopping down on the cot, I hold my head in my hands trying to absorb everything we have to do. All the while knowing the night runners have emerged outside, as they will every night. It's imperative that we clean them out of the area. Thoughts continue racing non-stop in my head as Lynn walks in and sits across from me.

"What's wrong, Jack?" she asks.

"I don't know. I sometimes feel that I can't do this. It just feels like too much and it's never-ending. We're going to get tired at this pace, overlook something, and then it's all over. It's going to catch up to us and trying to second-guess the night runners and their stupid ability to adapt is like trying to hold water in your hand. Seal something up and another place leaks," I say, wearily.

"Jack, you don't have to do it all yourself. You're trying to do it all and taking too much of the load," Lynn says.

"Good Lord, Lynn. I'm not doing anything. Everyone else is doing it. If we keep this pace and constant stress level, and we have to if we're going to survive, the mental breakdown will come soon. We're all going to have PTSD on top of everything else," I say.

"Believe it or not, these people look up to you and us in the leadership group to make the right choices. We've come this far and we'll make it. We just have to take it one day at a time. You're loading it all on yourself. You don't have to run around and be there all of the time. You're going to wear yourself out," Lynn says.

"I can't ask others to go into danger I'm not willing to put myself into as well. I've always felt more comfortable being in front and leading from there. That's just how I'm geared," I reply.

"I know, Jack. You just need to pace yourself. And when your flying toys get taken away, you'll be standing around wondering what the hell to do. That's the moment I'm both looking forward to and not. I know you and what happens when you have too much time on your hands," she says, smiling.

"Ha-ha…very funny. Maybe I'll learn to drive a sub," I answer, looking back and smiling. She always knows how to pull me out of a funk, which is exactly where I was. I can feel a renewal of energy. She's right, we'll just make it one day at a time and do the best we can.

"Oh, yeah, that's what needs to happen," Lynn says rolling her eyes. "Please give us plenty of warning before that occurs. I can see it now. 'Lynn, would you please come give me a push. I seem to have beached a nuclear missile sub'."

I chuckle and lie back on my cot. Lynn curls up next to

me with her arms wrapped around me. Peace and contentment flood through my body. The weight I felt before feels a lot lighter now. Thoughts still course through my head, but they're eventually pushed to the side as I lie next to her.

* * * * * *

Sandra wakes. The hard, wooden floor beneath her is cold and unyielding. Her pack surrounds her providing warmth. The sense of others waking enters her mind. The vast room is filled with other packs but there is still plenty of room for many more. She stirs and sits, readying herself for the nightly hunt. Although she doesn't notice it on a conscious level, the air is filled with the musky scent of unwashed bodies, the smell of her kind.

She rises and stretches, the kinks of sleeping on the hard floor working themselves out. Thinking of the young one inside, she ponders how the nightly hunt will go with so many. She knows she wants to take her pack up to the area around the two-legged one's lair. The tug on her mind is strong and she wants to look it over. She doesn't agree with Michael that they need to pull back. They should attack and eliminate any threat to the packs. However, she doesn't want to let him know she disagrees just yet. The intrigue with the other one in the two-legged lair is another reason she wants to go there. She doesn't know exactly what her feeling is, or why she has it, just that it exists. Feeling eyes on her, she turns to see Michael standing in the middle of the open area looking in her direction. The look he is giving her is one of perplexity, yet, with a searching aspect. She has the feeling he is analyzing her. She returns his gaze. Michael releases his stare after a moment, turning to the other pack leaders gathering around him.

* * * * * *

Michael rises from resting in the middle of the wooden floor. The jostle of others waking in the lair garners only a little of his attention. Part of his mind is busy with how to conduct the nightly hunt with so many to feed. He knows there isn't enough food in the local area for a pack of this size. They will have to spread out in order to not only feed for this night, but others. However, the greater part of his mind is on the female night runner, Sandra, who came in with her pack last night. He caught her tight-lipped expression indicating a disagreement with his notion that they need to pull back in order to save the pack from the two-legged ones. There's also something else about her that he can't quite figure out. He doesn't trust her implicitly. She seems to have something in mind, but he doesn't know exactly what it is from her thoughts. She, like him, seems to have the ability to shield herself when she wants.

He continues to look in her direction as she rises from her position and stretches. The good of the pack rests on his shoulders. He wasn't ready for the gathering yet, but here they are. The other pack leaders gather around him and he senses anxiety within each of them. After all, they came together in a moment of distress. His thoughts return to the night before; the streaks of light streaming down from the night sky. The images and sense of packs vanishing as those lights poured from seemingly nothing.

Every one of them felt the other packs' demise and they are nervous about the coming night. They all heard the thunderous explosions and saw the large flashes of light throughout the night. Michael wonders if the same thing will occur tonight. Without knowing what it was, he plans to keep the pack away from that area. He will disperse them to the other areas for the hunt. He knows he needs to break them into smaller groups for the hunt and send them into the outlying areas.

Sandra arrives in the circle of other pack leaders. He senses the young one she is carrying within her. There are others who carry young ones as well. These will be the future pack members and leaders, so they must be fed and protected. He had given a lot of thought during the time he isolated himself as to how to hunt and capture food, especially with larger packs. He sends images to the pack leaders of how to corner food, come at the food from different angles, and how to drive food into waiting pack members. He outlines areas for each and then sends them on their way with one last image; beware of the thing from above. If they hear it in the sky near them, they are to take cover in the closest building. For himself, he will go with a different pack each night.

* * * * * *

Sandra runs through the street. The sound of her pack close behind her echoes off the abandoned two-legged abodes on both sides of her. Most of the places they traveled this night have been burnt to the ground. In some, only the skeletal remains are seen while others have been razed to the ground. Trees, lining the street and cast in the shadows in the grayness of her sight pass by as she and her pack search for prey. Michael assigned her pack an area to cover for food. Feeling a persistent tug to the north and the two-legged lair, she has gradually turned her pack in that direction.

She rounds a corner and leads her pack even closer. The houses and trees suddenly give way to rubble and destroyed buildings. She stops and gazes out over this abrupt change in their surroundings. Glass and debris are scattered in the open areas in front of each building. Large chunks of the structures lie in the streets before her. She sees wisps of smoke rising from some places where the buildings once stood, and an acrid odor permeates the area. She recognizes the scent as similar to that emitted after the two-legged ones fire their guns. Caution grips her as she continues to survey the scene. She feels the restlessness of her pack standing still both behind her and to the side. They all remember the image sent by Michael of the danger above. They all felt the loss of packs last night.

She turns her gaze upward, half expecting to see the lights she was sent in the images. The night is silent. The droning she heard last night is absent. A shriek from afar carries over the night air. One of the packs has found food. She hears a call from even farther away – a call from one of the larger four-legged ones that also hunt in the night. The stillness returns.

Feeling like she is stepping over a boundary from one world to the next, she takes a cautious step out from the tree-lined street. She feels an increase in tension within those around her. Nothing happens. She steps again and then folds into her customary trot. The others follow. She keeps a constant eye and ear on the night sky. There is only the bright twinkling of the night lights high above.

Farther into the demolished area, she hears faint squeaks and scurries of smaller creatures. She picks up their scents and notices how prevalent they are. There is more than enough here to feed her pack. She turns into one of the open areas in front of the smoking remains of a building, avoiding the small and large chunks of scattered debris. She still wants to look at the lair which she knows is not far away, but her pack comes first. They must feed.

She sets them into the smoldering rubble to pick out the small, furry creatures. As they appear, many run into the small crevices, but there are many in the open areas that they run down. Shrieks from her pack fill the night. Quieter squeaks from their prey fill in the gaps of silence. Several members sit amidst the rubble and snack on their catch. Sandra grasps one of the furry rodents in her hands. She feels it squirm and wriggle to get away. A brush from the two-legged one that has haunted her all this time enters her mind.

She feels him nearby. The food she had in her hands drops to the ground forgotten. It squeals and runs away but is unnoticed by her. She detects the other and it fills her. The tug and intrigue increases until it's all she can think of. She stares into the distance, through the intervening ruins, directly toward the lair where she senses the two-legged one. Noticing her change, the others of her pack halt what they are doing and look at her questioningly. She shakes her head and sends them back to catching their food.

She glances down at her hands, surprised to see the food she had in them is gone. Looking around, she sees other prey across the street and, with startling speed, starts to run to catch it but is brought up short after only three steps. She feels the *one* again, only this time, there is a difference. She sees an image of another female – a two-legged one. She senses the feelings for this other female the *one* has for her. Anger and another constricting feeling (similar to what we would term jealousy) fill her. These raw emotions surprise her.

She heads immediately toward the two-legged lair calling to a few of her pack to join her. She has the rest wait to gather food, instructing them to feed themselves and kill enough prey for them when they return. Without waiting for the others join her, she sets off knowing they will catch up. She wants a look at the lair now. She wants to find a way in and kill this other that she now sees as a competitor. Startled by how she now perceives this other one that has periodically brushed her mind, deep down, she knows this is how she always felt. The surge of these new emotions adds to her surprise. Other thoughts and emotions, unknown before this moment, surge into her mind.

She hears the feet slapping on the pavement to her rear as the others catch up. Her long, brown hair, dirty and tangled, flops behind her as she picks up her pace. She winds through more scattered debris with the smell of smoke and the other acrid scent following her. The sense of the other one leaves, but she still can pinpoint where it came from. Before long, she comes to the end of the burnt and destroyed buildings. Before her lies a large road. Across it, high walls tower upward. She knows this is the place of the two-legged one and the lair of others of his kind.

The smells of the two-legged ones rise about the smoke and ash smell of the buildings around her. Other scents of large prey filter over the high walls as well. Her stomach rumbles reminding her that she hasn't eaten and thoughts of feeding her young one rise to the surface. She will scout the lair and return to feed. Killing the other female and having the two-legged one for her own are not far below the surface and have become the foundation for her thoughts and emotions. How she will get the other one is beyond her. She only knows that she wants him.

She leads her pack across the dark strip of road and up the far embankment, stopping just short of the top. The light-colored walls stretch high above her. Looking to her left, she sees the wall stretch off into the distance out of her line of sight. To her right, the wall continues a short distance before stopping. She heads along it and sees that the wall makes a corner and continues past her sight in this direction as well. Looking at the wall, she doesn't see anywhere that she can scale it. It appears to be too high to leap to the top, but she sends an image to one of her pack to make the attempt. The one she sent the image to starts a run at the wall.

A flash of light and explosion fills the night. The blast knocks her off her feet and she finds herself on the ground without knowing how she arrived there. Her mind is stunned from the concussion and her only thought is to flee; flee and safeguard her young one. Her mind is still too shocked to even know how to move let alone rise. Her senses gradually return with the exception that her ears are ringing loud enough to be painful. Sandra pushes herself up onto her elbows and spits dirt and pieces of grass out of her mouth. She feels the grit in her hair, on her face, and covering her body. Looking around, she sees the rest of her pack slowly rising from where they were blown to the ground.

She rises and shakes the debris off her. Looking to the source of the concussive blast, she sees wisps of smoke rising from a large hole in the ground. The night air is infused with the acrid scent she encountered earlier around the demolished buildings. She searches the immediate area for the one she sent to the wall and locates his body covered in clods of dirt. Not sensing his presence, she does see shreds of clothing lying about. Looking down at the ground close by where she is standing, she spots a foot. Sandra takes a step toward the crater and the body of her pack member but she stops, not wanting to go closer in case there are other things that caused the explosion. The protective instinct toward her young one takes hold and she shivers in fear. She turns and flees with the rest of her pack close on her heels.

*   *   *   *   *   *

Captain Leonard lies on his bunk cradling the back of his head with his hands. He flexes his sock-clad feet trying to ease some of the tension he feels while staring at the myriad of pipes affixed to the ceiling overhead. These mostly go unseen as his thoughts race. The information he gathered from the radio conversation today still seems so unreal. He can't push away the images of what he saw on his journey through the straits and sitting here just offshore from the base. The buildings still stand, but the complete lack of movement or people still baffles him. There must be a more plausible explanation than what he received even if it was indirectly verified by the SEAL Team leader.

He asked his communications officer and Chief Krandle to keep silent about the conversation. He knows he has to communicate something to the crew and his officers as they most assuredly know something is amiss but exactly what should he tell them. That is what is currently occupying his thoughts. Humankind gone in the blink of an eye and replaced by some new cannibalistic species. The infrastructure they once knew vanished. If he just springs that on them, they will think he has gone insane. He knows that is what he would think if his captain suddenly told him a story like it. And, if the casualties are as extensive as Captain Walker said, that would mean a lot of the crew's families would be gone. That news alone might break up their tight-knit group – and they need to be tightly knit right now. However, they still need some sort of explanation.

He'll brief his officers after the evening shift change and then make a general announcement. He'll tell the officers about the conversation but hold their silence as to the exact content. He will generalize the announcement to the crew in regards to what happened. He'll tell them that something occurred but that it isn't clear exactly what. He'll notify them that he will pass along details as he gets them. Until then, it's 'business as usual' aboard.

The two things he does know is that they will be meeting with this Captain Walker in the morning and that his first order of business will be to restock supplies from the warehouses. They'll have to surface, send a Zodiac in the morning to remove the security nets surrounding the mooring area, and dock the boat. Leonard did notice two missile boats tied up, so he'll take the other triangular berthing area.

Leonard glances over at the 24-hour clock hanging on the wall in his cramped quarters. Evening has just begun and the change of the watch will take place soon. The computer on his small desk adjacent to his bunk glows with a bluish tint. He pushes back the multitude of thoughts all vying for attention. He will just stay focused on the tasks at hand and tomorrow will hopefully bring more information. These thoughts are interrupted by static from the speaker mounted by the doorway hatch.

"Captain to the control room," the words echo in the small, mostly steel room.

Leonard swings his legs to the side of the bunk and sits. Lacing his shoes, he runs his hands down his khaki uniform attempting to smooth out the wrinkles. Turning on the water from the tiny sink in his private bathroom, he splashes his face to ease some of the weariness he feels. Drying with the small white towel hanging close by, he makes his way through the hatch to the control room.

Leonard waves away the ritual command of letting everyone know he has entered and makes his way to where his exec is peering through the periscope.

"What do you have?" Leonard asks.

"Movement onshore, sir," his exec answers, turning from the lens. "It started after sundown. There appears to be people running near the docks. I've only counted eight so far."

All attention in the control room is focused on their conversation. The crew appears to be manning their stations with their eyes on the controls, but Leonard knows their attention is attuned to him. The exec steps away from the periscope housing and Leonard takes his place.

The scope is turned to the night vision mode casting the shoreline in a green glow. The objects onshore appear crisp and, with the exception of the night vision, seem the same as they appeared in the daytime. Movement catches his eye and he increases the magnification. The image zooms in and he spots five people jogging together just before they turn between two buildings and vanish out of sight. *So, there are people around*, he thinks. *But why are they out at night instead of during the day*. His thoughts turn to the conversation today and the report by Krandle. Neither that nor his quick glimpse bode well, although he is still having a hard time rationalizing it in his mind.

He zooms back out and pans, hoping to catch a glimpse of others. He sees more movement and zooms in on them. Four others emerge into the open area in front of the docks. They come to a stop. Leonard zooms in closer. He watches as they turn their faces upward and appear to sniff the air. *What the hell?* he thinks, watching them. The one person in front of the other three opens his mouth wide and they all turn to the side with astonishing speed and run up one of the streets leading away from the dockside. *What the fuck is going on?* Leonard thinks, closing the handles and lowering the periscope.

"Have the officers meet me in the mess," Leonard tells his exec.

"Aye, aye, sir," his exec replies.

"Oh, and bring Chief Krandle," Leonard says.

"Will do, sir."

"Chief, you have the boat," Leonard says, stepping from the control room.

"Aye, aye, sir," his chief responds.

Leonard makes his way to the mess and sits, waiting for his officers to appear. They drift in singly and take seats after acknowledging him with a "sir". He returns each with a head nod. Chief Krandle steps in with the exec close on his heels.

"Everyone is here, sir," his exec says, turning to close the hatch.

"Gentlemen, you all know something has been amiss since we missed our rendezvous escort. Our route up the straits to here has only hammered in that point. I don't know what is going on, but here's what we know," Leonard says, starting off the meeting.

He continues to brief his observations and fully discloses the content of the radio communication along with the sightings just a few moments ago. While he has chosen to disclose everything, he hasn't reached a decision about what to tell the rest of the crew yet. Leonard asks Krandle to tell his story without mentioning the specifics of the mission itself. The officers sit in silence after hearing the information but are focused on Leonard with rapt attention.

"So, gentlemen, in conclusion, we know that something drastic has occurred during our transit, but we don't know what that is exactly. For now, we will dock the boat in the morning and prepare for our meeting with this Captain Walker. With the exception of the crew on watch, I want the rest stationed topside with arms after docking. We'll also send a small crew into the warehouses to begin restocking our supplies. I want us stocked and ready to go to sea as soon as possible if we need to," Leonard says.

"What about the rest of the crew, sir? What will we tell them? They know something is up and the rumor mill has already started making its rounds," one of the officers pipes up.

"I haven't decided yet. On one hand, they need to be kept in the loop to prevent the rumors, but we also need to keep ourselves together. If they know their families are in danger or possibly victims, we'll start losing people or they'll want us to go after them. We can't afford that kind of fracture," Leonard answers.

"We could keep the boat offshore so they can't go AWOL, sir," his exec chimes in.

"Duly noted, but that won't stop a fracture from happening internally," Leonard says. "Right now, I think we keep it general. Don't discuss this meeting or the contents of it with your people. I'll make an announcement shortly. Let's get ourselves prepared for the morning. Any questions?" Leonard looks around the cramped mess at each of his officers noting that each has a hundred questions in their eyes but none voice any.

"Okay, if there aren't any, except for those of you on duty, get some rest and I'll see you in the morning. Tomorrow will be an all-hands-on-deck once we dock," Leonard says.

They break up and Leonard heads back to the control room. Grabbing the microphone from overhead, he makes a boat-wide announcement.

"Attention, all hands. This is your captain speaking. As many of you are aware, we missed our rendezvous with our escort and are now lying off Bangor. Something transpired during our transit across the pond. We don't know exactly what yet, but we will dock in the morning, resupply, and meet with another military group to gather more intelligence. I'll pass information along when we know more. Until then, we are business as usual. That is all," Leonard says and hangs up the mic.

He then makes his way back to his quarters, slips off his shoes, and lies back staring at the ceiling once again with a hundred thoughts still running through his head.

* * * * * *

A Ripple on the Surface

Lynn lies next to Jack listening to his deep breathing and soft snores as he sleeps. Her arms are wrapped around his sleeping body and she knows just how tired he is by his soft snoring. She is tired herself, but her mind won't let her fall over the edge into sleep. Reaching down, she pulls the blankets over Jack where they slipped down and wraps her arms around him once again. Lying next to him, she feels contentment wash over her. A part of her still feels the deep disappointment of them not being able to relax and enjoy her coming back in peace.

Her thoughts wander to what that time would be like and the times they've had in the past. Lying here, it feels like the world outside of the wooden walls of their cubicle is just a bad dream and they'll wake from it soon. She wonders if a time of peace will actually happen or is this the best it will get. Their daily life is one of constantly striving to survive another day and pushing for peace and security. As optimistic as she sounded to Jack earlier, she wonders if that will actually occur. She wishes she could wave her hand and make it all go away. Even if she could only remove the threat of the night runners, she would be okay with just that much. They would deal with the aftermath of surviving, but they would at least be safe. *Well, moderately so*, she thinks.

Worry creeps into her mind thinking about the transformations in Jack. The physical ones. How will they affect him and are the changes complete? She hasn't noticed any alterations recently nor has he shown any signs of the once usual headaches. Thoughts wander. She envisions a time in the future when they are safe from the night runners. Where they can rebuild. Where she and Jack can live out their lives in peace and contentment. Build their place of safety and eradicate the threats. Let others run things and the two of them can just exist together. The gap between those thoughts and the reality around them seems so big.

She hears a small rap on the wooden frame of their

doorway covered by a blanket. *Well, speaking of reality*, she thinks, gently removing her arm wrapped around Jack. She removes her covers and rises trying to not wake him. Peeling the cover back from the doorway, she sees Watkins standing in the soft glow of the interior lighting. She holds a finger to her lips and nods toward the inside of her room asking Watkins to keep his voice low so as to not wake Jack.

"Sorry to bother you, but we have activity on the cameras," Watkins says in a whisper.

"I'll be with you in a sec," Lynn says.

She slips on her boots, makes her way out of the small room, and follows Watkins down to their little control room housing the radios and monitors. Watkins points to one of the monitors and Lynn sees a thermal image of several night runners gathered a short distance away from the northeastern corner of the wall.

"They arrived just a few minutes ago," Watkins says. "So far, they haven't moved much. They've just been standing there looking at the wall."

Lynn watches as the small group runs off to the side by the corner and stops once again. The night runner's movement vanishes from one monitor and appears on another. The fact that they appear to be looking at the wall in a calculated manner sends shivers up her spine. She sees one of the night runners, which appears to be a female although it's hard to tell on the thermal image, look down the wall one way and then the next. This heightens Lynn's worry and she feels goose bumps form on her arms.

"That's kind of creepy," Watkins says, standing just behind her shoulder.

"You're not fucking kidding," Lynn replies.

They both look on as one night runner begins running at the wall. The screen almost whites out completely and there is a muted roar from outside. The ground beneath her boots trembles ever so slightly. The screen clears and Lynn sees a hole that shows up warmer than the surrounding area. Small wisps of warmer smoke drift slowly upward. The image reveals the small pack of night runners lying on the ground. She sees a softer image of one night runner near the hole. Continuing to watch, Lynn sees the other night runners shakily pick themselves up. They soon turn and run off into the night.

"That'll teach 'em," Watkins says as they vanish beyond sight.

"I hope so. I really hope so," Lynn agrees. "Keep watch and wake me if you see anything else."

"Will do," Watkins responds.

Lynn glances at Watkins quickly before leaving to head back to her room. She ponders how Watkins will sometimes use titles and sometimes not. She's noticed that he will use them when they are gearing up for action or in it, but not when they are standing down. In the past, she would be correcting him, but…well…that's in the past, she shrugs. She enters her cubicle and quietly removes her boots. The chill of the night runner's actions still remain with her as she lies down. The images on the screen stay with her until she drifts off to sleep.

*   *   *   *   *   *

Sandra returns to her pack and they feed on the small, furry ones that are in mass amounts throughout the rubble of the structures. Seeing the sky above her lighten a degree, she gathers her pack and runs south to their new lair. They have eaten well and have found a significant source of food even if it is hard to catch. For a short time, she had her pack stand off a distance waiting for the prey to come out. Once the food became abundant and in the open once again, she and her pack pounced. She is one of the last packs to return and they enter the lair.

She sees Michael standing just inside the entry to the interior and senses his anger. She sees the image he sends her to join him. Directing her pack to find a place on the floor, she walks over to Michael. He glares at her as she makes her way to him.

In the vocal language, he asks, "Why did you take your

pack close to the two-legged lair when I specifically told you not to?"

"There was food in that direction. I followed the scent there," she answers.

Her voice still sounds harsh and comes out in a croak. Some words break like a child coming into puberty. Communicating in this manner makes her throat sore and feel raw.

"You are not to go there again unless I say so. Especially if there is the noise in the sky. We need to preserve the pack," Michael says in a hushed but firm tone.

"Then why not destroy them before they do the same to us?" Sandra asks, knowing if that happens, then her intent will be to locate and capture the two-legged one that haunts her thoughts. *After killing the female*, she adds to herself.

"We will, but for now, we will pull back and establish our hunting grounds. We will keep the pack safe and whole. You know that the two-legged ones are dangerous," Michael growls.

"That's exactly why we need to destroy them," Sandra snarls.

Sandra feels the tension between them build. She knows what she wants but also knows her pack is much smaller than the gathering Michael has brought together. She knows that Michael can and will call her pack away from her if he needs to. That will leave her helpless with her young one and will ruin her plans for the two-legged one. Sandra also knows that Michael would have no problem killing her if she wasn't carrying her young one.

"That will happen when we figure out how. And when I say. Now is the time to pull back, preserve the pack, hunt, and plan. We have a safe place and we will keep it that way," Michael says with another growl.

Grunting her displeasure, Sandra agrees but knows she will plan on her own. For now, she will watch and wait.

* * * * * *

I wake early feeling Lynn sleeping close behind me. The usual morning stupor I usually find myself in when waking vanishes in a moment as my mind registers what the day will bring. I ease up leaving the warmth of the covers for the chill of the interior. My head aches and feels foggy as if it is filled with cotton. I've felt this before in confined places with people sleeping. I'll have to check with Bannerman to see that we are airing this place out during the day and that the ventilation works. Of course, he has a million things on his plate as well. I make a note to see if he needs more help.

Rising so I don't wake Lynn, I slide on my boots, part the doorway curtain, and step into the building proper. Walking to and leaning on the metal pipe railing that circles the second story, I look over the quiet interior. I nod at Watkins standing across from me. The others of Alpha Team on watch are stationed on both the first and second floor. There aren't many others up and about this early.

I turn to see Robert and Michelle engaged in a conversation near the railing outside of the cubicle they've been sharing. It's apparent from their body language that, while not a heated discussion, they are at least having a serious one. I turn back to the interior, giving them a semblance of privacy. They talk for a moment longer and then I hear Robert's footsteps on the linoleum floor as he walks in my direction. I glance over and notice something close to a glare from Michelle as she looks at me for a second before going back in their room. Robert, with his black fatigues, vest, and M-4 slung across his back, leans on his elbows on the rail next to me.

He lets out a heavy sigh. "Trouble?" I ask.

"Nah. She's just a little pissed that I keep going out with you. She wants me to stay here with her," he answers.

"So that must be the twin laser beams she shot at me. She has a point you know. You should consider staying here with her," I say.

"Yeah, well, that's not going to happen. It's not that I don't want to, but maybe when this all settles down. Right now, I need to learn and get the experience, but she doesn't want to hear that. After all, old man, someone has to be there when you slow down," Robert says.

"Settle down? That may not happen in any of our lifetimes. I hope it does, though. I'm getting tired," I reply.

"Do you really think this pace will keep up?" he asks.

"I'm not sure. In some ways, I don't think we've even started. There's a shitload of night runners out there and we haven't the slightest notion of what they are capable of," I answer.

"Michelle isn't going to like that, just like she doesn't like the fact that we're flying off again soon," he says.

"Well, if it's any consolation, I'm having the same issue," I say, hearing the curtain part behind me. Lynn parks herself against the railing on the other side of me.

"What are you two boys talking about?" she asks.

"Nothing much. You know, the weather, the best deodorant to use, that sort of stuff," I answer.

"Uh, huh…and I suppose that the fact that Michelle and I aren't looking forward to you two flying out again soon never came up," she says.

"How do you do that? Do we really have a teleprompter on our foreheads?" I ask, startled at how she always knows what I'm thinking.

"We have our magical ways," she replies with a grin. "And to answer, yes you do. And yours, Jack, is bigger than most."

"You know I love you, right?" I say.

"Yes, I do, and love you, too," she replies. "Jack, there was something on the cameras last night I think you should see."

"What was it?"

"Just come look at the tape yourself before we head out," she says.

Robert, Lynn, and I walk downstairs into the control room. She pulls the recording out and starts playing it. She fast forwards until night runners appear on the screen. I watch for a few moments as the replay of what she saw plays.

"Shit! Are they actually casing the walls and looking the place over?" I ask, stunned by what I am seeing.

"That's what it looks like to me," Robert answers.

"I was thinking the same thing when I saw it last night," Lynn responds.

I continue to watch as the small band of night runners look at the walls. Lynn puts in another recording as the ones on screen move off to the side. They appear again and stop. I shiver and a sense of dread comes over me. I know not to underestimate the night runners, or anyone else for that matter, and didn't think I had been. The actions I am watching certainly indicate that I may have been. I hope this isn't a prelude to something and think about taking the AC-130 up tonight.

"We have to clear out the area," I say, watching a night runner take a run toward the camera and wall.

I continue watching as the explosion from the mine fills the screen and the subsequent night runner reaction. They vanish into the distance after moments of apparently being stunned. Lynn reaches over and hits the stop button but we continue to watch the blank screen for a few more moments. The fact that night runners will, no…can, openly observe and surveil doesn't leave me with a warm feeling. Cold dread creeps up my spine. As with the other packs I've observed, this one had an apparent leader. Perhaps it's the leaders that have the ability? Whatever the case, it seems they have a higher level of intelligence that I wasn't aware of. Yes, they can open doors and the thought of them being able to escape from the hospital comes to mind. Not that it ever really left.

"I'll go wake the others," Lynn says, jarring me from my thoughts.

"Okay, thanks, I'll meet you outside," I say.

Robert and I check that the outside is clear and step out to an overcast day. The moisture in the air after so many clear days brings a chill. It's barely light out and the parking lots are cast in a dim gray. The sun must just be peaking above the mountains but it doesn't look like we'll see much of it today. The air is still, with not a breeze stirring. The morning fits my mood after watching the video. I was only partially kidding when I told Robert that we may not see a secure peace in our lifetimes. Once again, it feels like we are barely treading water, but we are still alive. Looking at Robert sitting on the curb next to me, resolve sets in. I'll protect him, Bri, and Lynn to my dying breath. An image of Nic smiling fills my mind and fills me with sadness and longing to see her. Just to see my sweet girl once again. See her smile, hear her voice, and hug her just one more time. God, I miss her. My heart opens up and tears well in my eyes.

"So, what are we going to do?" Robert asks, breaking the silence of the morning.

"Kill every last one of the motherfuckers," I answer, looking over at him.

"I'm with you on that. But how?" he asks.

"We'll take the Spooky out and clear out the area. Scorched earth policy. Clear out every last place they can hide in. Strike fear in them. Make it so they won't want to come within miles of this place," I say.

What I don't mention is the fear they've struck in me. I've dealt with a lot of bad guys in my time but nothing like the night runners. Sure, it's been a while since we've had to endure nightly attacks and the barrage of their shrieks; but their ability to adapt so quickly, and the level of intelligence they seem to have worries me. The sheer number of them that the CDC statistics compiled is mind-boggling, particularly compared to the lack of our numbers. I feel deep down that it's only a matter of time before they come at us again; especially if Frank is right about them running low on food. Maybe we could leave food drops for them far away so they wouldn't think of coming here. I release that thought as it would sorely deplete our own resources. No, we have to clear them out of the area somehow.

Robert just looks at me. Team members begin to trickle out and toss their gear in Humvees. "Well, shall we go see what the sub captain has to say?" I say, patting him on the shoulder.

"Let's go do it," he replies. We head over to the Humvees for our journey north.

Sam the Unwise

The clouds remain over us on our journey to Fort Lewis. They don't have the look of foreshadowing rain but they are more evidence of the fall and coming winter. Time continues to tick away. With the exception of the continued signs of night runner adaptability, we seem to be doing well with our own advances. I just hope we haven't overlooked something drastic. It's not like we are playing a video game and can pull up our last save if we make a mistake.

We follow the familiar terrain of I-5 North. The leaves of the few deciduous trees in the area are turning red and yellow, giving color to the otherwise dreary gray day the Northwest is known for. It won't be long until the rains hit. And the shorter days. The grass in the median between the north and southbound lanes has grown tall, so much that the other lanes are hidden behind it. I look in the rear-view mirror and see five other Humvees climbing the hill behind. We take the first turn into Fort Lewis and make our way through the abandoned fort to the maintenance buildings.

I cast my mind out as we drive slowly through the myriad of buildings and adjacent fields. My second shock of the day follows. I don't sense a single night runner. I cast farther out and only find one small pack nestled in a building on the north end. This is puzzling as I sensed a few of them gathered on our last journey through. *Have they depleted their food here and moved on? Are they banding together somewhere else?* These thoughts occupy my mind as we progress through the main base and by the commissary. A deer walks into the road ahead, sees us, turns and leaps back in the direction from which it appeared. An occasional bird flutters across the road. *No, there's still food in the area.* As we pull into the maintenance area, I continue to puzzle over the absence of night runners.

We park and I join up with Lynn. The other team members exit and fan out in a perimeter. The sound of the Humvee engines idling mixes with that of the soldiers' boots running on the pavement. I feel the chill of the day seeping through my fatigues. It won't be long until we will have to start donning warmer clothing underneath. Lynn rubs her hands trying to keep them warm. I think about telling her about the absence of night runners but decide to bring it up later. Right now we need to focus on meeting with the sub.

"Well, do we take Bradleys, Strykers, or just transports up?" I ask.

"The Bradleys will just tear up the roads, and I'd feel more comfortable having some armament available. We haven't been up in that area as yet and don't know what to expect," she answers.

"Maybe we should just fly up. I'm pretty sure they have a small airfield there," I say.

"You said we could only carry two Humvees in the 130. That would take us forever to transport the five teams unless it's right next to where the sub will be," she responds.

"I don't think it's that far but it would still require a little hike. So Strykers it is then," I say.

"We can carry three teams in two Strykers, but let's take three Strykers and two Humvees, one ahead and one behind," Lynn says.

"Sounds good to me," I say.

Lynn turns and has three brought out of the maintenance building. The heavy whine of their diesel engines fills the air, overriding the idling Humvee engines. Lynn talks with the team leaders and has the teams form up into vehicles. I'll be in the lead Humvee with Robert, Gonzalez, and McCafferty. The rest of Red Team will ride in the first Stryker. Lynn will bring up the rear with Frank, Bannerman, and one other Black Team member. After test firing the .50 cal M2 machine guns mounted on top and checking the targeting systems, we start our convoy out of the maintenance area.

We backtrack to the main gate and turn north on the interstate. Cars begin to pile up in the right lanes similar to those in the Olympia area as we near one of the exits to one of the hospitals in the area. We track over to the far left lane and are able to squeeze by the stranded vehicles. Some, like those farther south, have their doors open as people must have tried to get to the hospital on foot. Our Humvee squirts through with little room to spare, but the wrenching sound of metal being ripped apart comes from the Stryker behind. I look in the rear-view and see sparks fly as one car door is torn off its hinges by the mammoth vehicle.

The Tacoma Mall lot is as empty as before. I look over the concrete barriers now separating the two lanes of traffic, searching for the car that was destroyed when I tossed the wrench out of the 130 seemingly so long ago. There are a couple of cars in the lot, but I can't make out that particular one. My thought momentarily drifts to Andrew. My guess is he either found his parents and stayed or didn't make it. I send him a quick thought of hope.

We take the Highway 16 exit and proceed through Tacoma toward the Narrows Bridge. Green exit signs track our progress. The signs indicate various Burger Kings, McDonald's, and Dairy Queens that won't ever dispense their fast food again. Seeing the signs reminds me of the movies I saw where archaic relics of the past would pass by, indications of a time that will never be again. So much has changed, the signs seem almost alien to me now.

I look over at the rooftops of the residential houses that line part of the highway. I think about the lives that once lived under those sheltering roofs. Bookshelves filled with books that will never be picked up and read again; once best sellers with rave reviews splashed against the front covers. The hoopla about their release now a forgotten memory of a world that once was. Photographs capturing happy moments with families and loved ones together now gathering dust. I look along the empty highway which once had cars stacked bumper-to-bumper as everyone tried to get to their nine-to-five jobs. The hectic rush in the mornings and evenings and days filled with the stress of having some project or another to complete. The honking and gestures from impatient drivers. Yes, that world definitely seems the alien one to me now.

We continue through the sections of Tacoma, residences giving way to businesses and back to residences. Rounding a corner of the highway, the Tacoma Narrows Bridge looms ahead. The light green twin suspension bridges running in a close parallel arch over the deep blue waters of the narrow strait between Tacoma and the Kitsap Peninsula. I radio the others in the convoy that we'll be stopping just prior to the approaches. Before crossing, I want to scope out the other side. It's hard to anticipate everything, but if we are able to see trouble before it happens, well, when is that ever a bad thing.

I pull into an open, paved area before the lanes split to the entrances of each bridge. Two of the Strykers stop behind in tandem and I see their .50 cals swivel to cover the sides. The other Stryker comes to a halt behind, covering the rear, with Lynn pulling her Humvee up and parking next to mine. The chill of the morning hits as I open the door and walk over to her window. There's still not a breath of air stirring. The rumble of the Strykers is the only sound. Standing at her window rubbing my arms to ward off the chill, I look to the bridges. Their arch prevents me from seeing the other side, nor can I look around them from the sides.

"What's up?" Lynn asks, rolling down her window.

"I want to take a look before we cross. I'll drive up to the middle and take a peek at the other side. I know there's a residential area just over the other side and a small airport close by to the left. I just want to make sure it's clear before we cross," I answer.

"Yeah, I knew there was an airport close by," she says.

"You did?" I ask. She merely points to the big green sign by the side of the road which says: Tacoma Narrows Airport, 1 ¼ mile.

"Yeah, I guess that would be a clue," I say, chuckling.

"Do you want me to come up with you on the second bridge?" she asks.

"Nah. Just hang back here and I'll radio if it's clear," I reply.

She nods and rolls up her window. I walk back to my

Humvee still rubbing my arms and looking at the gray clouds overhead. They aren't moving and it seems as if the world is holding its breath. As I climb back in, I hear the radio crackle with Lynn radioing the others.

"We're going to the top of the bridge and scope out the other side," I tell the others with me as I pull into the lanes of the bridge on the right.

"Hooah, sir," Gonzalez says beside me.

"Damn, do you just wait for the opportunity to say that?" I ask, looking over at her. She is staring straight ahead, but I see the corners of her mouth crawl up in a smile.

"My day wouldn't be complete without saying it to you at least once, sir," she says. "I like to watch you roll your eyes."

I hear Robert chuckle in the back seat. We pull onto the bridge and begin driving up the curved arch. The waters below are like the roads we've encountered – empty. This part of the waterway was always filled with white streaks of boats heading across the waves. Now, it's almost glass smooth with the occasional ripple.

We climb higher and just crest the topmost part of the bridge. Crack! A spider web of fractured glass appears on the windshield just on my side of the middle post. In my peripheral, I see Gonzalez's startled response as she ducks. My heart jumps and I crouch as well slamming on the brakes.

"Fuck! Is everyone around hostile?" I say, throwing the Humvee in reverse.

Adrenaline floods my system as I step on the accelerator and reverse quickly back down the slope of the bridge. My mind makes out that I saw a flash of light at the far end of the bridge just before the impact of the bullet on our windshield. I bring the Humvee to a stop when we are no longer visible over the top of the bridge.

"Everyone okay?" I ask quickly.

"Except for needing a new set of fatigues, I'm just fine, sir," Gonzalez replies.

"I'm good here," Robert says. "But I'll second the needing new fatigues."

"Good here, sir," I hear McCafferty, who is manning the M-240, shout from the open hatch.

"Okay, good, wait here," I say, grabbing a pair of binoculars, open the door, and step out onto the paved surface of the five-lane bridge.

There is a pedestrian walkway to the right side of the bridge and I run over to it making sure I am far below the line of sight from the far side of the bridge. I hop over the railing and slowly crouch up to a point just short of the top. Apparently seeing me back up hastily and run across the bridge, Lynn calls.

"Everything okay, Jack?" I hear her voice in my earpiece.

Hitting the push-to-talk, I answer, "Just peachy. Someone took a shot at us and I want to get eyes on the bastard."

"Is there another way around?" She asks.

"Not unless you or anyone here knows how to drive a ferry," I reply.

"African or European?" Lynn asks.

Great! I'm surrounded by comedians today. "Bravo, Mike," I respond.

"Awww.... you do care. What about just rolling the Strykers up?"

"We may just do that. Standby," I answer.

I lie down and crawl the rest of the way on the hard surface. The cold seeps through my sleeves and pant legs as I make my way to the crest. Ready to slide back down the crest in case someone sees me and wants to take a shot, I bring the binoculars up.

Down the curved arched roadway, on the far side of the bridge, I see a line of cars and trucks spanning across the lanes of both bridges. The magnified view brings everything into a sharp focus. Behind the cars blocking the lanes, I count twelve people lined up across the hoods, roofs, and trunks. All of them have rifles of some sort aimed toward where we appeared. Seven are aiming across the vehicles toward the bridge I am on and five have their weapons pointed up the span adjacent to me on the left.

I watch as several more cars enter the highway from a nearby ramp and park. Ten more people exit the vehicles, extract rifles and join the others behind the roadblock. I'm thinking they must have some form of communication and have a fortification somewhere near to be alive with the night runners about. How many more may be there is open to question. However, they've shown their intentions and I don't mean to stick around and jabber with them.

"Lynn, run a scan on the UHF frequencies. Pay particular attention to the four-sixty megahertz range," I say using my throat mic. "Let me know what you hear."

"Wilco, standby."

I'm thinking if they are communicating with radios, they'll be using the FRS channels common to most two-way radios. I am about to put the binoculars down and inch back when I spot another pickup truck appear from farther up the highway. It comes to a stop behind the blockade. A man exits and walks to the front of the truck. One of the people at the cars sees him and trots over. There's a lot of hand pointing toward our position and an obvious conversation is taking place. I zoom in closer on the two.

The one who trotted over, holding his rifle casually in one hand, appears to be doing the most talking with more hand gesturing. The driver of the truck shakes his head and, although I can't tell clearly from this distance, appears to start yelling at the other one. His body language indicates he is not happy. I don't think I would be either if one of my guys just plinked a round at a military vehicle from behind a flimsy roadblock. The driver pushes the other one toward the line of vehicles. Shaking his head again, he then stomps back to the truck. Swinging the door open, he reaches inside and brings something to his mouth.

"Jack, Lynn, over," I hear.

"Yeah, I'm here, go ahead," I respond.

"I just picked something up on four sixty-two dot seventy-one twenty-five," she says.

Bingo. "What did you hear?" I ask.

"Well, someone named Sam talking to Roger and he didn't sound too pleased. He told Roger to round up the troops and then get aloft to report what he sees because, and I quote, 'Numbnuts here just fired on a military vehicle'," Lynn answers.

"Okay, lock in that freq and monitor it," I say.

"Will do," Lynn responds.

Well, that's enough for me. We don't have time to play 'let's get to know one another' as we have to get up to Bangor. I also don't know what type of aircraft they have that they're sending aloft. I'm guessing some single-engine civilian type, but I really don't want to find out they have an A-10 stashed away or some World War Two fighter that's armed. I'll give the communication with them one shot, but I'm not dilly-dallying around. If they want to play games, we'll roll through them and be on our merry way. I take another quick look around to see if they have mines or some IEDs on the ground. I don't see any and inch backwards out of the line of sight, rise, and trot to the Humvee. Turning the vehicle around, I drive back to the end of the bridge and pull up next to Lynn. I gather the team leaders around detailing what waits for us over the rise of the bridge.

"So, what's the plan?" Lynn asks, stomping one boot on the ground to shake out the chill.

"Well, let's try this communication thing once and see if they won't open the pearly gates for us. If we get 'entrance denied', then we'll roll up and over them," I answer. I reach in the Humvee and grab the mic.

"Sam, this is Captain Walker on channel seven," I say. Silence.

"Sam, I know you can hear me and it's in your best interest to respond," I say, staring at the empty bridge ahead.

"This is Sam," I finally hear his words crackle over the speaker in the cab.

"Would you like to explain why I have a broken windshield?" I ask.

"Sorry for firing on you, captain. The boys are a little trigger happy," Sam answers.

"Yeah, you might want to get a handle on that," I say.

"Are you with the military?" he asks.

"Is that a serious question?" I ask in response. "And you shot without provocation."

"I do apologize, but we can't just have anyone coming through," he replies.

"Look, we just want to pass through. We're not looking for anything other than that and we're not just anybody," I say, getting irritated. Time is elapsing and we need to be moving on.

"I'd like to do that, captain, but we can't let you just go through. If we did that, then others would see and think they could try as well. They'd come in and try to take our supplies," Sam says.

"What others?" I ask.

"There are others in the area looking for any weakness and we can't afford for that to happen," he answers.

"Look, we have a safe place and you and your group can join under us," I say as a way or reconciling this situation.

"Thanks, but we have our own safe place here," he responds.

"Well, Sam, this is the only route, and we're coming through," I say.

"Sorry, sir. We can't let you do that military or not," Sam replies.

I hear the sound of a prop engine revving up across the water. *At least it's a prop*, I think, getting more irritated by the minute. I don't really want to unleash the .50 cals on them as they are only trying to protect their own as well, but we need to push through. I look up at the unmoving gray clouds overhead seeking an answer. They have none to give. I'm getting tired of this little tête-á-tête. It's getting us nowhere and I can't for the life of me figure out why they would want to stop us. Surely they know they have little chance. If that aircraft gets aloft, they'll know for sure. I ponder over whether to just let it describe what we have on this side, but I'm not a fan of just letting an aircraft roam overhead.

"Last chance, Sam," I say.

"I'm sorry, sir. You can go around to the south. There's a route to the north from there," he responds.

"Yeah, that's not happening. You either let us through or we're coming through," I say.

"Again, sorry, sir," Sam responds.

"It's your funeral, Sam," I reply, sighing and shaking my head in resignation.

Stubbornness is going to get him and lot of others killed. We could radio the sub to let them know that we're running late, but to go all of the way around would take us a couple of additional hours each way. Who knows how long our meeting is going to take, and we just don't have that kind of time before the sun hits the western horizon. I look again to the empty lanes of the bridge stretching across, sigh, and reach into the Humvee to replace the mic. I look over at Lynn who gives me a shrug of her shoulders as if to say 'we tried'.

"That could have gone better," I say in response to Lynn's shrug.

"It's not like we didn't give them a chance," Lynn says.

I still don't get it. We are on the very brink and need to pull together rather than play games. I can understand Sam's position though. I'm not certain I would let anyone roll through our area at will, but neither would I jeopardize our group with stubbornness. But given the option of strengthening our group with numbers to give us a better chance at survival, I would take it provided our safety and cohesiveness remained. But here we are, facing yet another group of people that we'll have to fight our way through.

This is different from out other situations, though. This isn't a group of marauders or bandits. This group across the span from us is just trying to protect their people and resources. Much like we are. *If we roll through them, are we any better than marauders seeking their own gain regardless of others?* I mean, we could radio Captain Leonard and head on the other route around the Puget Sound tomorrow. That will take us through a few small towns which could be blockaded as well. Either solution doesn't sit well with me. *Well, fuck. We did give them a chance and we are pressed for time. And they did fire upon us without provocation, accident or not.* I'm not happy with it, but we're proceeding along our route as planned.

"Jack, are you with us?" Lynn asks. I shake out of my thoughts and look at the others gathered around in the chill under the gray skies.

"Yeah, I'm here. Okay, here's what I'm thinking…but I'm open to suggestions. We take two Strykers in parallel up the bridge on the right with the other Stryker and the two Humvees astride on the left. We'll crest and fire into the road block creating a lane to pass through. Our field of fire will be limited due to the bridge superstructure. Make sure to keep our rounds away from the suspension wires. I'm not all that keen on bringing the bridge down with us parked on it. That belongs on the unfavorable situation list. You dump me in the water and I'm going to be a little upset. We open a lane through on each side and push through. Any questions?"

"What do you want to do about the aircraft?" Greg asks.

The Strykers idling nearby are blocking other sounds, but I still faintly hear the props of the aircraft in the distance carrying over the waters. It won't be long before it powers down the runway and gets aloft. I'm nervous about what they're about to put aloft but, by the sound of the engine, it isn't overly large. If it was an old World War Two bird, there would be a definite roar instead of the motor boat sound coming to us.

"I'm not a fan of letting it roam freely and give them free intel, but this should be over quickly. Lynn, you keep an eye on it, and if it comes at us, call out and we motor forward quickly and through. We can't shoot at it without taking out guide wires, so let's push forward to the other side. If it continues to come at us in a threatening manner, we take it out. I'm guessing there's another road block farther up the highway. If it follows at a distance, there's not much we can do but keep an eye on it," I answer. Heads nod in response.

"Anything else?" I ask, looking at each to see if there are any further questions or issues. No one says anything.

"Alright, if there's nothing else, then let's mount up," I

say.

*   *   *   *   *   *

McCafferty stands in the open turret of the Humvee gripping the M-240. She feels the cold through her gloves as they motor up the interstate. Turning and looking behind her, she sees the nose of the Stryker behind as they make their way through the line of cars in the lanes beside them. The balaclava she has wrapped around her head and the goggles do little to stop the chill from seeping through. The Humvee rocks as they drive over an object in the road. Her splayed feet on the gunners stand helps to keep her balanced, but her arm still knocks into the cold steel of the roof opening. Regaining her equilibrium, her thoughts wander.

She thinks of her parents and is filled with mixed emotions. There is joy at finding her dad alive and having him up here with her, but there is a tremendous sadness that settles in her heart thinking of her mom. The sorrow and grief threatens to overwhelm her and she feels warm tears fill her eyes. Keeping most of her attention focused on the area around her, images of her mom form in McCafferty's mind.

She remembers her mom puttering around the kitchen with flour covering her hands and in her hair from some baking project. She always had fresh pies and bread ready to deliver to neighbors or to take to church, the smell of fresh bread permeating the house. Her mom standing over the kitchen counter humming while kneading the dough. Memories surface of her mom tirelessly roaming about doing laundry, sweeping, and changing bed linens. She remembers her mom putting on her favorite dress for church and helping McCafferty with hers when she was young. There were the times when her mom took her out with her new bicycle and taught her to ride, picking her up the many times when she fell in the their dusty yard. Always dusting her off and giving her words of encouragement. Clapping when she managed to make it down the entire driveway on her own. The twinkle that always shone in her mother's eye. The memories of her mom waking early and herself waking to the aroma of breakfast wafting through the house. The peace and contentment McCafferty felt waking to the smell of bacon as it drifted in her room.

Although her dad felt he ruled the house and made the decisions, McCafferty always knew her mom actually did – but with a softer touch. Her mom never had a bad thing to say about anyone and would admonish her dad gently when he would make critical comments. McCafferty remembers going to the grocery store and her mom chatting with anyone and everyone in line. Now she is gone like so many others, just another on the long list of those lying in the emptiness of the world. McCafferty reaches under her goggles and wipes away the tears that are running down her cheeks.

"I love you, mom, and miss you so much," she whispers.

Although grieving for the loss of her mom and thankful for her dad making it, she is also thankful for those around her. Even though under constant tension and danger, she is relieved to have found herself in such good company in this strange new world. She is grateful for the camaraderie of Red Team and the bond they share; for Jack and Sergeant Connell. Grateful for Jack and his leadership, even though she mentally shakes her head at his plans and actions at times. She's glad for Sergeant Connell and respects her toughness in the same way she does Gonzalez. She has grown close to Gonzalez in the past few months and admires her quick wit and her ability to maintain her composure and humor in pressure situations. Yeah, she'll follow any of them to the ends of the earth. *Which*, she thinks, *is here and now.*

She knows they'll make it through this together, but she wonders if the stress won't get to them eventually. Her tours in Iraq and Afghanistan have shown her that, even with the best of them, the strain gets to everyone eventually. The hope arises in McCafferty that they reach a point of safety soon as she has seen an edginess grow among the other soldiers. She feels it within herself; jumping at any sudden noise.

The one thing she is most thankful for is that they don't

have to venture into any more darkened buildings. That creeped her out each and every time and filled her with more fear than she has ever known. The quiet was probably the worst part. A shiver runs down her spine as she remembers the buildings, the dark under the green glow with lasers tracking, the shuffle of footsteps on dusty floors, and the occasional whisper or quiet voice on the radio. The team or teams venturing farther into the building not knowing if there were any night runners within. She remembers the tension pulling her every nerve tight not knowing when or from where an attack would come. The attacks always came on suddenly and they were lucky if they had any advance warning by hearing something or catching a glimpse. Sometimes they were set upon by a mass of them which forced them out and other times by only four or five. Any thought of a night runner fills her instantly with an intense dread.

She pulls her focus back entirely to the area around her as a bridge looms ahead. It's actually two bridges running in parallel. The light green of the towers and suspension lines rise toward the gray clouds hovering overhead. The lanes widen as they rise upward and are lost from view as they reach the top to begin their downward arch on the other side. Her Humvee pulls to an opening in the middle just before the bridges. She braces for the stop keeping her weapon aimed at the topmost part of the spans, alternating between the two bridges. McCafferty first hears and then sees Sergeant Connell's Humvee pull up adjacent. Jack emerges from just in front and below her, walks over to the other Humvee, and talks with the first sergeant. Upon his return, she hears him tell them that they are going to the crest and scout the other side. She hears Gonzalez give a "Hooah" and smiles as she visualizes Jack's customary eye roll at the phrase. They all get a kick out of that and do it as often as they can without overdoing it. With him having spent some time with boots on the ground, Jack's not like the usual Air Force zoomies with their swagger and country club demeanor, but he shuns anything he sees as gung ho.

The Humvee lurches forward and they proceed slowly in

the middle lane up the arch of the bridge. McCafferty glances at the blue waters below, turned more leaden by the clouds overhead. She tenses as they approach the crest not knowing what to expect. The far side of the bridge is slowly revealed the closer to the top they come. A loud crack and bang coming from the windshield just ahead and below startles her. Hearing the whine of a ricocheting bullet as it passes just off her left and into the air above, her heart races with the sudden release of adrenaline and she cringes to her right before bringing the M-240 to bear to her immediate front.

McCafferty hears Jack shout "Fuck!" below her but the rest of his words are lost as she is thrown forward from a sudden halt. She is pressed there as the Humvee is thrown in reverse and begins to traverse quickly backwards. Pushing rearwards, she rights herself just as the vehicles comes to a stop and quickly brings the gun to bear once again. Ahead, only the top of the lanes are in view. She remembers catching a glimpse of a line of vehicles strewn across the bottom of the bridges on the far side before Jack drove them back below the crest.

"Everyone okay?" she hears Jack call out.

She hears Gonzalez' response and smiles although the near miss still has her heart racing. Inside, she couldn't agree more with needing a new set of fatigues. Her hands shake from the adrenaline. Expecting something or someone to appear at a moment's notice, she keeps her weapon trained on the empty lanes ahead of her.

"Good here, sir," she replies after hearing Robert answer.

"Okay, good, wait here," Jack says and exits the Humvee.

While keeping an eye to the front, she watches in her peripheral as Jack runs across the road and vaults a railing near the edge of the bridge. He almost disappears from sight as he first crouches and then crawls along the outer walkway. Her heart has slowed somewhat, but nowhere near normal, and she feels the chill creep back to her hands and face. Hearing the conversations between Jack and Sergeant Connell, she watches as Jack returns a few minutes later and they drive back to the group.

Rubbing her gloved hands together to shake off the chill, she observes the team leaders meet while keeping an eye on the gray lanes arching ahead. The adrenaline has subsided to an extent, but some remains as she knows action is imminent. Jack reaches in to grab the mic and she listens in on the conversation between him and whoever is sitting on the far side of the bridge. Having served in the sandbox a few times, she is used to this kind of action and the having to wait, but to have to do this here in her own country just feels strange. Her body and mind are tired after days of constant danger and not knowing what to expect from minute to minute. It's getting to her and she feels the weariness of it all. Her only hope is that they reach a point of stability where they can unwind soon. The only thing keeping them together right now is their camaraderie; their watching after each other.

She hears Jack's sigh as he hangs up the mic. She knows he must be tired as well and feels his exasperation. As if the night runners aren't enough, they have to deal with others. The chill settles deeper into her bones and the mental tiredness seems even more pronounced. The conversation made it clear that they are going into yet another battle. She shakes her head wondering what it is about human nature that creates these situations. *Can't they just see they have to be pulling together rather than isolating themselves?* She can almost understand the marauder mentality more than this situation. They're just bullies who take what they want and always have. Here, the two groups aren't that much different from one another and have much of the same ideas and goals. Mentally, she hopes that Jack will decide to take the other route mentioned. She's just doesn't want to be involved in yet another firefight. They are bucking the odds as it is and every engagement lowers those odds even more.

McCafferty ducks her head inside as Jack climbs in and relays the plan. She feels her heart beat faster, but it's inside a tired body and the familiar adrenaline surge doesn't appear. *They'll be through this quickly*, she tells herself, knowing the surge of adrenaline will come soon. Rising back through the opening, she checks to ensure her weapon is ready to go. They'll be paralleling the Stryker on the left bridge and she'll throw her rounds into the fray once they start. She feels exposed sitting up here but understands the need to gain fire superiority at the outset. That has been drilled into her head during countless other engagements. It still feels strange here but she trusts those around her and won't hesitate. She keeps her eye out as Jack mentioned they would be bugging out if there were any signs that the other group had rockets or some form of anti-armor.

The throaty growl of the Stryker diesels increases as the engines rev up and the big vehicles move online. Two Strykers move to the lanes leading up to the bridge on the right. The third moves to the middle of the left hand bridge. McCafferty grips the M-240 as the Humvee lurches and moves alongside. *There's the adrenaline,* she thinks as the chill of the day fades into the background. *It's go time.*

They begin to move forward. Her grip tightens as her entire focus is on the terrain slowly appearing as they near the crest. Inch by inch the trees and hills on the far side make their appearance. The line of cars she glimpsed seemingly hours ago will appear as her line of sight passes the top and begins to track downward. Her vision takes in the barrel pointing ahead and aligns it with the top of the roadway and the slowly appearing terrain beyond. The rumble of the engine next to her drowns out any other sounds although she thinks the thumping of her heart gives it competition. The tops of the vehicles on the far side come into view. Her breath quickens.

With a squeal, the Stryker next to her lurches as it pulls to a stop. McCafferty braces herself as Jack brings her Humvee to a stop as well and she sits staring along the dark gray lanes stretching ahead, arching downward to the cars and trucks across the roadway ahead. Small figures crouch behind trunks, hoods, and roof tops with their guns pointed her way. Feeling exposed, she swivels the gun back and forth watching and waiting for the first blink of light from beyond that signals gunfire. Glancing to the side, she sees the two Strykers adjacent on the other bridge. The smell of diesel exhaust drifts on the moist air and she can almost taste its acridness. Stillness descends as the two sides stare across the open space between them… waiting.

Movement below draws her attention as she sees Jack grab for the radio mic. Amid the rumble of the vehicles next to her sending tremors across the bridge and up through her feet, she barely hears Jack say, "Last chance, Sam."

Looking back to the front, she sees a miniscule flash of light from behind the cover of a car directly in front of her. Instinctively ducking, she catches sight of a spark flashing off the hull of the Stryker next to her. The whine of a bullet streaking off into the air behind causes her to flinch. Crouched, she hears Jack issue a "Stupid motherfuckers" almost under his breath. Rising back to her weapon, her ear piece crackles.

"I guess we have our answer. Let them have it," Jack says.

Loud, sharp, staccato bursts erupt next to her and from across the narrow expanse leading to the other bridge as the Strykers send their .50 caliber rounds streaking down the wide lanes. McCafferty swings her weapon and adds her 7.62mm rounds into the fray. Spurts of smoke leave the Stryker barrels as each round departs. Tracers stream above the dark gray asphalt and impact the glass and metal of the blockade vehicles attempting to halt their progress forward. Heavy thumps and the sight of glass shattering fill the far end of the ramp. Sparks fly where the heavy caliber rounds hit and punch through the thin metal. The dim light of the gray morning catches the shattered glass, sending sparkles as the pieces launch outward and tumble through the air. The stuffing from seat cushions puffs into the air where they are torn apart.

The rounds crash through the vehicles like butter. Large holes appear in the sides of the cars and trucks. Shards of metal are thrown outward from the collision of the heavy rounds and thin steel. Doors fly off their hinges, some falling straight to the ground. Stryker turrets whine as the guns track across the line of vehicles. Bullets crash through, impacting with bodies in their firing positions and strike the pavement beyond in a flash of sparks. A faint pink mist fills the air where rounds meet soft flesh and bone. Bodies are flung backwards heavily, crashing onto the pavement. Arms are severed or nearly severed from the heavy impacts. Heads explode spreading chunks of brain, flesh, and bone into the air.

The stillness of the morning is now broken by the staccato bursts of the heavy guns and the crash of impacting rounds. Feeling the vibration of the M-240 in her hands, McCafferty watches the devastation below. Faint sounds of metal screeching as if in agony reach her ears between bursts of fire. Those below scream as the violence is visited upon them and mix in with the vehicles being hammered. The back end of one car rears up from an explosion as rounds find the gas tank. It flips into the air and crashes down on top of a blue sedan next to it. Flames and smoke pour from the undercarriage. In mere seconds, the ground on the far side of the bridge is turned into a mass of torn metal, glass, and bodies. McCafferty watches as those still alive from the onslaught turn and flee to the sides. She lets up on the trigger as it becomes obvious those that made it through the few seconds of carnage are giving up and fleeing for their lives.

*   *   *   *   *   *

I watch the carnage and destruction on the ramp below. The screech of torn metal drifts into the Humvee above the sharp firing of the .50 cals and the chattering of the M-240 under McCafferty's care. The tracers of the larger caliber guns seem to hang in the air as they drift downward to impact with tremendous force. The tracers of the 7.62mm rounds mingle with the others. Metal is torn and thrown about to my front as the rounds tear their way through. I watch as a body leaning over one of the car roofs is picked up and thrown backward with force leaving just a pinkish mist floating where the body was. Those remaining behind the cars flee. The guns cease firing and, with the last of the shell casings tinkling on the metal floor of the Humvee, silence descends.

I barely hear the engines idling. My ears ring due to the din of the guns firing. I look down at the shredded vehicles ahead. A door falls from one of the cars to the ground, the sound lost. Except for the small flames licking the undercarriage of the flipped car and the smoke rising on the still air, nothing is moving. In just a matter of moments, the destruction is complete. I make out a couple of bodies lying on the pavement beyond the blockade. One person struggles to rise from the cold asphalt but gives up and slumps to the ground.

"Alright, let's push forward. Strykers in the lead. Lynn, follow and I'll bring up the rear. Watch to the sides for stragglers who might want to get a last shot in," I say with a heavy heart. I hear variations of "moving out" over the radio.

I still don't follow the logic of Sam not letting us through. Well, I do understand, but looking at the carnage below, it just seems like such a waste. I hear the heavy whine of the Stryker's engine rev up as it begins to pull ahead. I turn and pull on McCafferty's pants to get her attention. She looks through the opening and I motion for her to get inside. It seems over for the moment, but I don't want a stray bullet from the side causing any casualties as we pass through.

Lynn waits and then pulls her Humvee in behind the advancing Stryker. I watch as the Stryker turret swings to the left as it approaches the far side. Glancing over at the other two Humvees moving forward, I start ahead making sure I have spacing on Lynn. I don't see any of those that were at the blockade, nor do I see any flashes of light or any other indication that they are firing on us. The Stryker ahead plows through the gap left by the flipped car. Hitting two adjacent vehicles in the front and back respectively with a loud clang and a protesting squeal of metal, it shoves them back creating a larger path. Smoke from the smoldering car envelopes the Stryker causing it to vanish momentarily as it passes through.

The Strykers on the other bridge shove vehicles aside in the same manner. Lynn's Humvee follows the path through and vanishes from sight. Passing quickly through the lingering smoke, we emerge on the other side. Torn metal and shattered glass lie scattered on the pavement. Four bodies lie motionless amidst the devastation caused by the heavy bullets. Wet spots circle the bodies and run across the uneven lanes. I spot a severed arm near one of the mangled cars. As we continue on, I look to the sides watching for any indication they are waiting on our flanks. The only movement is the tail end of the truck Sam was driving heading down a side road toward the airport.

"Jack, we have an aircraft overhead on our seven tailing us," I hear Lynn say.

I take a quick look behind us and see a small single engine aircraft a few thousand feet up paralleling our route. I haven't heard any radio traffic on their channel in the past few minutes.

"Lynn, run another scan across the channels," I say.

"Wilco."

"We'll let it be for now. Everyone push on, but keep your eyes open. There's bound to be another roadblock ahead."

I don't want to have us stop to warn the aircraft away or take it down. I'm not a big fan of it above us but am willing to trade that for speed through the area for the time being. I'm sure it's radioing our position to any others who happen to be around. We continue on the highway in the opposite lanes keeping our spacing. I'm rather thankful I haven't seen any form of rockets as that would make a short end to our rendezvous with the sub.

"I've picked up radio chatter on four sixty-seven dot fifty-eight seventy-five," Lynn calls.

"And?" I ask.

"The aircraft is relaying our position to someone else and telling them to vacate. I'm assuming it's the aircraft calling as I can hear its engine in the background," she answers.

"Okay, lock it in. Let's continue forward and keep alert," I say. Passing by toll booths on our side of the highway, I see the Stryker ahead of us round a curve.

"We have another roadblock two hundred yards ahead. No sign of anyone," I hear it report.

"Hold up and blast a hole through. I don't want to be

surprised by any gifts they may have left behind. Watch to the sides," I respond.

I see Lynn's brake lights and bring our Humvee to a halt. McCafferty climbs back to man the M-240. Seconds later I hear the sharp chunk – chunk – chunk of the .50 cals opening up ahead. Minutes later I hear "It's clear" and I have everyone advance. The Strykers carve a way through the vehicles as before with Lynn and me following on the left. This already seems like a long day and it just began. I'm hoping we don't run into anything else along the way. Although our time table hasn't been upset to any great degree, I'm eager to get north and meet with Captain Leonard.

It's going to be a long day as I plan on taking the Spooky out tonight. There's still so much to do. It seems like the list just keeps getting longer and I'm not overly thrilled about the changes I've noticed in the night runners. Casting out briefly, I feel a few faint presences scattered throughout the area. Even with this recent action and the upcoming meeting with Leonard, the night runners still weigh heavily on my mind. I think again about telling the group, but I'm not sure of what their reaction will be. Lynn seems to think they'll be stunned at first but okay with it. Me, well, I don't want to chance that or create any division within our tight group. We need that right now, but they also deserve to know. Yes, I seem to have a life filled with quandaries. Sighing, I maneuver through the gap created by the Stryker and notice the aircraft turn back.

We pass by a warehouse park with a mass of tractor trailers; reminders of a time that has passed. Another residential neighborhood slides by and we are soon through the Gig Harbor area without any further incident. Fir trees and cedars begin to line the road on both sides. They are completely oblivious to what just occurred and anything going on with the few of us who are left. They will continue on just as they always have. I think about calling Sam on the radio to see if he wants join us and still may on the way back. Right now, my mind is on getting to our rendezvous and the meeting itself.

Beads of moisture begin to accumulate on the windshield

from low-lying mist in the air. The trees along the sides have a silvery tint from droplets clinging to their long branches. The lowering clouds create a world of gray and green. Some of the few deciduous trees have started to turn, lending some color, but it's almost washed out by the overcast day. Miles of trees pass by the windows with the windshield wiper getting an occasional swipe across to clear it.

Soon, the water of the bay leading into Bremerton appears. The highway swings around the tail end of the bay and the old aircraft carriers parked along carrier row come into view. They are now very much like the remainder of world; relics of a time past and sitting in their final resting place rusting away to nothingness.

Low lying clouds hang close to the still waters with the waves barely making an appearance. White specks of gulls hover close to the shoreline and a couple of teals pass across the waterway with their wingtips barely clearing the surface. Where once the waters were rife with traffic, and ferries plowed the sea lanes carrying tourists and commuters, nothing of that nature now stirs.

The road branches, carrying us away from the inlet and farther to the north. We swing into a column file and I take the lead once again. Bremerton fades behind and, passing a large mall, we leave this vestige of a once-flourishing civilization. Houses give way to more forested hills as we make our way closer to Bangor. I was expecting more roadblocks or other indications of survivors, but no one greets us. The pockets of other survivors we have found seem to be at random without any consistent factor that I can see.

We arrive at the entrance to Bangor. Not knowing what to expect, I feel a little nervous about meeting with Captain Leonard. I know I would enjoy having them join up with us but don't want to have a clash of personalities that could tear apart the close bond we have within our community. The sub could give us a potential for movement along the coastal areas and provide a power source should the ones we have fail for some reason. Besides having more people to help with survival and protection, it will give us more flexibility when the aircraft join the carriers and other vestiges of civilization sitting where they lie and slowly dissolve into rusting hulks. Mostly though, it's about drawing the remnants of humanity and survivors together.

We drive slowly through the entrance gates. The clouds are hovering on the tree tops, their highest points shrouded and lost in the gray. Droplets condense on the windshield. Making our way through the empty tree-lined streets, we arrive on a hill overlooking the docks and waterway. Two triangular concreted docks jut out into the water. The pier on the left houses what appears to be two large missile boats. On the right, I see the low lying black shape of an LA class fast attack sub. Small white objects are in a row as sailors line the deck. We have arrived.

* * * * * *

A Meeting of Minds

Captain Leonard wakes early. His rest was an edgy one with so much running through his head. It just seemed like his thoughts wouldn't shut down long enough for any beneficial sleep. He still doesn't know exactly what happened or is happening and his mind won't quite wrap around what Captain Walker or Chief Krandle have said. He wants to believe what they are saying, and watching the people onshore last night lends credibility to their stories, but this seems too much like the zombie stories a lot of his crew seems to be into.

Rising and swinging his legs over the edge of the bed, he dons his shoes and leaves his cramped quarters. Listening to the reports from the night watch, which is nothing much except for seeing more people running through the night, he peers through the scope at the lightening day. The low gray clouds hovering close to the waterline make visibility difficult as he turns through a three-sixty watching for signs of life. Nothing but an occasional flash of white as gulls dot the shoreline and pier. There is no evidence of those he saw last night.

The shore seems still…hesitant…waiting.

Leonard tells the crew to prepare to surface the boat. His chief has readied crews to board the Zodiacs to open the perimeter nets so they can slide inside and dock. He also had the chief ready other teams to go onshore to find supplies. That remains his priority – resupply his boat to be ready for any contingency. Depending on how the meeting today goes, and perhaps regardless of it, he needs to restock. He might head down the western seaboard and possibly to Hawaii hoping to gather some additional information along the way. His only worry is about their limited arms and lack of training. The fact that he has a SEAL Team alleviates this to some extent, but it remains a concern nonetheless. The crews sit at their stations in their white uniforms ready for the all-hands-on-deck greeting. Checking in with his communications center and verifying that no additional traffic has come in, he tells the office of the watch to surface the boat.

The *Santa Fe* slowly rises above the frigid waters of the Sound. Water pours off in sheets from the black surface with its anechoic coating. Waterfalls stream off the bridge cockpit through drain vents. The once dreaded, silent hunter of the seas rises from its hidden lair, baring itself to the observed world. Small and sleek, it appears like a ninja stepping out from a dark shadow.

On surfacing, the bridge crew races up the ladder. Opening the watertight hatch, they step onto the bridge and begin their lookout duties. On the lower deck, hatches open and crews emerge dragging inflatable Zodiacs onto the black surface. Readying the craft, they motor over to the floats bobbing on the calm waves to open the protective, submerged netting. After some time, they create a hole for the sub to motor through.

Leonard climbs and steps onto the bridge. The low clouds and early morning cast a dim light over the dark waters. Watching the crews work with the nets, he sees them create an opening. He orders the boat in. The sleek bow responds and, turning toward the docks, the *Santa Fe*, his pride and joy, rides slowly upon the dark waves of the inlet. Looking down, he sees some of his crew emerge from a hatch and line the deck with the few weapons onboard.

The *Santa Fe* glides slowly past the Zodiacs and eases up to the concrete dock. He sees the dormant missile boats tied to the adjacent pier and wonders if there are any other surviving boats. The lack of communications seems to indicate that he may be the only one although the others may be keeping a radio blackout. If there are any others, they should have responded to his attempts at communication although they may still be proceeding underwater. He'll keep the comm center manned and flash regular messages in an attempt to raise others.

The Zodiacs motor in and pull up to the dock. It takes some time but they eventually tie in with the dock and the gangway is lowered. The occasional cry of a gull, the drip of water still running down the sides of the boat, and the soft lap of waves against the concrete dock are the only sounds. The base remains silent and there is no sign of the people who ran through the night.

Looking at his watch, there's little time until their appointed rendezvous with Captain Walker. He calls down to have the chief ready the resupply teams. Several minutes later, the teams appear and begin making their way across the gangway. Leonard watches as they walk up the pier and disappear around a corner as they proceed toward one of the large warehouses in the distance. The remaining crew members climb the ladder and gather on the deck. Several rub the white sleeves of their uniforms as they attempt to ward off the chill.

Soft murmurs arise from the crowd above the faint slapping of waves and cry of birds flocking the area. Another faint sound arises on the moisture-laden air... vehicles approaching. The crews form up in a row, those with weapons are dispersed among them. Captain Leonard makes his way down and onto shore with CPO Krandle and his SEAL Team close behind. Standing on the dock, he looks up. On the rise above the docks, he sees a Humvee appear with more military vehicles behind. He watches with a sudden apprehension as they start down the road towards him.

* * * * * *

We start down the steep decline toward the docks. Although I'm not usually nervous about meeting anyone, and really never have been in the past – after all, we all put our pants on the same way – I feel apprehensive about this one. I'm not really sure why. It's not like we're going to trade gunfire, and I know I won't allow anything to disrupt the harmony of our group. Working together is the most important thing right now. Well...anytime. I just know it's going to be a hard sell with a submarine captain. I can almost feel the personality conflict. I try to keep my mind open as this may not be the case but anticipate it anyway. I'm not out to rule over anyone, nor do I have an ego so big that I think my way is the only way. Or our way for that matter. My main goal is for the safety of the group, with my kids coming first.

I eye the boomers sitting silently parked at the docks. My thoughts quickly go to the possibility of learning the systems and holing up there. Parking off shore and coming in for supplies. Those boats are pretty self-sufficient. Yeah, let's see the night runners swim the strong currents and try to penetrate those. That seems like an impossibility though. The systems will break down regardless of the long-term viability of the propulsion system. No, we have carved out our place and, although the night runners seem to be adapting amazingly fast, we'll have to make do with what we have. Still, I park the idea in the back of my mind.

I pull alongside the piers and park. The Strykers and Lynn's Humvee park in line behind. Opening the door, I hear a clang as the back doors of the Strykers drop. Lynn's shout of "Form up!" echoes across the silent base and adjacent waters. Boots pound across the pavement, muted to an extent by the moisture in the air, accompanied by the rattle of gear. The intrusions of noise are sudden but over quickly as the soldiers find their places. Robert and the rest of Red Team riding with me trot over and take their place in the formation. I'm left alone for a moment.

Shutting the door, which adds its metallic slam to the noise taking place, I glance down the dock seeing one man standing by the sub with a team behind him. The others gathered with him are dressed in camo uniforms marking them distinctly different than the sailors lining the low deck of the sub. I walk to the start of the dock and am joined by Frank and Bannerman. Lynn announces that all are present and accounted for before directing the teams to parade rest.

Silence descends, all sound seemingly absorbed by the gray cotton of clouds just overhead. I feel the moisture in the air condense on my face and in my hair. The fog is just a few scant feet over my head and the chill I felt before intensifies. I know it won't be long before my fatigues are completely damp. I feel the nervous energy build inside as I look down the dock where the other men stand. Again, I don't know where this feeling is coming from. I should be elated to find the crew and another group of survivors. I take a deep breath and feel the calm return. With a nod to Bannerman and Frank, I start walking down the wide concrete path.

Dressed in a dark pea coat with a braided officer's hat, the man whom I assume to be Captain Leonard starts towards us with his small group of six in tow. I look Leonard over as he approaches. Tall and thin with short-cropped dark hair lined with silver, he has the pale skin common with submariners. His angular face with deep lines in the corner of his blue-gray eyes, his long, thin nose, and his confident stride mark him as a man to be reckoned with. We meet a short distance down the pier.

I stop with Bannerman and Frank behind and to each side. He comes to a halt in front of us, his stance rigid. I know he expects a salute, but I stick out my hand not wanting to set a senior officer/subordinate tone.

"Jack Walker," I say, holding my hand out. He has a look of uncertainty which disappears quickly.

"Captain Raymond Leonard," he says returning my shake.

I don't miss the fact that he threw his rank in. I also note his quick glance at Bannerman and Frank noting their ranks. Another quick look of puzzlement crosses his face as, I assume, he is wondering why there is a major and colonel behind a captain. In the world past, due to his rank, Frank would have been the one in front talking. I observe the relaxed stance of the men behind Leonard taking everything in without being overly obvious. More interesting are the SEAL badges sewn into their fatigue tops.

"What unit are you with, captain?" Leonard asks, emphasizing the 'captain'.

"We're not with any particular unit. What you see is what's left of various units. Most here are from Army units, but we have a scattering of others. What exactly do you know about what happened?" I ask.

"Only what I've heard from you and the chief here," he

replies with a brief nod toward one of the men behind him.

I am about to ask what he's been told by the chief and the story there when I catch movement out of the corner of my eye. I look over to the side and see a group of men heading across an open area toward one of the large buildings nearby.

"Are those your men?" I ask, pointing to the men and fearing they are actually about to head into the structure.

"Yes, captain, they are. We're resupplying," Leonard answers, narrowing his eyes.

"Are they going into that building?" I ask, hoping for a negative reply.

"Yes. That one and several others in order to restock our supplies."

I turn back toward Leonard momentarily. "Seriously? You did hear what I said about going into buildings, right? About what happened and what is going on?"

Without waiting for a reply, I turn my head quickly back toward Lynn. She is standing in the center front of the teams watching our little group. Even from this distance, I see her eyebrows rise wondering about my quick movement. She knows me well and realizes that something is up.

"Lynn!" I shout and point toward the men about to enter a door into the warehouse. Lynn looks to where I am pointing. Seeing the men poised at the door in the near distance and knowing their intentions, she turns toward the teams standing at parade rest.

"Black, Blue, Charlie Teams on me," she shouts, knowing exactly what is about to unfold.

Amid a clatter of noise from weapons being readied, Lynn begins trotting toward the warehouse. With their boots pounding on the hard surface, the three teams follow. The eighteen men and women head toward the large building in an attempt to stop the inevitable yet knowing they won't be in time to stop the other group from entering.

I watch them race after and hear Lynn shout at the group from the sub to get their attention. I see no reaction from the people at the door and know Lynn won't be able to get there in time. I cast out quickly and sense night runners within the warehouse and in several buildings in the area. My only hope is that Lynn and the teams arrive in time in order to get those starting to enter out safely. The thought of putting the teams at risk entering a darkened building arises. I have a momentary thought of not putting them in harm's way, but there are people in danger. We are here and if we can help…well, then we have to.

"Lynn, there are night runners inside. Watch your asses in there. Assess the risk and get out if you need to," I say.

"Copy that, Jack," she replies over the radio.

This happens in mere moments. I hear a clatter of weapons directly behind me. Turning, I see the SEAL team has brought their weapons up. Not aiming at us, but definitely ready to do so. Looking over at the sub, I see several sailors lining the sub deck aiming weapons in our direction.

"Captain, those are my men and under my orders. We have every right to enter any facility on this base. As a matter of fact, being the ranking member here and with what you have told me, you are technically under my command. As far as I can see, I am the ranking officer on this base and therefore the acting base commander. You will tell your men to stand down," Leonard says. His head is thrust forward with his lips drawn tight with determination. His eyes narrow.

I hear movement from the remaining teams. Glancing behind, I see Greg has spread out the teams in reaction to the sailor's reaction. They have taken cover behind the vehicles. Soldiers climb in the Humvees to man the M-240s. Within seconds, the whine of the Stryker turrets reaches across the dock area as the guns are brought to bear. Tension fills the moisture-heavy air.

"Captain, they're not going to stop your people, they're going to try and rescue them," I say, holding up my hand to Greg telling him not to take any action. I turn back to Leonard.

"Rescue them? What do you mean rescue them?" Leonard asks, his voice rising.

"You heard when I told you about the night runners,

right? That building you just sent your men into is the perfect lair for them. They hide in darkened buildings. Your men will get torn apart inside. Did you send them in armed?" I ask.

Leonard stares at me for a moment. I can almost see the gears within turning. Whether he is thinking about his answer or absorbing the information is beyond me. The silence is virtually complete. Waves lap gently against the concrete dock. The cry of a lone gull drifts across the open waters. The faint sound of boots running on the ground as the teams race to the warehouse. The cotton gray of the clouds lie just overhead as if held up by the tension of the moment, muffling all sounds. Turning his head, Leonard gives a signal for the sailors to lower their weapons.

"No, Captain Walker, they are only armed with flashlights," he finally replies.

*   *   *   *   *   *

Lynn watches as Jack and the other group comes together. The teams behind her are in formation at parade rest. Although she doesn't think any violence will come from this meeting, she stands ready for anything. Everything she has gone through since waking and seeing her feverish roommate back in the sandbox has taught her to be ready for anything. The rules and the assumptions that governed society before everything went to hell have been thrown out of the window. Not only have they been thrown out, but they have been wiped out. The world is now filled with the unknown.

Night runners, bandits, small pockets of survivors, dwindling resources, and their own very survival fill this new world. Every day seems to bring something new, and to let down your guard for a moment is an invitation to potential disaster. They have made it far in a short period of time; but how long can they keep this up? There was a reason for soldiers to be rotated after a year. What will happen to them if they are still in this after a year…after two? *Will they constantly have to react to how the night runners adapt? How far will they be able to adapt? What is up with some seemingly turning back? Will that happen more? Could it be they only have to hold out for a certain time and all of the night runners will eventually become human again?* These thoughts hold her mind as she watches Jack, with Bannerman and Frank behind him, converse with this Captain Leonard.

Jack points off to the side and, after a second, turns quickly toward her. By his movement, she knows that he is worried about something. She has seen it enough times to instantly know something is wrong. The previous thoughts leave her mind. She tenses, ready to react to what is amiss.

"Lynn!" Jack shouts and points off to the side.

She looks and sees a group of people gathered near a door to a warehouse a short distance away. They appear to be about to enter. Immediately knowing they don't know the danger they are about to enter into and sensing that Jack's call was for her to gather teams to prevent or help them, she turns to the formation.

"Black, Blue, Charlie Teams on me," she shouts.

She makes sure the teams are ready and then begins trotting toward the large warehouse hearing the footfalls of the teams behind her. She knows immediately they won't be able to reach the people in time to prevent them from going in. Gathering her breath, she shouts out to them attempting to get their attention. No response. *Fuck*, she thinks and picks up her pace. She hopes she can reach them before they venture too far inside. If she can reach the door quickly, she can shout inside for them to get back out. She feels the heightened rush of adrenaline knowing she may have to enter into yet another darkened building. *This is fucking shit*, she thinks as she watches the last of the group disappear into the open door of the structure.

"Lynn, there are night runners inside. Watch your asses in there. Assess the risk and get out if you need to," she hears Jack on the radio.

"Copy that, Jack," she replies. *This shit just gets better and better.*

She knows what Jack is saying between the lines. If the risk to the teams is too great, he wants her to pull the teams out regardless of the situation. They had this discussion a while ago in the gym rescuing his kids and the others held captive. Some of those they had rescued wanted to go to the bathroom and she was to provide escort. Jack has told her to pull back if they were attacked and let the others fend for themselves. She argued that she wouldn't leave them defenseless…that's not what they were there for; they were there to protect. Jack had agreed with that, but losing the teams would leave everyone else without the protection they needed.

While the events of the past months have changed her way of thinking to a certain degree, she still feels that sense of protecting those that need it. It's a core part of her; help those that need help regardless of the risk. She understands Jack's concern. If they lose teams here, that would leave the compound with less to defend it, especially with the night runners showing their tremendous ability to adapt. This is the quandary she finds herself in – what is the acceptable level of risk? For her, there is no limit to the risk in order to help someone but who is it they are there to help – those in the compound or the ones directly in front of her. They both need levels of help. *Well, fuck it, I'll try to help the ones here to the level I can without losing the teams*, she thinks as they close on the building.

Lynn folds against the outside wall next to the open door. The clouds hang close to the tall roof of the cream-colored warehouse. Looking at the building closely for the first time, she realizes just what they are up against. The door she is next to is near the far left side with large sliding doors in the center of the building. This is evidently a large storage facility meant for trucks to enter and fill with supplies. Looking along the front of the structure, she notes the complete absence of windows. Quickly walking to the corner and peering along the wall there, she sees a similar sight; cream-colored sheet metal walls stretching high without a door or window to mar the surface. The inside will be pitch dark. She reaches up and feels for the

NVGs fastened securely to her helmet.

Turning back, she sees Horace, with her Blue Team against the wall on the other side of the door. Behind Horace, Mullins waits with Charlie Team. Her own Black Team is pressed against the wall on her side. All have their weapons ready to bring to bear. She knows each and every one of them dread heading into yet another darkened building. And Jack telling her there are night runners inside, well, she can take that one to the bank. A trickle of thought enters that he broadcast that in the open and it will be noted. Looking at the teams tense and ready, she feels her own tension drawn tight like a drawn bowstring.

Pressing the mic button on her throat mic, she says, "Horace, you have the right, Mullins the left. I'll take the center. Twenty feet in and be ready." Lynn watches Horace nod and Mullins give a thumbs up.

"Jack, do we have comms with the group inside? Are they armed and do they know we are coming in?" Lynn asks.

A moment passes before the answer comes, "No, they don't have any radios and aren't armed. Watch your ass."

"Isn't that your job?" she replies.

"It is and a wonderful job it is. The view is incredible," Jack answers.

"Good answer. See you in a sec, Lynn out."

Lynn settles herself by the doorway. Peering in, she notes that the darkness is nearly complete. The light from the opening extends only a few feet in before disappearing into an inky abyss. The sub tied to the pier a short distance away is forgotten as she looks into nothingness. Her heart races as she knows what lies within. She feels the tension quivering inside her yet, at the same time, she feels a certain calm settle in knowing that it's go time. The chill of the morning is lost as her entire attention is focused on the task at hand.

The shriek that emits from within startles her and causes her heart to jump. Night runners are indeed laired within and have either noticed her and her team or the others that entered only minutes ago. She swallows and takes a deep breath.

"Okay, ladies, that's our cue," she says. Flipping down her goggles and, bringing her M-4 to bear, she steps in the doorway.

She is immediately lost in the blackness, but her goggles bring everything into focus with a green glow. The interior is largely open. Several trucks are parked near the front and farther back with a few propane-driven forklifts scattered throughout. Large crates and boxes are stacked along the side and beyond the vehicles forming small mountains with aisles running farther back into the building between them. The back of the warehouse is lost behind the first large stacks.

Her head turns to the left and right; up and down. Searching. Anticipating night runners to immediately launch themselves at her. Her laser casts a thin beam of light everywhere her eyes look. Nothing. The quick rush of noise from clothing and boots follows her in as the others enter on her heels. She stops twenty feet in feeling the rest of Black Team fall in beside her. Her goggles pick up seventeen other laser beams as they dart about the interior. Toward the rear of building, several flashlights shine upward from amongst the boxes. Lynn catches a couple of flashes closer by. She wants to call out for those inside to leave, but they are too far to the rear of the warehouse. Any call will alert the night runners and bring them upon the hapless sailors inside.

"Okay, everyone, take is slow and easy. We're heading to the right along the front doors. Keep our current perimeter. Horace, when we reach the front doors, I want you to see if you can get them open," Lynn says over the radio.

"Copy that, first sergeant," Horace replies.

"Right behind you," Mullins responds.

"These people don't know we're in here, so watch your targets. Keep your eyes open. Move out," Lynn says.

Lynn can feel her heart thudding in her chest as they begin making their way along the front wall. Boots scuff on the gritty concrete floor along with the soft swish of clothing rubbing together. Thin beams of light streak out across the interior as they cover their individual sectors. An occasional murmur rises from the others inside as they apparently search out the area for supplies. She doesn't know why the group from the sub didn't just open the front doors. *Perhaps they don't know what they're dealing with*, she thinks, mentally willing them to keep their voices down. The last thing they need right now is to alert the night runners she knows reside within.

There was that first shriek that sounded out just before they entered, but the chorus that would usually follow didn't occur. She thinks again to call out to alert the other group that they are in, but that would definitely alert any night runners. She feels put in a difficult position. If they can get the doors open, she'll call out to them that they are in danger and for them make their way swiftly to her. The light shining in will give them an area of protection.

Twenty feet in and keeping their outer perimeter, a canvas covered supply truck blocks her immediate path. She turns the rear corner quickly and aims inside. Her barrel tracks left and right as she searches the interior. Fully expecting a shriek and a night runner to launch at her, she is relieved when the truck turns up empty. *Fuck I hate this*, she thinks, skirting the rear of the vehicle. *I just fucking hate being in these fucking buildings. Stupid motherfuckers! Why did they have to come inside?*

More murmurs of conversation arise from amongst the stacked crates as the teams make their way cautiously to the front sliding doors. Lynn wishes once again that those inside would just keep quiet. They've been lucky so far with the night runners, and she is actually amazed they haven't been set upon yet. Before, it didn't take long until the night runners were aware of them and assaulted. The fact that there are night runners inside, yet they haven't attacked, makes the quiet all that much more eerie. Surely they must smell them by now.

"We're at the doors, first sergeant. They look motor driven," Horace reports. Looking toward the short distance separating her from Blue Team, she eyes the large doors. From what she can see, they seem to roll on sizeable tracks.

"There must be a manual override. We'll hold here for a moment. See what you can do. Break. Jack, Lynn here," Lynn whispers into the radio.

"Go ahead," Jack replies.

"We're inside by the large doors trying to see if we can get them open. I can hear the other group deeper inside. Any idea exactly how many sailors are in here?" she asks.

"Standby," Jack replies. "Lynn, there are twelve crew members inside," the answer comes shortly.

"Copy that. Thanks, Jack." Several thumps interrupt the tense silence farther to the rear of the vast, dark interior.

"Okay, we're advancing up to the front of the vehicles. Mullins, you'll take the left and keep in line with us. Horace, keep trying the doors. You'll be in reserve. If something happens, pull Blue Team to the open door and hold a perimeter around it. We'll fold back to you. Remember, we have night runners in here, but there are also twelve sailors. Verify your targets," Lynn says.

With a positive response from both of the other teams, she spreads Black Team out and begins to advance slowly online. She observes Charlie Team advance and keep pace. Green laser beams dart in amongst the vehicles and over the crates beyond. Lynn keeps her head moving searching for the targets she knows are within. Step by step she moves forward, her heart beating harder and faster with each movement. Without the large door opened, her goal is to get to the sailors quietly and escort them out.

The air within is chilled and heavy with tension. Or perhaps that is her tension radiating outward to the surrounding environment. It becomes harder to pick up her feet the farther in she goes. The air feels thick and increases the more she moves inside. It's as if the very darkness itself has substance. She knows the intense adrenaline rush and dread of being inside a night runner lair. She also knows that it's easy for the fear to take control. If that happens, she'll be useless or dangerous to the others. With a deep, calming breath, she takes another step.

The randomly spaced supply trucks make it impossible for them all to remain within sight of each other. She steps between two trucks parked in line with each other. One other Black Team member follows her but now she can't see the others to either side. Scanning ahead, Lynn sees a dark spot on the ground just in front of the vehicle to her left. Looking closer, she notices it looks like a dark puddle with rivulets spreading out in several directions. She pauses and hears a wet sound coming from just in front of her.

"Black and Charlie team, hold up. I have something to my front. Standby," she says.

Going to one knee silently while keeping her M-4 at the ready, Lynn looks under the truck toward the front. Her heartbeat picks up even more and jumps into her throat at the sight. Lying on the ground just under the front bumper is a person dressed in the jeans and work shirt of a navy crew member. A flashlight lies beside the unmoving form illuminating the side of the body. Dark stains cover the shirt and ground beside. While the sight of the body startles her, it's the movement around the body that causes her to tense up.

Lynn sees a pair of legs kneeling on her side by the still body with more movement on the other side. The bottom of the truck cuts off any further view. The wet sounds continue and she knows immediately what it is – chewing. This must have been the shriek they heard just before entering and she hopes these are the only two night runners within. The sailor must have been put on a watch or just wandered off by his or herself in their search. She watches as a head comes into view and lowers to the dead sailor.

Keeping her eyes glued to the scene in front of her, Lynn slowly moves her hand to her throat mic. "I have two night runners and a dead body three meters to my twelve o'clock in front of the truck," she whispers. "Keep alert for others. Mullins, can you get a shot at them?"

"I can't see anything from my position but I'll work my way forward," Mullin's whispers his reply.

"Copy that. No sound."

The night runner with its head lowered sinks its teeth into flesh and, with a wet, tearing sound, rips off a chunk. It begins to raise its head back and halts suddenly...pauses...the chunk of flesh drops from its bloodied mouth. Lynn freezes. She feels that the pounding of her heart can be heard for miles. The night runner sniffs the air and looks directly at her. It lowers its head farther. Their eyes lock. Lynn's mouth turns dry as another burst of adrenaline floods her system.

The night runner's eyes glow through her goggles, sending a deep chill along her spine. Time pauses. An eternity passes as they stare at each other. The absolute silence of the moment encompasses her; folds around her like a cloak. Not a muscle twitches or breath is taken. They kneel staring at each other like statues frozen in an instant of time. Then, like a speeding locomotive emerging from a tunnel, normal time resumes. She hears a low, deep growl emit from the creature in front of her. The other night runner freezes in its motion then, suddenly, a second head appears to stare under the truck. The second night runner stares hard and then snarls, baring its blood-stained teeth. With astonishing speed, both rise and come around the front of the truck.

Taken aback by their startling speed and emergence, Lynn begins raising the barrel of her weapon. Both night runners round the truck just scant feet in front of her and charge in her direction. Knowing she won't be able to bring her weapon to bear in time, she launches herself backwards from her kneeling position in order to gain her more separation and time. The move brings her M-4 up quicker and she squeezes the trigger.

Rounds exit the moving barrel with muted coughs as they pass through her suppressor. The light from her firing flashes on the sides and undercarriage of the truck beside her. Still in the air falling backward, she watches as her bullets impact the nearest night runner in the thigh and stitch upward. Hitting the hard floor on her rear end, she is jarred and slides backwards on the seat of her pants.

The first round hits just above the left knee of the night runner. Entering the soft flesh, the bullet begins to tumble upward. Missing the femur, it rips upward through the thigh and exits the top of the hip taking massive amounts of tissue with it. The second round hits square in the middle of the thigh and slams into the femur. The tremendous force of the impact shatters the thick bone. The next bullet collides powerfully with the pelvis. Hitting the top of the pelvic bone, the bullet splits with both pieces angling farther up. Ripping through sections of the intestines, both shards exit just under the lower rib cage in the back. Blood sprays into the air from the entrance and exit wounds

Being so close to the night runner, Lynn feels a splash of warmth against her cheek. The injured night runner is spun completely around from the impacts and falls to the ground next to her. She feels the crash through the hard floor and hears a whoosh as the air leaves its lungs from the collision with the concrete. Her slide backwards comes to halt. The other night runner is almost upon her. She looks up. Through her goggles, she sees the bared teeth and glowing eyes above her just beyond her outstretched feet. The night runner leaps into the air, flying toward her with outstretched arms.

Time slows. Lynn brings her M-4 up angling it across her body. Her vision is filled with the wild eyes and snarling face of the night runner. Arms reach out to her with fingers curled. The lips and chin of the enraged creature are streaked with fresh blood. Pulled back lips and open mouth frozen in a snarl reveals stained teeth. In the clarity of the moment, Lynn notices a gold cap covering one of the upper incisors. Saliva and blood drips from the side of its mouth. The night runner draws closer inch by inch.

Keeping her M-4 between her and the creature hurtling in slow motion towards her, she thrusts out with her weapon. Rolling at the moment of impact of her carbine against the night runner, she slams the body down next to her on the solid floor. The creature hits hard and emits a grunt. Its head lands with a sharp crack. Lynn uses her momentum and continues her roll, rising to her knees. The night runner appears momentarily stunned and she gathers her feet under her pulling her M-4 up with her.

Turning her carbine, she pumps a single round into its head. Blood splashes upward from the impact and the night runner collapses and settles solidly onto the floor. A pool of blood forms quickly around its head. A firm tug on her pants nearly knocks her off balance. Stepping to the side to maintain her equilibrium, she looks down to see a hand of the first night runner reaching out and firmly gripping her pants near the hem. The pale face is off to the side of her and, looking again into its eyes, she sees a mixture of hunger and pain in them.

A muted cough from nearby sounds and a strobe of light illuminates the night runner and area around. The night runner twitches and a shower of blood erupts from underneath its chin. The glow of the eyes fades. It twitches twice more and is still.

Lynn quickly turns and looks around. She notes that only seconds have passed since discovering the body. Silence returns and she realizes that she didn't hear the familiar shriek of discovery from either of the night runners. This confuses her but she is thankful that the cry of alarm wasn't sounded. Looking at her team mate standing a few feet away, she nods her thanks for his taking care of the downed night runner.

Adrenaline courses through her body leaving her both tight and relaxed. She notices her panting breath and works to bring her breathing back to normal. The smell of body odor, blood, and feces wafts to her nose.

"Okay, let's get back on line and move to the front of the vehicles. Stay alert," she instructs the others over the radio.

Cautiously walking to the front of the truck next to her, she steps over the puddle of blood trickling slowly along the uneven surface. The mutilated and torn body of the sailor lies on its back. The upper part of the shirt is darkly stained. She observes that most of the facial tissue is missing, revealing muscles, tendons, and bone. The throat has been ripped away and lifeless eyes stare blankly at the tall ceiling above that is lost in the darkness.

An open area stands between her position in front of the trucks and the beginning of the large, stacked crates and boxes. Flashlights continue to wave in the air at various points in the depths of the building. She hears the persistent murmurs of the group from the sub. In the background, she picks up soft thuds emanating from the same general area.

From her position and looking toward the top of the crates, she catches a flash of movement. Directly in front of her, something moved in the air across an aisle formed between the stacked crates. Due to the height of the stacks, Lynn can't see much of the tops. Concentrating on the edges, she witnesses more quick and subtle movements causing a measure of dread and fear to surface once again. *That has to be night runners*, she thinks. The fact that there are night runners moving about without the familiar shrieks sends yet another cold shiver to race down her spine.

"Night runners on top of the crates," she says into the radio. Thin points of light move upward with her call. They streak down aisles and on top of the stacks.

It's time to do something. She is hesitant about taking the teams down the aisles. With night runners on the crates above, those aisles will become death traps. She knows her only choice is to shout to the group from the sub to make their way to her. The movements she saw indicate that the night runners are moving toward those inside, if they're not already there.

"*Santa Fe* crew members, this is Sergeant Connell. You are in immediate danger. Make your way quickly to the front doors. We'll cover you," Lynn shouts.

A loud shriek penetrates and echoes in the vast interior. More follow, filling the warehouse with their reverberations. Terror-filled screams begin from far back in the warehouse. Flashlight beams wave frantically in the air.

"Charlie and Black Teams, form a perimeter on me. Horace, get those doors open now," Lynn says.

"Working on it, first sergeant," Horace replies.

"We have friendlies out there so watch your target," Lynn says, cautioning against itchy trigger fingers.

The once nearly silent interior is filled with shrieks and screams. The screams are a mix of fear and pain. Movement in her peripheral catches her attention and she swings her M-4 toward it. Light bounces on the floor off to her right. The wavering beam is an indication that someone is running with a flashlight in their hand. Others in her teams have seen the same thing as lasers converge on the aisle entrance.

"Keep an eye on your sectors. Possible friendlies approaching on the right," Lynn says.

Several of the thin points of light leave the point of convergence and swing back to the other aisles and crates. Two figures emerge from the aisle racing toward the front of the building with flashlights in their hands. Just behind them, three night runners give chase.

"Open fire," Lynn shouts. "You two, make for the open door."

The muted coughs of several M-4s opening up are lost in the din. Tracers streak out and converge on the first two night runners quickly closing the distance on the sailors running for their lives. One night runner drops immediately forward onto its face from multiple bullets striking it. The second spins a one-eighty and slams onto the hard surface of the floor. The third attempts to close in, but its forward momentum is halted as weapons are focused on it. It stops and stands upright as if it hit an invisible wall. Its shirt puffs in multiple locations as a second series of bullets hit forcefully and topple it backward. The two sailors alter their direction of flight toward the rectangle of light of the open door.

Light flashes from an aisle directly ahead of Lynn. Beams from flashlights are focused on the ground. Behind the lights, she can barely make out four sailors speeding her way.

Movement on the crates above the four running figures captures her attention. Before she can bring her M-4 to bear, a shrieking night runner leaps down from above crashing onto a sailor bringing up the rear. They both go down, colliding hard with the floor. The surprised scream of the submariner rises momentarily above the cacophony of noise before being abruptly cut off. The three remaining sailors cut off her view of what happens next. The three exit the aisle and are brought up short as their lights shine on Lynn and the few team members close to her.

"Keep moving! Head toward the door," Lynn shouts. The three continue to stand in place as if stunned.

"Move!" Lynn shouts again.

She watches as one shakes his head quickly as if coming out of a trance. They dart to the side and begin running once again. Lynn puts them out of her mind as they race past her position.

Looking back down the aisle, she sees the night runner that leapt down crouched over the still form of the sailor. Quickly centering her crosshair on its chest, she squeezes the trigger and feels the familiar light kick against her shoulder as she sends rounds streaking outward. She sees the torn and stained shirt of the night runner puff out as her bullets pass through it to strike flesh and bone. It falls heavily on the body it was feasting on. Behind the now downed night runner, Lynn sees more night runners streaking toward her. She catches the movement of more on the edges of the stacked crates above. She imagines the other aisles would give the same picture. The gathering horde of night runners will soon exit the aisles and leap from the tall stacks. She knows that they'll soon be beset and in for a fight.

"Horace, those doors if you please," Lynn says.

"Working on it," Horace replies.

"Black and Charlie teams, be ready to pull back on my command. Horace, if we have to pull back, head for the open doorway," Lynn says, watching the oncoming night runners quickly closing in.

They emerge from the aisles almost before she knows it. Multiple night runners pour into the open space ahead and jump from the stacked crates forming a waterfall of leaping figures. A horde of shrieks and screams grows exponentially, overwhelming any other sound. The space in front of the two teams fills quickly. The area is lit by quick and continuous strobes of light as the soldiers open fire. The leading night runners fall to the ground adding screams of pain to the clamor. More bound over the fallen.

"Start pulling back in line now," Lynn calls over the radio.

The level of noise echoing inside is deafening. Shell casings bounce on the concrete surface but go unheard. Magazines clatter as the soldiers reload. Mouths open to call "reloading" but the words are lost amidst the thunderous roar of the night runners. Step by step the teams fall back, splitting as they make their way between the vehicles. Even though night runners fall to the ground by the dozens, due to their numbers, they slowly close the gap.

Lynn clicks the mag release dropping yet another empty mag to the ground. Slamming in a fresh mag, she continues to add her fire into the advancing mass of night runners. Another step backward takes her to the rear of one of the trucks. A thin beam lights the area in front of her causing the night runners caught in its path to throw their arms in front of their faces. Those caught in the widening beam fall to the ground writhing in agony. Slowly but surely, the band of light grows. The ones behind and on the sides turn and flee.

The shrieks diminish in volume as the night runners race back into the darkness of the warehouse leaving their dead and dying behind. Daylight pours in lighting the front of the building. The injured night runners, crawling slowly along the floor, scream in pain and slump to the ground. Lynn raises her goggles and, with a look to ensure the attack is over, turns to see Blue Team push the sliding doors the rest of the way open.

Turning back, she shouts, "Anyone left alive, make your way to the doors." Nothing but several shrieks returns her call.

"Okay, let's get the fuck out of here," she yells.

Walking outside, the day looks the same, taking on a surreal aspect. The gray clouds still hover just above the tall roof just as they did when she entered. She feels the intense adrenaline begin to ebb leaving her feeling weary. They've made it through yet another encounter. She sees Jack with the rest of Red Team and Greg with his team standing in front. Huddled together off to the side, she spies the five sailors she saw exit the aisles. Of the twelve who went in, they are the only ones who made it out. With a heavy sigh, she gathers everyone up and begins a slow walk to meet Jack who is standing ready with the rest of the teams to back her up if she needed.

*   *   *   *   *   *

I watch as Lynn and the other teams fold against the outside wall by and open doorway ready to enter. A faint, solitary shriek drifts upward from the building. I think about calling Lynn and having her return, but she's the one there and it's her call. Her core instinct to help others worries me at times. I know her propensity to put herself in danger in order to assist those in need. However, I also know she cares deeply about her soldiers and won't put them in a position that will risk them unnecessarily.

The tension that was so prevalent just moments ago subsides as we all focus on the warehouse, watching the scene about to unfold. Glancing at Captain Leonard, I see his eyes narrowed in concentration. I wonder if he thinks that we are still trying to interfere, or if he believes we are truly trying to help. Perhaps he realizes he made a mistake and is looking to see the outcome. I'm guessing he cares about his people, so it may be he just doesn't realize the danger he sent his people into.

I listen as Lynn briefs the teams and watch as she readies herself and steps inside. I feel anxiety in the pit of my stomach as she disappears knowing full well what possibly waits inside. I'm sure my call telling Lynn that there are night runners inside is going to raise a few eyebrows. I noticed Leonard's quick glance when I made the call. I said that in the clear over an open channel, so everyone is going to run that through their minds. But there's no way I'm going to hold something like that back when it can help. That's Lynn down there. It's all I can do not to run over and be the one to go inside. If it comes up, I suppose I'm going to have to explain that radio call. Perhaps it's time to tell the command group.

The other teams rush through the open door one by one, flowing like a black wave until they vanish into the dark opening. I feel a sinking feeling in the pit of my stomach watching the last of them disappear knowing well the fear and dread of being in a possible night runner lair. I'm thankful for the distribution center in that we can very much limit any further excursions into darkened buildings.

Minutes pass with only the short radio calls from Lynn to the other teams and some calls requesting information on those inside. One comes that grabs my attention. It is one I was rather expecting to hear at some point given that night runners are holed up within the warehouse building.

"Black and Charlie team, hold up. I have something to my front. Standby," I hear Lynn say.

Another minute and then, "I have two night runners and a dead body three meters to my twelve o'clock in front of the truck," Lynn whispers on the radio. "Keep alert for others. Mullins, can you get a shot at them?"

I look to Captain Leonard and say, "If you'll excuse me, I have my people to attend to." He turns his head briefly to nod before gazing back to the warehouse.

I take a few steps and hear from behind me, "Captain Walker, we'd be happy to help if you need?"

Turning, I see one of the SEAL Team members standing slightly off to the side. Captain Leonard turns sharply to the chief but doesn't say anything.

"We can always use the help, Chief…Krandle is it?"

"Yes, sir," Krandle responds.

"Like I said, we can always use the help, but we don't have any spare comm gear or NVGs," I say.

"I understand, sir" Krandle says with a nod.

Leonard looks at the chief with a hard stare before returning his focus back to the large cream structure that his men are currently in… along with our teams. I tell Frank and Bannerman to wait with Leonard and make my way to where Greg is standing with Red and Echo Teams. They are more relaxed but still in their covered positions behind the vehicles and manning the weapons. Greg walks to meet me.

"You've heard the calls?" I ask, to which, he nods.

"I want us to be in a position to support Lynn if they run into trouble," I say.

"Probably wouldn't be a bad idea. Any worries about the boys in white?" Greg asks nodding toward the captain and the sub.

"Not for the time being. I'm not sure their Captain is a big fan of me. I don't think he believes what is going on but I don't think they'll cause any problems. I think he's trying to digest it all just like we had to," I answer.

"That can't be easy."

"No and I'm not sure I have yet."

"That's because you're an old man," Greg says.

"At least I didn't fall out of the ugly tree and get hit by every branch on the way down," I respond.

"Look who's calling who ugly," he replies, leaning over me trying to be intimidating.

"Hey, I'm not the one kids point at and mistake for a sea cow when swimming...just sayin'." Humor is one way we disperse the tension of knowing our teammates have entered a night runner lair.

Lynn's call of, "Night runners on top of the crates," interrupts our little tête-á-tête, prompting action on our part.

"Red Team, Blue Team, form up on me," I shout.

We form up and begin trotting toward the distant warehouse. As we draw closer, my throat tightens and heart rate accelerates hearing a din of shrieks emanating from within. I head toward the open side door when I see the large doors begin to slide open. The sound of shrieks increases through the thin aperture that is growing wider by the second. It's hard to make out who is pushing the doors apart, but I see a full team shoving on the large, heavy doors. The screams within change in tone from rage to screams of pain.

With the doors mostly open, I see Lynn and several of the other team members that entered standing in a line deeper inside the building. Scores of night runners lie scattered on the gray painted concrete floor. Some caught in the light arch in pain before slumping back to the ground. A group of five men huddle together outside off to the side. I observe Lynn lower her weapon and shout something into the interior. She stares into the darkness waiting for something.

Finally, she shouts, "Okay, let's get the fuck out of here!" Turning, she heads in my direction.

As she draws near, I see the weariness of the post-adrenaline phase of combat etched in her eyes. There is of course the bone-deep weariness we all carry from the struggle to survive on a constant basis. It brings a bleached out quality to the eyes that tells of having to endure stress over a long period. It's the look of frontline veterans returning from a combat tour overseas and something I've observed in all of us. I also notice a splash of blood on her cheek which sparks additional concern.

"Yours or someone else's?" I ask, nodding to her cheek as she stops in front of me.

"What?" Lynn tilts her head.

"The extra bit of rouge on your cheek you managed to pick up."

"Oh, someone else's," she says as she reaches to her cheek. She then wipes the spots of blood with her sleeve leaving a light red smear.

"Better?" she asks, finishing.

I look at the streaks and shake my head. "Yeah, um, much better."

"Jack, you're such a horrible liar," Lynn says, making another attempt which only makes it worse. I decide it's in my best interest to not say anything else.

"So, what happened in there?" I ask, nodding toward the bodies covering the warehouse floor. Lynn proceeds to give me the cliff notes version of what happened.

"How was your little chat?" she asks, finishing.

"It was interesting…and is bound to get even more so after this."

I look over at the remaining sailors gathered together and nod for them to start heading back to their captain. They look plenty shaken but they start walking slowly, periodically looking over their shoulders at the building. Lynn directs several team members to head back inside to gather empty mags lying on the floor in the lit area. We then begin walking across the wide, empty lot and up the drive to the piers. Two firefights and it's still morning. Yeah, it's already been a long day, and we still have a long night ahead of us. I'm quite ready to wake up from this nightmare.

"I can't believe he sent his people in after what we told him," Lynn says as we slowly make our way back.

"I'm not sure he understands the situation, but I bet he's ready to listen now," I reply.

"He'd better. That's all I have to say. That was not fun."

"I'm just glad you're okay," I say, putting my arm around her and giving her a quick hug.

I leave Lynn and the other teams by the vehicles and walk down the dock toward where Captain Leonard and the others are still standing. The surviving members of his crew have just left his side and are making their way to the docked sub. I close up to where Bannerman, Frank, Leonard, and Krandle and his team are standing.

"I owe you my thanks, Captain Walker," Leonard says. "My men briefed me on what happened inside. Their story seems a bit far-fetched, and if I hadn't been standing here myself, I wouldn't have believed it. It still seems a little too unreal."

"Believe me, captain, it was a lot for us to swallow in the beginning as well," I reply. "I'm sorry for the people you lost."

Leonard merely nods and turns to Krandle, "I owe you my apologies for doubting you as well, chief."

"I'm not sure I still believe it myself, sir," Krandle responds.

"I'm guessing you're ready to listen now," I say.

"I am, Captain Walker," Leonard replies with a nod.

"Yeah, about that," I say and proceed to tell our story.

Captain Leonard listens as I tell him about the happenings as far as we know; leaving nothing out. He has a nod here and there along with several episodes where he tightens his eyes. I feel like I'm telling a children's horror story as I listen to myself tell of the events of the past few months. It seems unreal to me as I tell it…and I lived it. I notice his lips tighten as I mention I was prior service and wasn't in when it all went down but, to his credit, he doesn't say anything. I mention our compound and our efforts to gather survivors and clear the area of night runners. After seeming to run my mouth for days on end, I finally bring him up to speed on where we stand now. I'm not usually much of a talker, and I totally feel that I've used up my words for the next several months if not a year. I finish by inviting him and his crew to join us.

"I think that's a great idea for us to join up. As far as I can tell, I'm now the base commander here. We can fortify this location and you can bring your people up. We can begin rebuilding here and can certainly use your expertise," Leonard says.

"Oh boy, here we go," I hear Bannerman mutter. I don't think anyone else heard it, but it was fairly clear to me.

"Captain, I know where you're coming from, but there isn't any government anymore. That part of the world is gone," I say.

"Captain Walker, I know you may be a civilian now, but the others with you are still part of the government. We're the government until we meet up with any still operating in an official capacity," Leonard replies.

"Leonard," I say, purposely using his name rather than rank, "there aren't anything but small, scattered groups to 'govern'."

"Then we govern them. I'm the ranking officer at the moment, and we'll just have to keep the government alive in that manner," he says.

"There…isn't…any…government…to keep alive. We have opted to go with a functional command. You know, to have the best chance of survival. What you saw here," I say, sweeping my arm toward the warehouse, "doesn't even come close to what is going on. These night runners are rampant and are as wily a foe as you can ever imagine. There are also bands of marauders about. Now, you are welcome to join us, and of course we'd have you on the leadership team, but we have a harmony within our group that I won't have messed with. Every day here is a fight for survival and we need the cohesiveness that we have in order to survive. I get where you're coming from, truly I do, but right now we need to establish a safe haven and we can move onto other things once we have that."

I notice Krandle give a slight nod at my little speech. I see Leonard's jaws clench and the veins in his head begin to stand out. I'm quite sure he isn't used to being talked to in this manner, but to be honest, that's not my concern. Frankly, I'm tired and this morning hasn't improved my mood much. I understand his position and might act exactly as he is if our positions were reversed. It must be fucking confusing as hell to just walk into this situation. However, my main concern is for the people with us, and I won't sacrifice what we have for anything. It's not that I even remotely think I'm the best for the job and will willingly follow anyone who has more experience. As a matter of fact, I'd welcome it with open arms, but until that happens, this is where we are.

"Walker," yeah, I notice his dropping the rank, "I plan to restock and head down the western seaboard and possibly to Hawaii to see the situation there. Know that this conversation isn't over."

"You can't be planning to go back into the warehouse or any others, are you? You just lost seven out of the twelve men you sent in," I say. I feel bad for even mentioning that, but it's necessary for him to actually understand the inherent danger that buildings present.

"We need to resupply," he responds.

"Walk with me if you will," I say.

"Where are we going?"

"You need to see firsthand what we are facing," I say to which he gives a small nod.

We begin to walk down to the warehouse. I signal Lynn to bring Black and Red Teams with us. Krandle walks behind with his SEAL Team. Standing back from us, but close enough to see into the interior through the now wide open sliding doors. We see dozens of dead night runners lying across the gray floor.

"That, captain, is only some of what your men walked into. Lynn, how many would you say were inside?" I ask.

"That's about a quarter of 'em," she answers. I hear Krandle give a low whistle.

Leonard looks on, turning his head left and right. I can almost hear the gears turning as he sees firsthand what I was talking about.

"And this is in every building?" he finally asks.

"No, not in every one. There is sometimes less, sometimes more, sometimes none at all. It all depends on how they group together and where they lair up. We haven't found a trend as yet. But, yes, this is what we are facing," I answer. "Now…you can gather what you can as long as it's in the light. And I mean daylight," I continue.

"That doesn't give us much," he says, eyeballing perhaps four stacks of goods that are in the daylight pouring in the open doorway. "Perhaps you could provide cover for us if we had to go in farther."

"No fucking way! We're not going back in there. Especially with what just happened. Those aisles are fucking death traps," Lynn speaks up.

Leonard turns sharply to Lynn. "Sergeant, now see…"

"Captain Leonard, we have some supplies. If you'll make out a list of what you need, we'll see what we can send. We'll make a convoy run up here with them," I say, interrupting him and forestalling and argument. "Just give the list to Bannerman here before we leave and we can have it back up here within a couple of days." I look to Bannerman for approval of the timeline and he nods.

"Okay, Walker, that will be fine," Leonard says.

"Call me Jack," I say.

The morning heads towards noon as Leonard consults with his crew and then meets us on the dock giving Bannerman his requested supply list. "We may be able to supply this but will have to make some substitutions," he says after looking it over.

"That will be fine, Major," Leonard replies.

"We can have this to you in three days providing the route is clear," Bannerman says.

"What about if you tied up in Tacoma or Olympia?" That would make it easier, and we wouldn't have to worry about blocked roads or someone ambushing us to take the supplies," Frank says.

"I think we can accommodate that. That is if the docks are clear. And thank you again," Leonard responds.

"I have a question if you don't mind. Well, actually several. Are their fuel rods being stored here?" I ask.

"That's classified information, Jack," Leonard answers.

"Seriously?! I'm pretty sure classified went out with the first waves of the dead. I'd like to know if we are in danger of them melting down," I say.

Leonard mulls it over for a few seconds before replying, "No, there aren't any stored here. There used to be, but they were moved."

"What about the rods in those subs?" I ask, pointing to the two missile boats docked nearby.

"I'm sure they are shut down but, yes, those might be a problem over time," he answers.

"What about scuttling them offshore? We'd use them for a power supply, but we just don't have the expertise if you are planning on your trip down the coast. And if something happened..." I say leaving the question floating.

"That would have to be done far offshore with the prevailing currents and winds, but it could be done," Leonard replies, pondering.

"Do you think you and your crew could do that?" I ask.

"Perhaps, but I'd like to get away as soon as we can. We can discuss that when we return. Amongst other things," Leonard says pointedly.

"I'm so looking forward to that," I say sarcastically, to which Leonard actually smiles. "You know, a thought just occurred. If you are thinking about setting ashore, what are you planning to do if you find survivors?"

"There's not much we can do really. Our space is limited. We can direct them to your location if you'd like," Leonard answers.

"That may do more harm than good with them having to find shelter for the night and with bandits around. They also may not want to depending on the distance, but the more we can gather, the better off we'll be," I say.

"Well, if we find any and make contact, we'll let them know," he replies.

That causes an uneasy feeling as you never know what type of groups he may encounter. We just may find ourselves beset upon by marauders looking to take over our compound. However, increasing our numbers will also increase our knowledge base. We are in dire need of medical personnel and a scientist or two wouldn't hurt. Actually, we are in need of a wide range of experts.

Chief Krandle steps forward and says, "Captain Walker, sir, we'd like to join up with you, but if Captain Leonard is planning to set ashore anywhere, he's going to need us."

"Chief, we'd be more than happy to have you anytime, but I think you're right, Captain Leonard is going to need you," I reply.

"Chief, you are under my command, so you're not at liberty to discuss where you will or will not go," Leonard says, rounding on Krandle.

"Technically, sir, and with all due respect, being under your command ended the moment we stepped onshore. We were under your operational command while onboard, but we are now effectively back under SWC Group One. With that said, sir, we'd like to accompany you and assist under the caveat that we can accept or decline any mission you have for us based on the risk factor," Krandle replies, standing at attention.

Leonard stares hard at the chief for several moments. "That is acceptable. Glad to have you aboard," he finally says.

"One last thing. How do you want to stay in

communication if you are in fact heading down the seaboard?" I ask.

"We could use satellite comms or phones," Leonard suggests.

"I'm not sure about the viability of satellite communications, but we can try the phones. If not, then we can just use the UHF when you draw closer," I say. I look to Bannerman who merely nods. The unspoken dialogue is to whether he can acquire satellite phones.

"Alright. And we'll make our way around the sound and try the ports. We'll let you know where we decide to park," Leonard states.

"Sounds good. We'll see you in a couple of days," I say. Handshakes are made all around.

And with that, we part ways. The teams gather back into the vehicles and, climbing the hill toward the base entrance, the docks and docked sub disappear from sight.

A Secret Revealed

We begin retracing our route back to base with the only caveat that we hold up short of the second road block we encountered on the way in. The scenery and weather remains much the same. The gray skies are low over the treetops and the silver dew drops are heavy on the fir and cedar branches. Close to where we went through the second line of vehicles blockading the road, the Strykers take the lead and we halt.

I switch to the channel we previously had locked that Sam was using. "Sam, this is Captain Walker, how do you read?"

A moment passes in silence. There is just the vibration and rumble of the Humvee. Robert is now in the front seat with McCafferty in the back. Gonzalez is taking her turn on the M-240.

"Sam, I know you're there. Let's not play games again," I say into the radio.

"Go ahead, captain," I hear him finally respond.

"We're coming through again. Are we going to have any trouble this time?" I ask.

"No, Captain Walker, if anything's to be said, it's that we learned our lesson. I'll let the lads know you're coming and to let you pass," Sam replies.

"Any further thoughts about joining us?"

"I don't think we really have much of a choice, do we. We'll be set upon on all sides now if we stay, so, if the offer still stands, I think we might take you up on that," he answers.

"Have your folks gather what they need and whatever supplies you want to bring. We'll meet you at the bridge entrance. Make sure everyone knows to keep their itchy trigger fingers under wraps. I wouldn't want anything bad to happen because of one jittery soul," I say.

"We'll do that. It'll take us while to gather everyone and our things."

"We'll wait. Just don't take too long. See you there."

I radio the conversation to the rest of the teams but warn them to keep alert. With that, we move slowly up the road and park a short distance from the wrecked vehicles still spanning the width of the highway. The bodies have been removed and no one is in sight. We park the Strykers in a triangle pointing outward with the Humvees in the center. I have Lynn call Cabela's to fill them in. With the vehicles idling, we wait.

"I was kind of hoping the SEAL Team would have joined us. It seems we could really use them," Robert says as we wait.

"Yeah, I thought the same thing and was this close to trying to talk them into it," I say, holding my pointer finger a hair's breadth from my thumb. "We really could use their expertise. However, Captain Leonard needs them even more. They are his only combat force with training. They would be a welcome addition, especially seeing the night runners seem to be adapting quickly."

"Ah, sir, we don't need 'em. We have Red Team and we can handle a bunch of sweaty runners," Gonzalez says, poking her head through the opening.

"Please tell me you don't have a 'hooah' coming somewhere," I plead.

"What would ever give you that indication, sir?" she responds.

"Good. I'm glad to hear it," I say.

"Hooah, sir," she says with a wink and disappears back through the open hatch.

An hour passes and the clouds thin in places showing a hint of sun above. Sam finally radios that they are ready and making their way to us. A line of vehicles, trucks, cars, and moving vans, appear from a side road and enter the highway with Sam's pickup in the lead. Sam parks, steps out, and walks over to us.

"I hope there are no hard feelings, captain," he says extending his hand.

"None here and I hope for the same on your end," I say, accepting his shake.

"No. We have one grieving wife that will have to be

cared for. She went into hysterics, but the doc sedated her," he states.

"You have a doctor with you?" I ask.

"More of a family doctor, but yeah," he replies.

"Good to have. We only have medics with us and could certainly use him or her."

"I'm sure he'd be happy to help. So, what would you like for us to do?"

"Just follow along. I'll have some units behind you in case someone breaks down and for protection. We're pretty cramped at the moment, but we'll see you situated once we arrive. How many are with you?" I ask.

"I don't have a firm count, but we have about forty all told," he answers.

I direct one Stryker and Lynn to bring up the rear of our now larger caravan. We set out across the bridges and south toward home. I can't believe it's only early afternoon as it feels like a couple of days have passed. I plan to meet with the group when we return and then settle in for a nap. The day is only partially over. There is a night flight to take, and I want us to be rested for another long night of work. Each step we take brings us closer to an eventual safe haven. If something like that can even exist.

We snake south down I-5 and through the gates. I have McCafferty and Gonzalez exit on our entrance to the parking lots to direct the vehicles following into a farther lot. I pull into the lot where the other Humvees are parked. The Strykers park adjacent. The large maintenance and vehicle storage garage Bannerman had started is near completion and we'll soon park our vehicles under cover. We'll then bring down additional vehicles from Fort Lewis and store them here. Those will be in addition to the ones we now have in the hangars and maintenance buildings up north.

The new group gathers just outside in the chilly, damp weather. With Frank's assistance, Bannerman makes his way to orient them and assign them places. I know I'm going to hear about the overcrowding and barracks at our meeting. And, to be honest, with the new additions, it's time we address it. With the winter and shorter days coming, meaning longer periods crowded indoors, tempers will flare. Bannerman was right to bring this up early on. It just seemed like there was always something else to do. There still is and I don't see how we are going to be able to do this with everything else, but we also have more hands to help. And, we now have a doctor and another pilot. Not that the pilot aspect will be useful for much longer, but we can rig speakers up to a light aircraft and cover more ground in our search for other survivors.

With Sam's group, we are now around two hundred and fifty people. I'm not sure of the exact number on a sub, but if Captain Leonard joins us after his trip, that number could reach four hundred. That's enough to do some serious work in a hurry. I almost wish that Leonard wasn't heading back out. Although it would be nice to have more intelligence on what is going on in other places, he has a crew trained in a variety of useful areas. It will be nice when he returns. Hopefully he will see for himself what is going on and relax some on the rank thing. I once again wish there was someone with qualifications to take over. I'd like to just take a backseat for a while, on the other hand, I also know that isn't in my mentality. No, we push on, build a secure place around us, make it survivable in the long-term, and then I'm grabbing my fishing pole. Yep, with a hammock and a cooler at my side. I sigh at the pleasant thought knowing that's what it is – just a daydream of things that will never be. I close my door and head inside with Robert.

* * * * * *

Captain Raymond Leonard watches as the Strykers and Humvees carrying Captain Walker's troops drive up the paved street and vanish over the ridge. The sounds of the vehicles gradually fade until only the sounds of the lapping waves are heard. He thinks over the interesting morning and conversation. Interesting is putting it mildly. He lost seven crew members today because of his decision. He realizes now that he dove beneath the waves off the Philippine shore and rose to a completely different world, one he would never have imagined possible and doesn't quite understand. The world he once knew and loved being a part of has disappeared to become an alien one. He has a fleeting thought of staying until he understands better what they are facing, but he needs to see it for himself, and not just this little corner. His mind still can't wrap around the idea that this is worldwide.

"Come on, chief, let's get below," he says, turning toward the gangway.

"Aye, aye, sir," Krandle replies, turning with him.

Back on the bridge, Leonard watches as the crew leaves the deck to the stations or quarters below with the exception of those casting the lines off. Backing slowly away from the docks he has docked at for years, he clears the nets and turns the *Santa Fe* into the channel. As they make their way across the gentle waves, he briefs his XO on the events. Leonard knows that the scuttlebutt will be making its rounds among the crew about now.

"Are we going to close the nets, sir?" his XO asks.

"No. There's no real need now," Leonard states, understanding the finality of his statement. With those words, his mind shifts away from the world he was has known.

"Sir, shall we prepare to dive the boat?" The XO asks.

A melancholic feeling settles within Leonard. "No, XO, we'll make the run on the surface. I want to see things with my own eyes and feel the fresh breeze for once. It's not often that we've had the chance to do this and I want to enjoy it."

The sad feeling departs to an extent as he looks over the black hull of his boat making its way into the strait. The pride he has always had with his sub rises as does his love of the sea; his love of all waters. It's in his bones, and he's loved every minute at sea regardless of the situation or mission. He's always run a tight ship and it shows. He's proud of his boat and his crew. They've made it through many sticky situations before and they'll make it through this one. Fresh supplies will be his only problem. Maybe they can keep coming back here and restocking. He's not sure how many supplies Captain Walker and his soldiers have, but they seem confident enough with what they have. He likes the captain, but turning over command, his command, to someone else goes against every fiber he has. *Maybe that will change*, he thinks as the fir-clad shore slides slowly by. *They seem to be able to handle themselves well, even if a little on the cocky side, including that sergeant he had in charge.* He chuckles as he knows that definition applies to him as well.

"I'm going below for a moment to make an announcement. Keep us off the rocks, please," Leonard says to his XO with a grin.

"Aye, aye, sir."

In the control room, Captain Raymond Leonard, commander of the fast attack sub, *Santa Fe*, picks up the mic about to make the strangest announcement of his life. For one of the few times ever, he feels at a loss for words. There's so much to say…yet so little.

"Attention, all hands, this is the captain speaking. I'm sure you have all heard a story or two by now. I would delay this until the stories get really good and run a contest on the best one, but I'm sure the one I'm about to tell you tops them all…

"As you may already know, we lost seven good men today. Men we lived beside, laughed with, and counted on. There will be services held on deck at 15:00. Now, for the rest. At some point during our transit across the pond, the world was stricken by a flu pandemic. The resulting vaccine caused a seventy percent mortality rate worldwide. A further almost thirty percent have met with changes that render them hostile and ferocious. They can apparently only survive at night and live in the leftover darkened buildings. A mere one percent of the population has survived. We have met with a surviving military unit and are traveling to be resupplied. Following that, we will sail down the western seaboard to investigate. I know that many of you will be worried about families, and we will gather information as we can. Right now, we have to stick together as we always have if we are to survive. We are each other's family. I know you will each do your duty as you always have. That is all."

He hangs up the mic knowing that it will be difficult for a lot of them. Most of the crew are young and will have wives, kids, and parents that will weigh on their minds. Some will want to jump ship when they put into ports. He'll have to post lookouts to prevent that and talk with the chaplain. He can't have the crew leaving. If too many in critical positions leave, it will leave him and the others stranded. *We have to prevent that at all costs*, he thinks, climbing back to the bridge. He gives a momentary thought to his own mom and sister so far away in Kansas. He silently sends a prayer aloft for their safety.

* * * * * *

The captain's announcement fades away. Vance Krandle sits with his team in the enlisted mess. They crowd around one table staring at the speaker before glancing at each other. Silence accompanies the end of the speech as each is lost in their own thoughts pondering the implications of what they just heard. CPO Krandle's thoughts go back to that fateful evening seemingly years ago when he watched Gold Team get taken down. He replays the events and remembers the hordes that easily overwhelmed his teammates.

His memory jumps to seeing the dozens of creatures that Captain Walker and his teams call night runners lying in the warehouse. Knowing what they were facing, the sergeant still went into the warehouse to save the sailors inside. That took a lot of guts, and he's not sure he could have done the same. Well, he knows he would have, but he wouldn't have been comfortable with it. He still has nightmares of that night in the Philippines when he and Gold Team were taken by surprise. He also knows that the captain and his people they met only a short while ago have their act together and know what they are doing. He wonders briefly if he made the right choice in staying. There is a very thin line between loyalty and survival.

It's only the camaraderie of fellow soldiers and the desire to help those in need that keeps the fear at bay. It's a desire that lies deep within the core of a person. That very thing is why he and his team are sitting where they are. He knows that the submariners will need them.

"Do you think we should have stayed with that Captain Walker and his crew?" his point man says, breaking the silence.

"You know why we're here and why we're needed. We'll join up with them soon enough," Krandle answers and proceeds to tell the deal he made with Captain Leonard.

"What about our families? Do you think we'll be able to call them or be given time to go see about them?" the point man continues.

"I don't know. I'm sure the captain will let us make the attempt if there's time. And, from what I gather, there isn't any electricity, so that means no calls. But right now, our place is here and we'll continue to look after each other as we always have," he answers. They've always been tight and all nod at the reply.

"So…any clue as to what we'll be doing?" Krandle's XO asks.

"My guess is we'll be reconning ashore wherever the captain decides to investigate," he responds.

"And the ROE (Rules of engagement)?"

"We'll define that as we proceed. It's pretty apparent we don't want to be ashore at night, and there may be civilians to think about. We are not going into darkened buildings if we can at all help it. You saw the warehouse. If we're fired upon, that's an obvious one, but we'll try to make contact first. However, under no circumstances will we endanger the team. If possible, we pull out if engaged," Krandle answers.

"So, we're playing it by ear then?" the XO states.

"Pretty much."

"That sounds super fun," the point man says sarcastically. "I hope we brought plenty of ammo."

"Stow it, Speer. And I'll be talking with the captain to put in a request for ammo and spare parts."

Krandle looks around the table at his team. Speer, his point man and their resident joker, grew up hunting in the Ozarks. He can track with the best of them, but his attitude and seemingly constant sarcasm grate on Vance at times. However, when on a mission, he keeps that at bay and there isn't a better point man in the business. He is at home in the outdoors.

Ortiz runs slack (second position) and the little Puerto Rican is the picture of fury incarnate under fire. Perhaps it has something to do with his growing up in the East LA area. It has taken Krandle a while to bring that aspect of him under control, but he has been able to tame that to an extent. Krandle walks third in line and likes to carry his own radio.

Blanchard, the designated medic is a skinny, quiet, unassuming kid from South Chicago. That quietness is belied by an internal fortitude. He will, without hesitation, venture into the thickest of combat to help a fellow teammate. Blanchard is also the one mostly on the end of Speer's barbs to which he will look up and merely shrug. Speer will sometimes go at great lengths to invoke a reaction from Blanchard but has been unsuccessful to date. Of course, their tightness makes these attempts good-natured without causing a fracture within the group.

His XO, Franklin, walks fifth in line and carries the spare radio. The black petty officer from Atlanta is one sharp tack and will make a fine team leader someday. Well, would have. His actions and speech seem slow and he is often thought of that way. That is until he spins circles around those who make that assumption regarding his logic and thinking.

Bringing up the rear is Miller. A full-blooded Sioux who grew up in South Dakota. He rarely speaks and even then, his replies are only a few words. Krandle is sure there are weeks when Miller's word count never exceeds double digits. But he is a master at covering their back trail. There were times when they had to backtrack and were unable to do so via any signs of their passage. He is that good.

Together, they make one hell of a fine team. They are fortunate to have been able to work together and be a team for some time. They have fused into a single organism, each knowing the other's thoughts and actions; knowing each other's strengths and weaknesses. If anyone can make it through what they are facing, it's them; and Krandle feels fortunate to be a part of them.

Downing the last of the sludge the bubbleheads call coffee, Krandle says, "Okay, ladies, let's see if we can go topside and take a look."

*   *   *   *   *   *

Feeling tired and drained from the busy morning, there's nothing I want more than to drop down and take a nap. However, I pull the command group together in order catch everyone up on today's events. Those who went with on our excursion slump wearily into their chairs. There is a clatter of noise as Sam's group arrives inside and arrangements are made for them. With the new arrivals, it becomes increasingly cramped. Bannerman and Frank arrive and both sit with heavy sighs. I proceed to give an overview of the morning and ask Bannerman to include weapons and ammo in the supplies being readied to deliver to Captain Leonard and his crew.

"We can do that. What would you like sent?" Bannerman asks.

"Radio Leonard and see what he needs. Talk with Krandle and the SEAL Team and see what they'd like," I answer.

"I'll see to it. Now, with the new arrivals—" Bannerman starts.

"Let me guess. We're going to talk quarters," I interrupt.

"Well, it's way past time. There's no way we're going to be able to house everyone in here for the long run," he replies.

"Okay, I agree. We need to develop a secure, permanent place for us all. I think the base housing is still out of the equation with the night runner adaptations, so we need to build something here. Are we going to be able start on those with all that is going on?" I ask.

"That depends. We'll have the inner wall up in about a week or so. We can focus on the guard towers and have them up shortly or we can disperse our activities between the towers and quarters. I think it's important to have the quarters up quick, or we're going to start seeing problems crop up," Bannerman says.

"I agree. We're going to want them finished before winter. At least in my opinion," Drescoll adds.

"It seems it's pretty important to have towers up fairly soon. If what you say is true about the night runners changing, and the fact that they're going to have more hours of night during the winter, we'll want our defenses in place," Robert adds.

"How long until the wall is finished?" Lynn asks.

"About a week or so depending on the weather," Bannerman answers.

"And how long to get the towers in place if we focus on them?" Lynn prods further.

"That may take another week or two. We'll have to let the concrete in the upended storage containers set before we can start on the upper levels," Bannerman replies.

"And the quarters?" Lynn asks.

"Now that will probably take a while. It depends on the design we come up with. I'm thinking we could build them like apartments. Some can support families and others individuals, couples, or roommates," Bannerman responds.

"So, let's talk about the design then," I say.

We spend the next hour discussing a secure design. We come up with building apartment style complexes on top of concrete filled storage containers to have them off the ground. The buildings will have retractable stairs and ramps for their entrance. A hoist and pulley system will be incorporated with a garage-like facility for bringing supplies and heavy objects into each building. Retractable ramps will run between the buildings in case we need to pull back into another building with ramps eventually running to the Cabela's roof. This will be our final redoubt in case the apartments become overrun. Overhangs will surround the bottom of the quarters so the night runners can't scale them from underneath. Steel shutters with firing ports are to be hinged on each of the windows and doors.

"That's going to take some time to put up," Bannerman says after we complete the design phase.

"Like how long?" I ask.

"I couldn't even hazard a guess. A lot of our projects are nearing completion, so we should be able to put a lot of hands to work on it, but as far as how long it will take to complete enough buildings to house everyone, I have no idea," Bannerman replies.

"If you want my opinion, I think the towers have to do with the safety of the group and the quarters are, while not really a nicety, they don't match up with providing for our security," Greg says.

"I couldn't agree more," I say. "Anyone else have different ideas?"

The opinions are mixed among us as we ponder different ramifications of each. We eventually arrive at completing the towers and have some people assigned to begin filling the containers with concrete and laying them in place. I also mention Roger, the pilot who was with Sam and his group, and my thoughts of rigging up loudspeakers to a light engine aircraft to help out with the search for additional survivors in the area. Frank comments that he'll talk with him and incorporate him into the search.

"You know, I have to say that standing at the narrows today gave me an idea about putting a moat around the compound," Frank adds as the conversation subsides.

"A moat? Really? I'm not sure having stagnant water like that is a good idea. That will breed all sorts of bacteria," Lynn says.

"True, we don't have to fill it, but if we dig a ditch, say twenty feet wide and twenty feet deep, it could trap any night runners who try to get close to the walls. We could put a drawbridge at the front entrance and that would seal us away," Frank replies.

"Wouldn't that fill up with water during the winter months?" Drescoll asks.

"We could line it with concrete and put sump pumps to drain it," Robert adds.

"Okay, but I don't think that's a very viable option. I mean, building a ditch like that all of the way around the compound isn't a very plausible solution. That's four miles of ditch you're talking about," Greg comments.

"What about just around the inner walls? We could run the ditch under the existing walls and just encircle the inner compound," Franks says.

"I suppose that might be viable and we could build a drain field and pump the water into it," Bannerman states.

"We have the mine field we've put up. Do you really think that's necessary?" Drescoll asks.

"My thinking is that they could push through and once they make a path through the mine field, then they could reach the walls. The night runners have shown themselves to be relentless regardless of the numbers they lose," Franks says.

"The night runners could come up with a way to build a bridge across it," I comment.

"Really?! Do you think they could do that?" Drescoll asks, incredulously.

"Who knows? They've been pretty innovative in the past. Just look at the hospital. Each of our innovations seems to spur their own. We are, in effect, sponsoring their adaptability by the very nature of trying to keep them out. It's a cycle. We need to stay at least two steps ahead and think of their possible adaptations," I answer.

"Are you saying we don't build something because of what it may spur on the night runner side?" Drescoll asks.

"No. I'm not saying we stop coming up with and adopting solutions, we just need to think ahead to any possible night runner reaction, regardless of how far-fetched it might seem," I reply. "I think our best solution lies with clearing them out."

"Well, that's true and I completely agree with that. So,

what do we do about the ditch?" Drescoll says.

"I don't think we have the resources right now to do that, the towers, and build the quarters," Bannerman chimes in. "I think we need to concentrate on the towers and quarters."

"I agree, but I don't want to completely drop Frank's notion of a moat. I think it's a great idea and not only because of the night runners. If Leonard is truly going to let others he encounters know about our location, we may experience trouble at some point from a large group of marauders. We need to prepare ourselves for that eventuality. And that's regardless of who Leonard meets. I think someone, at some point, is going to find us and decide they'd like our little garden for themselves," I say.

"That's true. I've thought about that myself. We might want to bring more Strykers down," Frank says.

"We're close to being finished with the vehicle storage building and can bring them down and store them when it's complete," Bannerman replies.

We begin to wind down our meeting when Horace speaks up. "Sir, I'm just curious, how did you know there were night runners inside of the warehouse?"

And, there's the bomb! It goes off with little sound but she may as well have tossed a grenade in our midst. I feel my heart beat increase more than it would if I was inside of a night runner-infested building. My initial thought is to scream shrilly and run from the building. My second thought is to suddenly go deaf, but Lynn knows that one. I've tried that one in the past with little success. I was thinking of telling them anyway but the worry of their reaction has kept my lips sealed.

My cheeks puff out as I forcefully blow air through my pursed lips. "I suppose it's time I tell you a story. Grab some popcorn and make yourselves comfortable as I have a bit of one to tell," I answer

I proceed to tell them the changes I seem to have undergone. I can't tell them too much really as I really don't understand it myself. Jaws hit the ground and disbelief crowds everyone's eyes as I spin my tale. The silence within the group is complete as I finish. The sounds of people shuffling and arranging their belongings within the building rise in stark detail but are unheard in our little circle. Telling what happened and the changes that occurred makes it sound like quite the fabrication. I hear myself as the words come reluctantly from my mouth and I don't believe it. I wait for the first burst of laughter or "that's a good one, Jack" but am only met with stares as the thoughts churn inside each head. I worry about their reaction.

"So, wait a minute. First of all, you mean to tell us that the night runners communicate amongst themselves in some sort of telepathic manner? And that you can sense and 'hear' them?" Drescoll asks, breaking the tense silence.

"It appears so," I say.

"Then we can use that," Drescoll states.

"To some degree, however, they can sense and 'hear' me when I open up like that. It's not as great a tool as you might think," I reply.

"But still. You know if night runners are in a building before we go in," he comments.

"It's not as accurate as that. I didn't sense anything in the building when we picked up our chutes but they were in there. For whatever reason, it seems to be a hit or miss kind of thing, and I don't want to rely on it being definitive," I respond.

"Fair enough, but why didn't you tell us this before?" Franks asks.

"Because I don't really understand it myself and wanted to know more about it before bringing it up. Plus, in all honesty, I didn't know what your reaction would be. And I still don't," I answer.

"You have to know we're not going to think ill of you, Jack. We're a team and that goes no matter what. We may not agree on everything, but we still need to operate as a single entity and, honestly, I don't think we'd be here if it wasn't for the experience you bring. That goes for the expertise we all bring. I think I speak for everyone here," Frank states. I look at each to see them nod in agreement.

"Thanks, everyone. I appreciate that and apologize for keeping that from you. It's just strange coming to terms with not only that, but everything around us as well."

"Completely understandable," Drescoll says. "So, I have another question."

"Go ahead," I say with some trepidation.

"You say you can hear better and see in the dark like the night runners. Do you have their strength and agility as well?"

"First, I'm not sure the extent the night runners can hear, see, or smell, so I can't really talk to any comparison. It does seem they are still more advanced in those areas, though. I don't think I could sniff out a single person in a building. So, I'd have to apply that to other areas as well. Why do you ask?"

"Well, I was thinking…if you had the same abilities, we could test them and therefore know what abilities and limitations the night runners have," Drescoll says.

The big "duh" goes off in my head. *How did I not think of something as plain and simple as that before?* However, I've seen what the night runners can do, and I seriously doubt I am able to do what they can do. It is worth looking at, though. I almost wish I had their exact abilities and knew how to use them. Then we could test out our defenses, to see if the walls are the right height and if other defensive measure we take will keep the night runners at bay.

"That's an excellent point and I'll be honest that I never thought of doing that before. We'll keep it in mind in the future, but remember, I don't think anything I have measures up to what the night runners have," I respond.

I look at Robert and Bri who continue to stare at me as if I'd just sprouted wings. I can't say as I blame them, or anyone else's reaction for that matter. I'm sure it was a shock, but I am glad for the understanding. I'll talk with them later about it, but right now, with the meeting breaking up, Robert and I need to get with Frank, plot out the targets for the night, and get some rest.

*   *   *   *   *   *

Night runners streak in through the broken door. The chase has been a long one playing cat and mouse with this particular pack. I've tried to keep the sprints to minimum to lessen the sweating. I know their ability to find me via scent and have used everything at my disposal to keep ahead of them. Pack after pack has found me throughout the night as I try to make my way to a secure shelter. I wrack my mind to figure out why I'm out here at night but I fail to remember why. All I know is that I'm close to being spent and only have a partial mag left in my M-4. If my count is close to being correct, there are only four rounds remaining. After that, the knives at my side are all I have.

I'm spent, and it's all I can do to keep my panting breath from giving me away. Behind what used to be a customer service desk in a store I can't remember, I hide behind the partition peeking out through a narrow gap. Eleven night runners that rushed in only moments before hard on my heels stand only a few scant feet away. They stand with their noses in the air trying to catch a scent. I hear their low growls deep in their throats and smell the strong, acrid odor of their unwashed bodies. My choice of hiding spots is iffy at best and I'm surprised I allowed myself to choose it. My only way out is through the night runners.

I slowly glance to my side and see Lynn hugging the cabinets below the counter. Her wide eyes tell of our situation. Somewhere along the way, she lost her NVGs. She's been relying on me and, when outside, the half-moon to guide her way. I turn gradually back to the milling night runners while fingering the M-4 trigger guard. Four rounds, eleven night runners. Not the greatest of odds. I wish Lynn had a few left but her ammo was spent during our busy night of eluding numerous packs. Close calls and endless running has marked out progress toward shelter. We're close but this looks like it's as close as we're going to get. We might as well be a hundred miles away.

With my heart beating hard in my chest, I'm out of ideas. It's either sit and wait for them to pass hoping they don't detect us, or launch at them. Lynn is in the dark, so it will be up to me. If I do manage to take them out in a quick, surprise attack – and the odds are against that – then the noise will surely bring others. It might gain us time however and allow us to get near our elusive sanctuary. I feel Lynn's hand on my shoulder and she begins to shake me. Gently at first, but with ever increasing strength.

"Jack," she says.

I can't believe she is putting us at risk by moving and talking out loud. I shift to remove her hand and try to silence her.

"Jack."

The night runners turn and shriek.

"Jack, it's time."

I jerk awake and come close head-butting Lynn as I sit bolt upright. My heart is hammering in my chest and I break out in a cold sweat.

"Jesus, Jack, what the fuck?" Lynn says, rocking back to avoid my sudden movement.

"What? Fuck," I say, momentarily confused as to where I am or what's going on.

"Jack. Jack, it's okay," she says, putting a hand on my shoulder. I feel my heart rate begin to decrease as I become aware that I had a nightmare and am sitting safely on my cot in our little cubicle.

"Sorry. Are you okay?" I ask.

"Yeah. The question is, are you?"

"Yeah. Just a fucking nightmare. I'm guessing it's time to get up," I say.

"Well, it is, but do you think you should venture out tonight? Maybe you should rest and give it a go tomorrow night."

"I'm good. It was just a dream and I'd rather not head back there so quickly, thanks." I reply.

"Sometimes I'm not sure which is worse. The nightmare outside or the ones in our head," Lynn says, understanding.

The Rain Cometh

We've all had the nightmares that follow extensive time in combat or nerve-wracking environments. The realness of them seems to sometimes match the reality of the waking world. The intensity of them leaves one feeling more tired than when you went to sleep. With my racing heart calmed to almost normal and the adrenaline fading, I rise, slip on my boots, lean over to give Lynn a kiss, and make my way down to the first floor.

Robert and Craig meet me at one of the wooden tables to go over our plan for the evening's flight. Our main goal is to knock down more of the structures in the area. We'll keep a sharp lookout for any night runners on the prowl. If we find any, we'll break off from clearing the buildings to pursue them. Frank has circled the service stations and libraries. We'll need those resources intact. The one fear I have of leaving those structures standing is that any night runners in the area will certainly use them as lairs so that we can be pretty assured of encountering them when we decide to enter. The service stations are small for the most part and easily cleared. The two major libraries in the area are a different story altogether.

With our maps marked, Robert briefs Red Team and the others assisting with reloading on the operations for the evening. He will be directing the fire control again tonight. We gather our gear and head out to begin the drive north. The breaks in the clouds I noticed earlier have disappeared but the overcast has lifted. We'll have to keep an eye out for that. Although we can operate in any weather and see through the clouds, I do not want to land in bad weather without runway lighting. We can navigate just fine and set our own approaches, but it's the lights that allow us to find the runway with low ceilings. I don't mind shooting an approach to get to a lower altitude, but I don't want to have to fly it down to minimums. It could make for a short evening.

A very light breeze has sprung up which will make the

formation of fog more difficult. If we had the calm winds we experienced earlier in the day, I would most likely call off tonight's flight. As autumn sets in, we'll have more of this type of weather which will limit our ability to fly. The gray is a darker shade as the day begins its wind down toward dusk. We could just take out the buildings during the day and make it easier but I want to catch as many night runners as we can and that means flying at night. It may also give us more information as to where they are located, where they hunt, and possibly the numbers we are facing.

"Are you ready for this?" I ask Robert as we pile our gear in one of the Humvees.

"You're kidding, right?! Of course I am. Not to make light of what we are doing, but I get to direct fire for a howitzer, a 40mm auto-cannon, and a Gatling gun. I wouldn't miss it for anything. You know, it's funny, I expected something much different, but it's not so different than the games we used to play. More complicated, yes, but really not that much different," he answers.

"As long as you keep in mind what we're doing and why," I say.

"Of course. How could I ever forget? Every day reminds me," he states.

"How are you doing, Bri?" I ask as she walks up toting her gear.

"I could use more of a nap but I'm ready," she replies.

I seriously don't think I'll ever get used to seeing my young daughter – who once tumbled on the mats in her cheerleading outfit – in fatigues and toting an M-4 like it belonged. I once again reach out for a sliver of hope that this won't always be the case. I hope they won't have to face this for their entire lives. And, along with that, I hope that their lives are long-lived ones. My hope being that at least they outlive me. No parent should outlive their child. I feel the hole in my heart thinking once more of Nic. Her death seems both so long ago and just yesterday. A sad feeling washes over me. I just want to sit on the pavement and lose myself for a moment. My sweet,

sweet girl…gone…forever.

"Dad, are you okay?" Bri asks.

"Yeah, I'm fine. Let's load up and head north," I respond, shaking loose from memories.

The drive north is like every other one we've taken, driven mostly in silence as we become lost in our own thoughts and contemplate the night ahead. I keep an eye on the overcast watching for any signs of it lowering. The fog can roll in quickly this close to so much water but with the breeze, we should be okay. Driving through the base that once looked and felt like a ghost town, the melancholic feeling that accompanied such trips is absent. It is replaced by an almost feeling of normalcy. I don't know if this is a good sign or bad. It is, however, a suggestion that we are adapting mentally to our situation. Now if we can keep PTSD at bay.

Rolling up to the aircraft, we quickly stow our gear and take our stations. Not too many words are exchanged as we all know what we have to do. Going through the pre-flight checks, I hope the aircraft will remain intact and not develop any mechanical issues. We've put a few hours on it and lack for any maintenance and it's a long way to go to get another one. Although we don't have a long time left for our ability to fly anyway, I don't want to take the time to fetch another one. The Spooky is the ideal weapon for this environment.

We start up without any problems and all systems check out. We taxi to the runway and lift off into the darkening sky. Although the ceiling is high enough for us to shoot an approach and pop out at a reasonable height to find the runway, we will have to venture into the clouds for our runs. This won't hamper our operations in any way though. I'll just head north on occasion and shoot an approach to verify we still have an adequate ceiling height.

I hear Robert running through the systems checks and I set the repeater scope up front to mimic the IR scope. The ground shows up with differing degrees of grays and blacks. Anything white will indicate something quite warm and most likely indicate the small, moving forms of night runners afoot under us. So far, I don't see anything moving, but the sun hasn't yet set below the western rim. It's just the heavy drone of the four engines and the white of the clouds outside streaming by the windows. We have darkened the cockpit so I can only observe the white wisps close by. I have to admit I am happy to be in the cockpit again; the day's events lost for the moment. I set a course for the first of the buildings we chose earlier. We might as well get an early start on our evening's work.

Robert sets our first target and I begin an orbit. He clears the 105mm howitzer to fire. I glance at the repeater scope and watch the targeted building disappear in a flash of light. Smoke and debris rocket up and outward from the impact. Craig X's the target off the map as Robert sets up the next one. The sky outside turns a darker shade of gray and then goes black as night folds upon us. Our evening has begun in earnest.

We begin to circle over another strip mall a couple of miles to the southeast of Cabela's when our repeater screen shows white on the edges. It zooms out and is filled by small white objects filling the streets and scattering in all directions. There are hordes of them, to the point that I can't even begin to guess how many. One moment there was nothing and then enough to turn the screen almost a solid white to the side. I'm taken aback by the vast numbers.

"Robert?" I say over the intercom.

"I see 'em. Engaging," he responds.

I bank and head toward the center of the mass spreading out in all directions. The count on the screen has way passed the hundreds mark and more into the many thousands. I knew the math of how many night runners must be in the area from the CDC statistics and the previous population, but seeing a horde like this fills me with a very deep dread. A hypothetical number in your head and seeing the actual visual representation are two very different things. Looking at the screen zoom in as we head toward the scattering night runners, I wonder how we managed to stay alive this long. We've never encountered packs in these numbers anywhere. I'm guessing they must have gathered together recently and am thankful we didn't venture in a lair of this size. If we managed to get deep inside a building housing this many night runners, it would be over before it started.

Could our leveling the place have caused them to bunch together like this...or is there some other reason? Is this one of the instances where we have triggered an adaptation on their part? These thoughts run through my head as the white mass becomes individual forms and smaller packs as they run farther into the night.

"Are we recording this?" I ask Robert.

"Yeah, Dad, I have the recorders on," he answers.

"Good. Frank is going to want to see this."

Robert sets up on a large pack as we drift over their position. He marks them and I start to orbit. Tracers stream downward into their midst. Their running forms, white on the screen, elongate as they fall to the street. Streaks from ricochets peel off into the night and impact the surrounding buildings. Only a couple make it through the devastation and disappear into a side structure. Robert swiftly locates and marks another target. This is definitely what you would call a target rich environment.

The next pack selected is even larger than the last one and more spread out. Seeing that, Robert opts for the 40mm auto-cannon. I feel the solid thuds of the rounds departing. Flashes appear on the ground in the midst of the fleeing figures and walks through them leaving torn bodies in the wake. The once almost solid white screen clears seemingly in an instant as if a switch were thrown. I cast out for any signal but only receive fuzzy images. I'm guessing it must be the distance although I've been able to 'see' night runners from greater distances at times. I just don't get this and wish I knew more about how to use it. I wonder if that is even possible. It seems to be a hit or miss type of thing. *Is it me or do the night runners experience this as well?* I think watching the white figures on the screen disperse and vanish.

"Did you mark the buildings they vanished into?" I ask Robert as I level the aircraft out.

"I marked a few, but it seems they went into whatever

buildings were the closest," he answers.

"Okay, let's target all of the buildings in the area making sure we keep away from any of the structures Frank marked," I say.

"Way ahead of you," Robert says as he call out and targets one of the buildings nearby.

We begin systematically taking on the surrounding structures with the 105mm. One by one, buildings are turned into rubble. In several instances, we observe night runners emerge from the structures once the first shells hit. We quickly set up the Gatling gun and take them down when we can. In some instances, night runners exit the adjacent buildings we are shelling or even ones farther away. They don't stay in the open long enough for us to engage them directly, but we mark the buildings. I would like to hit their lair, but it was impossible to see which one they emerged from.

Over time, I notice a certain trend, and that is that we are pushing them farther to the southeast and away from our compound; our sanctuary that I feel we are only holding onto by our fingernails. Seeing this many night runners, thousands upon thousands of them, strengthens this feeling that we are barely holding on. However, we continue pushing them out. The more area we can clear, the better I feel about our chances.

We continue to hammer away at the structures in the area where the night runners vanished. They aren't the buildings we designated for the night, but the emergence of the night runners changed any plans we had. A small thought creeps into my tired mind wondering what adaptations the night runners will possible make from this slaughter. We drone through the night, periodically venturing back to McChord to shoot approaches verifying that the weather isn't closing in on us. It wouldn't do to have a night like this only to pile it in on landing. Of course, there is never a good time to pile it in. That will be avoidance number one. Setting up orbit after orbit, we reduce building after building to rubble until we expend our 105mm ammo. We then patrol farther out looking for any night runner packs that are on the prowl. Finding none in the

Olympia area, we head north to scout the areas around the bases. Nothing. It's as if the night runners, which once dominated our screens, disappeared from the night. Overall, I feel good about our night's work as I set up for our approach into McChord and land. After reporting into the compound, we seal up the Spooky and try to grab some shuteye.

* * * * * *

Michael rises with the coming of the night. The lair he found for the packs is serving them well. It is a little cramped with all that have responded to his call but it provides warmth from the chill of the days that seem to be coming with more regularity. The pack has grown so much that he's had to find lairs for some of them in the outlying buildings. Tonight, he will scatter the packs in all directions but with the warning not to venture close to the two-legged lair. He needs to find prime hunting grounds to feed so many. More have joined and it's important they find enough food. He'll stay in communication with them throughout the night in order to ascertain the best places to find food. Some he will send into the surrounding buildings to find the alternate food source he found a while ago. That will hopefully provide during in lean times.

He exits on the tail of the others as they lope off into the night. They crowd the doors as they try to leave all at once, but eventually they all manage to depart. The sound of so many feet pounding on the hard surface rebounds off the surrounding buildings like a roar, eventually fading as they disperse. As the sound dwindles, he sees a flash of light off into the distance that illuminates the buildings, casting them into silhouettes. Immediately following is the sharp crack of an explosion, muted by the distance. He freezes in his tracks. He remembers the same sounds on another night when he felt the loss of several packs and decided to call the remaining ones together.

With a large pack surrounding him on the grounds of the lair, he listens. Before long, he hears a droning in the sky drawing closer. Looking up, he sees the clouds hanging low.

The moisture he felt falling from them several times before is lacking. Perhaps their closeness will allow him to see what it is in the sky that makes such sounds and has decimated their numbers. He's not sure he wants to see it, but if he does, maybe he can find a way to avoid it, or at least understand it better.

The droning increases in volume, but he can't see anything as yet. Becoming nervous, he draws back closer to the lair ready to issue a warning to the packs. Suddenly, from out of the nearby clouds, Michael witnesses a stream of fire erupt and pour down toward the ground. His mind is suddenly filled with the agony from several pack members and they vanish from his thoughts. *It's back,* he thinks and sends a warning for everyone to get out of the streets and into cover. The droning moves off to his right and more streaks of light appear. With them, more of his pack disappears. Off to the side, he sees Sandra running toward him with her large pack in tow. Giving him a glance that he doesn't understand, she runs past him and into the lair. With a last look at the overcast sky still spitting fire toward the ground, he turns and follows her in with those around him entering on his heels.

Without being able to see the streaks from inside, he still feels more packs leave his thoughts. They are being wiped out. Several loud explosions begin which shake the floor he is standing on. He feels the panic of the packs remaining as they lie huddled in various structures. With each ground-shaking boom, more members vanish. He knows that thousands of his kind still live but they are disappearing pack by pack. He thinks of sending them out into the night to flee whatever is above them unleashing this devastation but knows that will be sending them to their death. There is no right answer.

He senses the terror overcome some of the packs and they leave the buildings. They are almost immediately overcome which essentially verifies that the right decision is to stay indoors. Surely they can't destroy every building in the area. They just have to weather the night. They may have to move farther from the two-legged lair as he is certain they are the ones responsible for this. With the decimation of the packs, his fear turns to anger. He will figure out a way to end this. For now, it may mean venturing much farther away and finding a new lair. He hates to abandon this one, but they were set upon almost immediately and he knows there is no way they can sustain this for many nights. It's not only the loss of their numbers, but also the lost evening of finding food. Those that do make it through the night will go hungry. Yes, the answer lies in getting farther away until he figures out a way to take out the two-legged ones. They will pay for this.

He senses Sandra draw close and feels anger and disgust emanating from her. He knows this is, like his own anger, derived from fear. He knows of her protectiveness of her young one, but there is something else lying just below the surface that he can't figure out. No, his trust of her isn't anywhere remotely complete. He needs her and her pack though. He wants them to be part of a larger essence and hopes that trust eventually comes.

"We need to do something about this," Sandra says using the vocal speech.

"I don't want to hear it," he replies, answering in the same vocal communication. The others standing nearby back away, sensing their anger and giving them room. Soon, he and Sandra are standing alone near the exit doors.

"We are being destroyed. We need to attack the two-legged ones," she says, ignoring his reply. They both feel the floor shake as another explosion in the near distance signals the loss of more of their kind.

"Like I said before, we can't fight what we can't see or get into. What we need to do is pull farther back before we lose the pack. We need to find suitable hunting grounds and a lair that is safe. Only then can we regroup and find a way to destroy the two-legged ones," he responds.

"No. We are losing more of the packs and the longer we wait, the more we'll lose. We must find a way in and kill them," she says.

She says this knowing full well that she intends only to capture the female she saw with the one two-legged one. The yearning for him remains strong. She isn't certain why she has this feeling, only that she does. It is enough to override all but her most basic instincts, including the need to protect the young one inside her. Sandra will use the female to lure him close and then capture him. She has no idea what she will do with him but thinks by capturing him, that he will become hers. This urge is so strong she is surprised but vanquishes any questions she has about her feelings or motivations.

"I said no. We must do everything to keep the pack united and preserved. And that will be achieved by getting farther away. We will find a new hunting ground. We are being wiped out here so we must leave soon. Tonight if we can," he says.

Sandra emits a low growl of displeasure. "Yes, we are being killed here and that will continue. That is precisely the reason we need to attack."

Michael rounds on her and emits a low, dangerous growl of his own. With child or not, she is threatening his leadership, and that, he will not tolerate.

"How?" he says calmly and quietly but with and underlying menace. "How do you plan to attack something you can't see and is out of reach? How do you plan to attack something you can't get into? You've seen the high walls. How are you going to get over them without annihilating what remains of us?"

His question is punctuated by another loud explosion. More pack members vanish from the ranks. He hopes that their lair won't be the recipient of whatever is causing those explosions.

Sandra feels at a loss for an answer to his question. She knows there has to be a way in but can't think of one at the moment. Her thought was to launch pack after pack at the wall and hope they could gain entrance by building a wall of bodies to climb over. This 'plan' has invaded her thoughts from time to time, but she doesn't have enough in her own pack to accomplish this. The loss of one of her pack members to that explosion near the walls makes her hesitate as well. Her head had ached all of the next day. Knowing she will eventually find a way in, she grunts in agreement with Michael. *For now*, she thinks. In the meantime, she will wait and watch.

The blasts tearing the night apart eventually cease. Michael is hesitant about going out, wondering if it's a trap and fearful lest the thing in the sky returns. He cautiously steps outside. The droning that was once prevalent in the night sky is gone, leaving only the aftermath of the hours of explosions ringing in his ears. Many have survived the night, more than he had hoped. Many more. But many died this night as well. They must move while they have the chance. He waits for several moments before issuing the call for the survivors to gather.

As the packs lope through the night returning to the lair, the thought occurs to Michael that they could gather more food than they are able to eat on certain nights and store it for the times when they have to hole up. That way, they won't go hungry if they are unable to hunt for some reason. He knows that the prey they chase down spoils easily, so maybe he could send packs out to gather some of the alternate food to store at the lair. Yes, he will see to that on subsequent nights. Tonight, they will journey farther away and find another lair. They will be hungry, but tomorrow night, they will be out on the hunt again.

* * * * * *

Alan wakes and finds himself standing on the first floor of the compound that took him in a while ago. For a moment, he is confused and not sure how he arrived here. This isn't the first time he's suddenly found himself away from his small cubicle in the middle of the night. Many other nights have been ones full of nightmares in which he wakes drenched in sweat and wondering where the strange visions came from. His dreams have been filled with images of running endlessly through the night and ghastly moments of tearing into the bloody bowels of living people. His terror-filled nightmares end with him suddenly bolting upright and shivering uncontrollably. His blankets are crumpled and lying on the floor, his pillow soaked from night sweats.

Other nights have ended just like this one, waking in some part of the building confused and disoriented. In a way, this is better. He isn't stuck with the sickening images. On nights like this one, he has the distinct impression he was on his way out and doesn't know why, only that there is that definite pull to do so. That is the one thing that fills him with dread. *What if I didn't wake?* Well, the walls actually protect the immediate grounds, so he would be safe but *why the hell does he feel the desire to be out?*

With the disoriented feeling fading, he makes his way back toward the escalator and his cot. The people here have treated him well since finding him outside of the gates. The memory of that day resurfaces and he relives those terror-filled moments when fleeing from those shrieking creatures in that dark building. The others here filled him in on the changes in the world. Those still seem like a fairy tale story, but waking in that dark room with the overpowering, musky odor of sweat and unwashed bodies lying next to him…his inability to see clearly but fleeing from those pounding footsteps and ungodly shrieks…launching into the daylight only to find himself alone. Night runners the ones here call them. And they tell him that they believe he might have been one of them. That's the part that seems so far-fetched.

Waking the few times downstairs, like he did tonight, reminds him of waking in that room. For the first few seconds when he does, he thinks he's back in that place. Fear fills him and he feels that he must flee. He hopes time eases his dreams and he finds a time when he doesn't wake in a different place. Lying back on his cot, he hopes the dreams don't return and that he can actually get some sleep. The one thing more frightening than the images of his dreams is that, on waking, he has the sensation that he actually enjoyed the experience within his dreams; he hates the thrill he remembers feeling.

Cressman watches as Alan returns upstairs. It's not uncommon for some people to become restless and stroll through the building during the night. She's noticed Alan walking around quite a few of the nights she's been on watch. Thinking nothing of it, she returns to watching the entrances.

* * * * * *

The dark outside gradually lightens with the coming day. We only managed a few hours of sleep, but for one of the first times out at night and sheltering in a 130, we aren't bombarded by shrieks and slams against the fuselage from night runners. It was almost scary with its silence. Seeing the thousands of night runners show up on our screens and the suddenness of it makes me believe they are gathering in greater numbers. *I guess that's a natural evolution. I mean, we are doing it*, I think, watching from the cockpit as the overcast morning gradually lightens.

I'm still awed by the sheer number of night runners in the area. *If they weren't the only packs out, how many of the fuckers are there?* I'm just thankful we were able to get the walls up in short order and our defenses in place. That many night runners could have gone through us like butter if we hadn't prepared quickly. I'm also thankful they didn't gather in a horde like they are now. It would have been over in a short period of time if they had. Even if we had been holed up in the 130, their relentless attacks would have eventually torn through. I'm also fucking thankful they can only come out at night. Again, humankind would have fallen within the first day if they were able to be out any time like us.

The coming of the day reminds me that we've made it through another one. We've managed to keep one step ahead for yet another turn of the world. And last night, we managed to hit them and hit them hard. At least in our immediate area. Their numbers here make me wonder what it is like in the bigger cities. I can't imagine the size of gatherings, say, in the Seattle area. Seeing the gathering like the one last night makes me feel that the odds of finding any other surviving souls are drastically low. Yet, we continue to find them in the oddest of places.

A fearful thought occurs, *What if there is a vast gathering of all of the night runners across the entire area. What if the night runners in the Seattle, Tacoma, and Olympia area gather together in one huge pack?* The thought causes a deep shiver of fear. There's no way we could combat such a horde as that. While we might have the ammo stocked at Fort Lewis, we wouldn't get a chance to expend anything close to enough before being overrun. I'll bring that idea up when we meet next. We may need to develop other ideas to combat it.

With the day light enough to venture outside safely, we make our way to the vehicles. We'll resupply the Spooky and ready it for another night of work before we travel back south. Driving over and maneuvering the heavy shells from the armory into the back of a supply truck, we manage to restock the AC-130. I pull the tapes and close up the aircraft feeling the tiredness of the long day yesterday and the flight last night. What we saw raises many questions, but it was also encouraging to see that we were able to push the night runners farther away. It also felt good to be able to take the fight to them. Perhaps if we can keep that up, we can keep them off balance gaining us more time to fortify. I even think about just taking the Spooky aloft and observing their behavior over a few nights. Any intelligence we can gather will only aid us.

The exuberance we had on the first night out is replaced by one of weariness as we drive south back to Cabela's. I see that same tired look in Robert's eyes as he rides along beside me, but there is also a presence of a certain light. Pride…confidence…the sense of accomplishment, they all shine through. I also noticed the ease with which Bri carried herself. It's as if she was born to be in that seat. And her confidence with her training and experiences has shown itself as well. Glancing into the back, I see she is leaning her head against the door with her eyes closed – fast asleep. I hate this world that I have to bring them up in, but I couldn't be more proud of them. This is a very dangerous environment we find ourselves in but they have adapted well. Again, I hope we find a measure of peace before the constant stress begins to show itself outwardly. We can't afford to make big mistakes. I can't afford to make mistakes.

Nearing the off ramp that will take us to Cabela's, I wave at several semis with their accompanying escorts heading in the opposite direction. I'm guessing they are on their way to the distribution center to pick up supplies for Captain Leonard and his crew. The feeling of a nap grows stronger as we draw closer. There is still the debriefing for our flight and then meeting with the group to talk over the night's events, but then it's oblivion for me.

I pull in and park seeing people in the training phases on the firing ranges. It won't be long until we have another group graduating. Then, depending on what Lynn sees, we may be able to increase our team numbers. With the view of the massed night runners last night, we could definitely use as many as we can get. I climb out of the driver's seat with my bones feeling like they are made mostly of Jell-O. My flight suit smells as bad as I feel. I think that is the only thing keeping me awake right now. Kind of like carrying my own smelling salts. Lynn walks over from one of the training groups and greets me with a hug.

"I love you, Jack, but you're making my eyes water," she says into my ear.

"Awww…that happy to see me, eh?" I reply.

"Well, I am, but I guarantee that flight suit of yours is going to run away screaming when you take it off. I take that back, it's already screaming and it will only run away."

"It's my new anti-personnel device," I say, chuckling.

"Congratulations. It's working. Now go shower and I'll meet you inside shortly. I'm guessing you want to get the group together to meet," she says, pulling away with a kiss.

"Yeah. It was an interesting night, and I want to get everyone's take on it before I slip into a coma. See ya in a few," I reply.

Lynn nods and trots back to the training group. With Robert on one side of me and Bri on the other, we head inside. I've seen it a hundred times and thought about it as many, but seeing them walk along with M-4s over their shoulders like it was nothing out of the ordinary still seems surreal to me. In a world filled with the bizarre, it just strikes me as odd and is just a sign of the times we now live in.

Craig and the others of the flight follow in with their gear and we meet up by the table we briefed at the evening prior. Frank joins us as we lay our marked maps out on the table. He has been taking notes from our markings to add to the master map he has in the back of the operations room.

"First of all, I want to say nicely done to everyone. Robert, good job picking up and changing targets on the fly. It can be overwhelming when targets come up suddenly like that and in such numbers. Nice job sorting it out and picking out one group at a time. And noting the buildings they ran into. I can't say enough about the job everyone did tonight," I say.

I watch as the confidence I saw in Robert solidifies. There's a definite light shining through and he has picked up the mantle of leadership well. Yes, there is more to learn but I notice that a definite foundation has been built. I'm happy to see it as who knows just how long I have here. I want to make sure both Robert and Bri have the skills it takes to survive in this world we find ourselves trapped in. I feel more secure seeing those roots take hold and grow.

"So, with that said, what can we do better?" I ask. Silence among the group ensues. It's the usual response to question like that.

"How were our reload times?" I ask, trying to prompt a discussion.

"I thought they were fine. We didn't lose any targets because of it," Robert replies.

"Okay, true. Any difficulties designating targets and getting the guns to bear? How was the lead on the moving targets?" I ask further.

"I thought we coordinated well and it seemed our first rounds hit where we wanted," McCafferty chimes in.

"Dad, what about hitting multiple targets? I've been looking over the systems and we can designate and fire on two separate targets at once. At least if they are in close proximity.

We could've hit more of the packs when they were in the open if we did that," Robert says.

"Do you think we're ready for that?" I ask in return.

"I think we can do it. And we could have accounted for more night runners if we had that going tonight," he answers.

"You know that if we fuck it up, then we stand the chance of missing the lot of them as we come back around," I say.

"I know, but I think we can do it," he replies.

"Okay, you take the fire control crew and run through the systems. Take them through dry runs after we get some sleep. If we decide to head out again tonight, we'll leave early and practice on the range," I say.

"Okay, Dad."

"Anything else?" I ask.

No one replies and we separate, some heading to the showers and others drifting upstairs for a bite to eat. Before leaving the table, I wrap my arm around Bri's shoulder. "I just want to say very nice job tonight. You handle those systems like you were born for it. I'm very proud of you." She looks up and gives me a smile of appreciation.

"Thanks, Dad. It's not that hard and I love flying with you," she says.

Her smile warms my heart. I head off to the showers to try and remove some of the stink I'm carrying around with me. It suddenly dawns on me that the reason everyone didn't talk during the debriefing is because they wanted to get away from my proximity as soon as they could. I can't say as I blame them much as I'm trying to get away from me just as quick as possible.

The hot water flowing over me not only cleans the grime off but I also feel some of the stress that formed over the past couple of days flow down the drain. I still feel tired but lighter and more refreshed. Finishing, I dress and head upstairs to catch a bite before meeting with the group. I'm then finding my cot and fading off for a year-long sleep.

Sitting with Robert, Bri, and the rest of Red Team, I listen as they tell various war stories; both recent and past. Although the kitchen crew manages to make quite tasty meals, I barely notice as thoughts race through my head. The thoughts are very scattered with none sticking around for very long before being replaced by another. I glance toward the front door and the daylight pouring in through the entrance windows.

I notice, in an abstract manner, the periphery close in. The gray light filtering in seems to zoom into focus, and I feel myself rush forward into the light as if speeding through a tunnel. The light vanishes.

"Jack...Jack...come back, Jack," I hear Lynn say as if from a distance.

I feel the reverse of what drew me into my reverie; rushing backward through a tunnel. My surroundings slowly resolve and clarity returns. I shake my head clearing the reverie.

"Welcome back," Lynn says.

"Wow! That was bizarre," I say, looking down to the half-eaten sandwich sitting in my hand.

"What?" Lynn asks.

"Oh, nothing," I reply. "Are we ready?"

"Yeah, everyone is gathered," she answers.

(For the story and world where Jack ventured to during this dream-like state, look for the collaboration novella with Mark Tufo, "A Shrouded World", where Jack meets Michael Talbot.)

Plodding over to our meeting area, I have Frank bring up a monitor and tape player. I put in the tapes we recorded last night and show them the sudden appearance of the night runners.

"Holy shit!" Drescoll exclaims as the screen turns white in almost the blink of an eye. "There must be thousands of them."

I look at the rest of our group with their jaws hanging open at the sight. Frank asks for a rewind and plays it in slow motion, watching their emergence. He begins taking notes. Several smiles paint the faces of the group as the tape plays forward to our engagements. The flashes and prone bodies are portrayed on the screen in stark detail. I feel a moment of sorrow as these were once humans and, at least on the screen, they don't look any different. An image of Nic flashes through my head and the sorrow is short-lived. As I said to Bri seemingly so long ago, we can never feel sorrow for these creatures. They are as dangerous a foe as humankind has ever faced. The tape finishes.

"So, it appears the night runners have gathered into much larger packs," Frank says. "If I were to hazard a guess, those we saw on the screen would pretty much represent the entire number of night runners in the area."

"Do you really think so?" I ask.

"Well, I want to take a closer look today to get an exact count, but with the percentages we have from the CDC and knowing the previous population, I would say it's close to the amount we'd expect. I mean, there have been losses, but from what I saw, I would say they have all gathered together. I can give a better answer after I look it over."

"Okay, let's look at it another way. How many survivors do you think there really are? Forgive the pun, but what's your frank assessment?" I ask.

"Like I've never heard that one before. Well, again taking the percentages into account against the presumed losses, I would venture there is less than one-half of one percent left. I have been trying to come up with a trend regarding locations for the survivors, but if there is one, I haven't found it. My best guess, based on the factors of night runner gatherings, is most are in rural areas, but we've found survivors in the urban districts as well. It may be that we have primarily conducted our searches there. We may want to extend our searches into the rural areas but my feeling is that, seeing the ones in the rural regions will most likely survive longer, we should still concentrate our searches to the urban areas," he replies.

"What about with the large gathering?" I continue my query.

"Well, if they are gathering in hordes like that, I would put the chances of other survivors where they are at close to nil.

Those left alive will be found and, with those numbers, will be quickly overrun," Frank replies.

"And the chances of similar gatherings like those we saw last night?"

"If it's happening here, then I would say we'd have to expect it elsewhere. It seems to be in their nature to gather. With what we've witnessed in our outings, it seems that the night runners gather around a leader. We don't know how that is chosen. It could be strength, intelligence, or some other factor. If they have gathered together in that large of a pack, then I would guess it would have to be around a very strong leader," Frank responds.

I think back to the strong ones I felt across a distance a while ago. What he says makes sense. The stronger the leader in the area, the larger the gathering. A thought occurs that if we could locate and take out the leader, then perhaps the pack will scatter. That may not be a good thing though. It may be easier if they gather in one place. Locate that place and we could either attack it in strength from afar or know that the other areas were clear. Of course, if we did take out the pack leader, it may be that another would just step in. We know so little.

"Let's take it a step farther. What if the night runners we saw last night gathered with the greater numbers in Tacoma and Seattle?" I ask.

I seem to be full of questions but I want everyone's thoughts. The thought of encountering such a vast number of night runners worries me to no end. And worry is putting it mildly. It scares me to death. What I saw last night is scary enough. I can't imagine a horde numbering in the hundreds of thousands. My questions cause silence among us as we ponder the ramifications. We all saw the video and imagine a gathering of ten times that number.

Frank rubs his chin lost in thought. "I don't see that happening to be honest, Jack," he eventually says. "From what we've seen of the packs before our cameras were destroyed, the night runners seem to be driven by their need to hunt and by the prey nearby. A much larger gathering wouldn't be able to feed itself. And despite the size of a given area, the hunting grounds will still only support a certain number of predators depending on the food source available. If they gather in greater numbers, the vicinity will become devoid of prey in a short time. They couldn't sustain themselves. Now, while they may be able to migrate, they are limited in that ability by their only being able to be out at night. I really don't see them gathering beyond what we see on the tape, and I'm not sure if a pack that size can sustain itself for very long here. It may be that they can, but if that's so, it certainly won't be able to support many more."

What he says is true and makes me feel a little better. "So, the number of night runners we may encounter in a certain area will be determined by the number of prey and by the previous population?" Lynn says.

"That's my feeling," Frank states.

"It's my feeling that we are pushing them back by searching them out at night and by demolishing any buildings that would house them. We definitely saw them being pushed farther to the southeast last night. I feel the need to keep this up, but our time is limited. It's only a matter of time before the jet fuel becomes too contaminated to use and we have to prioritize what we want to do with that time. We are achieving results here, but we also made a promise to the soldiers to look for their families. Which priority do we take?" I ask.

"I think we focus on our attacks in the local area," Horace says. "I think the morale factor will be improved by knowing we are taking action and securing the local neighborhood."

"I disagree. While I'm in complete agreement with the fact that we are achieving results here, we owe it to the others to do what we said and search for their families. You mentioned morale and I feel that we will be better served by showing we care. And, as you mentioned, Jack, we made a promise," Drescoll states.

The debate continues with valid points on both sides. I feel we are pushing the night runners out of the area but feel conflicted regarding continuing our attacks versus searching for the families. Yes, we did promise, and holding the faith of others is important, but where does that promise lie when the safety of others may be in jeopardy. Seeing the vast numbers of night runners last night eroded some of the security I felt we were building.

I mention that we have enough ammo for the 105mm stored at Fort Lewis for leveling the local area but not enough for places like Seattle and the surrounding areas. We don't have to rely solely on the Spooky as we can use C-4 and maybe learn to use the heavy calibers of the tanks, but the AC-130 certainly makes shorter work of it.

We eventually arrive at agreement to continue to use the AC-130 during the night until Captain Leonard arrives. We'll then evaluate our progress and priorities at that point. The consensus seems to be to attack for the next couple of nights and then determine our route in the search for families. We all know that time is of the essence and that every day we delay lessens their chance of survival, but our survival here ranks highest on our priority list. Once we have a certain measure of security, we can then head out in our search. Weather will be a contributing factor for heading out across the distances.

I also mention not finding any night runners in the areas we have already demolished and the absence of them around the Fort Lewis and McChord areas.

"That means the hospital will be clear, right?" Drescoll asks. "We could use some of the equipment inside, especially as we have a doctor on board now."

"I suppose so, but just because we didn't pick any up on the screen doesn't mean they aren't there," I reply.

"Can you sense them if we get close?" he asks.

"I can try, but as I mentioned earlier, it doesn't really seem to work that way. It's more of a hit or miss type of thing. I couldn't sense much of anything below us tonight and there were a shit ton of them. Of course, the distance may have been a factor, but I'm not going to rely on it being an accurate indication."

We talk over a few other items and then break for the

day. I head off to find my pillow as my eyes are closing on their own. Nodding to Robert and Bri as they trudge toward to their wooden cubicles, I draw the curtains back and barely make it to my cot before collapsing.

Waking early in the afternoon from a deep, restful sleep, I grab a bite and trudge downstairs to the table. Frank meets me and we go over the map, marking buildings. I notice he has selected several in the area we visited last night.

"I looked at the tape a few times and marked some of the larger buildings that remain where the night runners ran into last night. The big one here," he says, pointing to a coliseum of Saint Martin's College, "is where a majority of them emerged from. I would target it first and before dark. If they are still in there, we could get a number of them while they are still inside."

"Okay, we'll concentrate in that area. Good job," I reply, running my finger along the buildings he's marked. With his hand covering a wide yawn, Robert joins us.

"Careful," I say, "you'll unhinge your jaw."

"It feels like it," Robert responds, breaking into another yawn which, of course, becomes contagious.

"Other large groups emerged from these buildings," Frank says, pointing out other campus buildings, to which Robert and I nod.

"Now here's the part that you may not like," Frank continues. "I couldn't get an accurate count, but by my estimate, the numbers we saw last night were over ten thousand and could be as many as fifteen thousand."

I know we saw a lot on the screen, so many that the screen literally turned white, but I had no idea there were that many. I am stunned into silence. Again, the theoretical number that must be out there that we can summon up in our head isn't like physically seeing that many. It's like when I'd see something on the news that mentioned a billion dollars. It's easy to conceptualize because it's something imaginary, but trying to actually visualize a billion of something is mighty hard to do.

Frank looks at Robert and me staring at the maps with

our jaws scraping the ground. "If we take the estimates we found from CDC reports and combine that with the area population, that puts the total number of night runners in the area somewhere around sixty thousand. If we take an attrition percentage from starvation, combat, and other factors, and I don't even know what number to use, but let's use a fifty percent attrition factor, then that leaves thirty thousand remaining in the local area. That means those we saw last night only represent half...or less...of those left."

"I can't imagine what the larger areas like Seattle would be like," Robert comments.

"What will be interesting is to see whether a pack of this size can stay together considering the food they'll need. My guess is that they'll have to migrate to some extent or cover a wide area," Frank says.

"What about the other fifteen or so thousand in the area? Where do you think they'll be located and do you think they'll eventually join up with those we saw last night? As far as that goes, do you think they've established other large groups?" I ask.

"I'm not sure to be honest. I'm guessing there were a few that migrated outward into the countryside. I imagine those will be in smaller groups just because there aren't that many places to house larger packs. And, I have no idea whether they'll join up or if there are other large groups. For the most part, up until now, we've only observed small packs of five to seven and larger groups of up to twenty or so. We don't have any information on how they group or why, but it does seem they have the tendency to congregate," Frank answers. "Like I mentioned, they may group together based on prey or leadership. We'll just have to watch and see."

The others on the flight crew begin to arrive singly or in small groups. I brief the overall flight for our practice runs up at Fort Lewis and for the night. Robert briefs the systems and changes for selecting and firing on two targets simultaneously. That will be utilizing both the 40mm auto-cannon and Gatling gun in unison. The 105mm howitzer will be used for single targets, those being the buildings. With everyone hovering around the large map with the buildings for the night marked, I point out the targets mentioning Frank's briefing about where the night runners emerged from and his estimate of numbers.

"We're going to conduct practice runs this afternoon over the ranges, land to refuel and rearm, and then we're taking off again during daylight to destroy the campus buildings in the hopes of catching those night runners we witnessed last night inside," I say. Smiles light up around the table thinking of being able to catch that many night runners indoors.

"We'll then patrol the rest of the evening looking for night runners on the prowl and taking out the remainder of the marked buildings. The weather looks better than last night, but we'll be keeping an eye on it. Be ready as night falls to engage any night runners emerging. Any questions?" I ask. There aren't any so we gather our gear and fold into the vehicles the same as last night.

Taking off, we circle one of the large Fort Lewis ranges. It takes a while to get the coordination for multiple target selection and firing. After quite a few runs, the crews are able to put their rounds on the selected targets. It's not as good as when we run the single targets but our rounds eventually impact close to the ones selected. I'm not too sure about using this as our first option, but if the night runners emerge like they did last night, then close is good enough. Our 40mm and 20mm rounds will decimate their ranks. I'm eager to see the devastation we'll bring upon the night runners. This time, we'll be ready for their emergence. They kind of took us by surprise last night and, although Robert reacted quickly, we could have taken out a far greater number. Their numbers worry me, okay, they scare the shit out of me, and I'm all for reducing those. Zero would be good number.

We land to rearm and refuel. The cloud cover has broken, letting the sun shine through in intervals. If it clears and the winds calm down, there is a chance of fog forming so we'll have to watch for that. It will be easier given that we'll be able to fly under the weather and have a clear visual of the region. Feeling the sun warm my shoulders as it casts its rays through a break in the clouds, I hook up the fuel lines from the truck Robert drove over. We stand next to each other as the volatile fuel runs through the thick, rubber hoses and into the selected tanks. The high-revving truck is loud, but we manage to shout about the noise.

"Are you sure about running multiple targets tonight?" I ask, shouting above the truck noise.

"Yeah, I think we have it down," he answers.

"You know we can't afford to lose any time or be off target if they emerge suddenly like last night," I say.

"Dad, we've got it. It took us a while to work the coordination, but we can do it," he replies.

"Okay. Just don't forget the leads."

"No worries, Dad, we'll handle it and bring the rain down on their heads," Robert says with a smile.

I shake my head remembering my own youth and enthusiasm; it's hard to hide a smile hearing it from my own son. There was a time when I used to use those same words. The others return with a fresh load of ammo just as we are reeling up the last of the hose. Bri walks out from the rear of the aircraft readjusting the M-4 on her shoulder, a weapon she has used several times.

"The gauges all show fuel although the right wing outer fuel gauge stuck for a moment. I tapped it and it ran up to full," she says as Robert drives the fuel truck over by the base operations building.

"Keep an eye on it. It may stick on the way down as well," I say, thinking we may have to switch the gauge out with one from the HC-130 parked next to us.

The specific fuel tank and gauge are the same between the aircraft so it should be an easy change out. It is, however, a reminder that everything will eventually fail and that the fuel becoming unusable may not be the only limiting factor on our ability to fly.

"I will, Dad," she replies.

Loaded up again, we climb into our positions and take

A NEW WORLD: DISSENSION

off into the afternoon sky. It's going to be another long night but at least we'll have some action to keep us occupied rather than just boring holes through the sky. I feel a heightened degree of anticipation knowing we are about to hammer a large night runner lair. I'm also looking forward to the start of the night when we may have the chance to 'bring the rain' with the emergence of the night runners. With the hope of a seeing a large number of them again, I turn the Spooky south listening to Robert and the crew run through their checks and bring the systems online.

We set up and orbit around the Saint Martin's campus. It's daylight with the clouds breaking farther apart. The late afternoon sky drifts through the windshield as we circle. I glance down at the large arena that Frank indicated housed a majority of the night runner horde we saw. The light of day will allow me to watch the awe-inspiring sight of the 105mm rounds impacting.

Robert sets up the target and clears the gunner to fire. Making sure to keep a stable platform for the crews in back, I look down just in time to witness the impact. With a yellow and orange flash, the first round collides against one side of the structure. The point of impact disappears in a cloud of smoke and dust that rockets upward quickly. Brick and large chunks of the building are hurtled outward into the surrounding parking lot. As we circle, gaining a different vantage point, I see a portion of the building has collapsed into a pile of debris. Robert waits for the call that the weapon is reloaded and clear before issuing the command to fire once again.

The picture is repeated until nothing is left of the facility except a smoking pile of debris. Small and large chunks of the building are scattered over a vast area of the parking lots. We move onto the other campus buildings leaving the area around the library intact.

"Any sign of bodies?" I ask, watching the devastation below.

The repeater scope I have dialed in zooms for a closer look at the rubble. I can only glance down at it in intervals, but I don't see anything that resembles a body or parts of bodies amongst the wreckage.

"I don't see any from here," Robert reports after a moment.

"Alright. Keep an eye out, but let's move on," I say.

The sun moves on toward the western horizon turning from a yellow to an orange ball sitting just above the silhouette of the Olympic Mountains. The waves of the South Sound sparkle as the rays bounce off their crests. The campus below lies in smoldering ruins. I radio the base notifying Frank of our progress and for him to have a team prepared to recon the campus below us tomorrow to search for bodies. Although we don't see any through our cameras, we need the intelligence to see how successful we are. Frank will need that info to update his intel on the remaining night runners in the area. I cast my thoughts outward and 'see' nothing. It's blank without even a hint of a night runner about. I wish I understood this 'ability' better.

We drone on, taking out some of the marked buildings as the sun sinks lower behind the mountains. My eagerness to catch the emerging night runners increases with each inch the sun lowers. It vanishes with a bright orange band of light spreading behind the hills, highlighting the underside of the remaining clouds. I tell Robert and the crew to be ready. The guns are loaded and wait for the order to rain death below. The cameras zoom out ready to catch the appearance of the packs. Seeing we may have taken down a central lair, the remaining packs could materialize from anywhere. The orange sunset changes to purple and then darkness dominates the landscape.

I can almost feel everyone holding their breath expecting the screens to light up like last night. The silence within the aircraft matches the quiet that seems to emanate from the ground. It's as if the world is having a final silent moment waiting for two forces to collide. The sunset fades into darkness yet the screens remain empty. There is no sign of any night runners escaping their lairs to run into the night. I cast outward once again and feel the same emptiness. We've either annihilated the night runners in their vast lair or they've moved somewhere else. Or it may be something altogether different.

"Okay folks, let's press on to the other buildings. Stay alert for any night runners on the prowl. Be ready, but it's apparent we aren't getting the show we had last night," I say over the radio. I listen as Robert sets up the next target and I contact Frank with the news.

The remainder of the evening is clearing building after building. We don't see a single night runner all night and I don't know whether I should feel worried or relieved. Depleting our 105mm rounds, I head over the base area searching for any night runners out hunting, but we come up empty. To all intents and purposes, the area seems to be clear. I know that can't be true given the numbers that Frank said must still be around. I open myself and push outward in the hopes of feeling something, even lowering our altitude in case the distance is a factor. I don't sense anything all night. We land and shut down a little after midnight, sealing the aircraft up and stretch out where we can in order to catch some sleep.

* * * * * *

Michael rises feeling the others of the pack begin to stir with the coming of the night. They lost a lot of the pack the night prior, but a greater majority of them survived the exploding buildings and that which hunted them from above. He ran the packs far away from the devastation and found a series of buildings which would suffice for their lair. He had to split the pack into different buildings but they were roomy and will provide warmth and shelter. He feels their current location will place them far enough away from the two-legged ones to provide an increased margin of safety.

Running far through the night in their escape, he felt their fear and hunger. Tonight, they will set out on the hunt and search for food. Some he will send to find new hunting grounds. Others he will have search for the alternate foods prevalent in many of the abandoned two-legged places. He will have those supplies brought back to stock the lair if they encounter lean times. They will also have food if they are unable to hunt because of the thing in the sky that brings death. If they know that is out and about, he will keep them indoors and they will feed from the supplies.

Michael senses the hesitation of the pack members as darkness falls and they step cautiously out into the unknown. They are far from their normal hunting grounds, but he smells fresh scents on the night air as he stands by the entrance watching the packs emerge. He sees them glance upward toward the sky before trotting off with their individual groups. Faint blasts echo in the night from distant explosions, lighting up the sky in intervals. The skyline flashes before the muted booms reach them. He warns each group to take cover if the explosions draw closer or they hear the droning from above.

The building empties with Sandra leaving with one of the last groups. He catches a look from her before she trots off with her large pack. Hers is one of the packs he designated to search the buildings for food they can stock. Michael isn't exactly sure of what her look means, but he knows it isn't one challenging him. He would have taken action if it was. He can't allow any challenge to his leadership now that he has gathered so many together. The result would break the gathering apart and they may find themselves in competition with each other rather than cooperating. With the danger surrounding them on a nightly basis, he won't let that happen. He has allowed Sandra's arguments only because of the size of her pack and the fact that she has a young one, but there is a line that he won't allow to be crossed. Giving a low growl of frustration, mixed with eagerness to be on the hunt, he lopes off into the night with others chasing down the scent of a large prey in the area.

* * * * * *

The night runner lopes down the tree-lined street with the other five of his pack running behind seeking out the elusive scent of prey in the chill of the night. He was told to take his pack out to search for good hunting grounds; feed his pack and then locate areas where prey is in abundance so the packs can feed on subsequent nights.

They are hungry from not being able to feed the night before. Images quickly surface of last night and having to stay hidden in the building along with several other packs while booming explosions rocked the area around him. He had felt fear as some of the other packs vanished from his thoughts with each tremendous blast and had wondered if the next would be on the structure he was hiding in. The sheer terror of hunkering down in a corner with the others of his small pack squatting next to him; all of them jumping with each impact. The ground-shaking blasts drew closer and closer until he was sure the next would bring the walls down around him and the others. There were several moments when he wanted to just rise and flee into the night. The one who leads them all sent a message to keep hidden and that's the only thing that kept him shivering in the corner, thinking his time was limited. He felt relieved when the loud explosions stopped and he took his first tentative steps outside. There was a great fear that he would be cut down like the others he felt earlier. Then there was the long run through the rest of the night, tired and hungry, to find their current lair.

The distant rumbles and quick flashes of light make him nervous and have him constantly looking up toward the star-lit sky. He expects the streams of light he saw before quickly entering the building to streak down on him and his pack. However, his pack has to feed and as long as the booms remain muted in the distance, he'll stay out and continue the hunt. They need to eat and the pack as a whole need to find adequate hunting grounds. If the crashes begin to draw closer, he'll take them inside one of the structures. For now though, he'll test the area for scents and track down any prey.

A few streets farther down with the slap of their feet on the hard path, he stops where two paths come together and lifts his nose into the air. A musky scent drifts on the night air and reaches his finely-tuned sense of smell. It's from another predator and sometimes prey. It's one of the four-legged ones that they've also found running in packs. They're a dangerous foe but they are food. The odor mixes with others of its kind and he can tell it's coming from one of the larger packs. The scent grows stronger.

He looks around at the five others he has in his pack. They need to eat, but he knows he doesn't have the numbers if the four-legged furry ones are in a large enough pack. Deciding to find other prey, he notes the location and presses farther into the night.

A few streets beyond, he stops. The scents swirling through the numerous streets and abandoned two-legged lairs makes it difficult to determine a particular direction but the smell he picked up earlier of the furry four-legged ones is definitely stronger. He turns to see if he can see them but the streets remain as empty as they have been all night. The others in his pack have their noses in the air as they also detect the increase. Although they are showing some nervousness, there is also a degree of eagerness. That aroma means food even if it does also mean a fight. He detects even more of the mixed, musty smells. It's a larger pack but he can't determine just how large. Still wanting to find other food sources, he turns away from where he thinks the scent is coming from and begins trotting again.

Hungry and tired, he stops once again a short time later as the musky scents become even stronger. He has the sudden feeling they are being followed. A light breeze causes the branches to the side of the street to sway ever so slightly. The odor of the four-legged ones out on the prowl becomes stronger and then lighter depending on the flow of the wind. The street is filled with a soft rustle as another light gust blows through the leaf-clad trees. Faintly, caught upon the swirls of air, he hears the soft padding of many feet. They aren't the heavy footfalls of another pack but those of smaller animals. That, coupled with the increasing scent tells him that something is nearing.

He is wary of the small number he has with him. He has fought the ferocious four-legged ones in the past, but those were small in number and he was the one chasing them. The fact that they are following his small pack leaves him with a wary feeling. The sounds of the padded footfalls increases and then go silent. He stands in the middle of the street looking up and down the hard path and into the strips of land between the surrounding structures but sees nothing. His pack draws nearer and they huddle closer together. He feels them begin to get anxious, their eyes darting in all directions and raising their noses high into the air. The gusts die for a moment and he picks up the faint sound of panting. Whatever it happens to be is near.

He is at a loss as to which direction to go. He wants to continue his hunt but isn't sure which way he should venture. There is also the hunger gnawing at his stomach. They are a match for most anything and the caution he feels is balanced by eagerness. There is food close by, but prey doesn't normally track its predator. Dark shadows of the things the two-legged ones once used for transport line the sides of the path he is on. He passes several as he cautiously steps toward where two other hard paths meet.

The sound of the soft footfalls begins once more as he nears the corner of the street. This time he can clearly discern their direction and, coming to a halt, looks down one of the side roads. The largest pack of four-legged ones he has ever seen comes into view trotting down the center of the street. A low growl issues from his throat as he senses the threat. They outnumber his small pack three-to-one and they aren't some of the smaller of their kind he has chased down in the past. These are some of the biggest he's ever seen.

A low growl still vibrates in his throat and he hears the others of his pack emitting the same. Edging out into the middle of the intersection to face the four-legged ones that are covered in fur; the large pack of animals halt with every head locked onto him and the ones with him. The large animal in front of the others hunches down and he hears a low growl similar to his emanate from it. Several other four-legged ones join in and he notices the hair on their haunches raised with their ears drawn back. A fight is coming and he feels the excitement of it surface, underwritten by a measure of worry. It's not quite like the overwhelming thrill of the chase, but it's similar. A pack this large will not be easy to take down, but the adrenaline that courses through his body fills him.

The four-legged one in front and several behind it edge forward. Several farther behind separate and race off to the side and are soon lost from sight in the tall grass covering the areas in front of the deserted lairs. He marks their progress to either side of the hard path by the tops of the grass swaying to the side and being trampled down. Those soon emerge and form smaller groups on both sides of his small pack. He knows this tactic, having been taught to do this very thing from their overall pack leader. These four-legged ones will hit them from multiple sides at once. He sends a picture to his pack members letting them know this and for them to position themselves toward these smaller groups.

As the four-legged ones slink closer, his growl increases in intensity warning them. He hunches forward, readying himself for the inevitable attack. The three groups surrounding them continue to edge forward mixing their own low growls in with those of his pack. The hair along the backs of the four-legged ones stand on end with their tails posted low to the ground. Every one of them has their lips pulled back revealing their dangerous, long canines meant to rip, shred, and tear. Only a few feet away from him, the other leader hunches down and runs forward a few steps, then launches high into the air.

The other four-legged ones charge in on the heels of their leader. Their growls combine with those from his own pack and the once still of the night erupts into a din of howls and snarls. He steps quickly to the side and pushes the leaping four-legged leader aside into the path of a couple others rushing in. Quickly turning back, he grabs another leaping form that is nearly upon him and slams it to the ground adding a pained yelp to the mixed clamor of noise. Not able to take the split second necessary to rend the four-legged one, he turns to take a third springing figure square in the chest.

Grabbing the one as it attempts to tear at his throat, he

feels the hot breath and sees the gnashing teeth inches away. The four-legged one is rocking its head back and forth violently trying to break from his grasp and sink its long teeth into the soft flesh of his neck. The impact of the animal causes him to lose his balance and he feels himself toppling backward. If he falls, he knows, that for him, this fight will end almost before it started.

Holding the side of the four-legged one's neck with a firm grip, and with the last of his balance, he jumps into the air twisting as he goes down putting the snarling one below him. Timing it just right, he pushes outward with all of his might. The head of the creature hits the hard ground with a crack. It emits a quick, pained yelp and goes limp. He quickly rises and notes that the other four-legged ones have drawn back. They still encircle his small pack, but their initial onslaught is over.

His head rapidly turns from side to side looking for other leaping figures but all have retreated a few feet away. He notes one of his pack members is on the ground unmoving. Four of the four-legged ones lie still around them including the one he just finished off. The sweet smell of blood rises on the night air filling him with a deep lust for more. He sees injured four-legged ones limping behind the packs still surrounding him. Others prowl back and forth, but the leader locks eyes on him and snarls; his teeth bared. This fight is long from over.

He wanted this open area so he could see an attack from any direction but now he realizes he would have been better served by having something at his back. He isn't used to being the one attacked, so this didn't register until now. He looks to the surrounding buildings and thinks of climbing one of the fences and getting on one of the roofs. The height will keep the four-legged ones at bay until he can think of something else. The problem is that he'd have to go through the line surrounding him and his four remaining pack members. The safety of the structures might as well be a long night's run away. Rumbles continue to echo off in the distance with quick bursts of light illuminating the night sky. His plight makes the activity in the distance seem even farther away.

Without warning, the four-legged attack in unison once again. One moment they are growling and milling about, the next launching themselves into the air at him and the others. The area is once again filled with snarling, twisting bodies. It's all he can do to keep the leaping figures off him. He is dancing to the sides, throwing jumping and bounding figures from him. Screams of pain from both the four-legged ones and his pack rise up over the din. It seems like the four-legged ones keep materializing out of nowhere. As he was avoiding one, another latches onto his arm. The hurt is immediate and intense, sending white hot pain rocketing into his head.

The four-legged one, with its teeth buried deep in his forearm, is shaking its head from side to side, ripping into and tearing the soft tissue and muscle. His arm feels close to snapping from the intense pressure. He reaches down to pry the snarling mouth from his arm but he can't pull it free. Punching downward with all of his strength, his fist lands heavily on the long snout. He feels more than hears the crunch as the bone of the four-legged one gives way sending a spray of blood out its nostrils. The creature lets go with a strangled yelp and streaks off into the night with its tail between its legs. His arm burns with pain as he turns to face his next attacker.

Momentarily clear of furry bodies leaping toward him, he turns in time to see another of his pack members go down and realizes there are now only two of them left. One struggles nearby with the jaws of one of the large four-legged ones clamped about his throat. The pack leader kicks out hard connecting directly with the rib cage of the four-legged one feeling the ribs give way. It surrenders its hold and staggers to the side. He looks down and realizes it is too late for his pack member. Blood runs freely from his torn throat forming a deep pool beside him. Twitching a few times, he goes limp and the blood flow slows to a trickle.

The four-legged ones continue to press their attack despite losing close to half of their own. The iron smell of blood fills the air creating a feeding frenzy of sorts. Mixed in is a myriad of odors; blood, feces, bodies torn apart. The pavement is slick with body fluids as they run to the lower ground and slowly make their way to the gutters. The last remaining member goes down surrounded by furry bodies and shrieking in pain.

He realizes his time is now measured in moments and takes off down the street. Feeling the warm blood trickling down his arm, he hears the sound of running paws behind him. He vaults up and over one of the abandoned, dark transport things sitting by the side of the hard path feeling the cold metallic surface under his hands and feet. Landing in the tall grass on the other side in a crouch, he hears the howls behind him, closing the distance. He is used to being on the other side of the chase. The tables have been turned.

With his heart racing in his chest, he looks at a wooden fence just a short distance away. *If I can just make it*, he thinks in a series of picture images representing safety. Springing quickly forward, he makes for the fence and the measure of protection it represents. The snarls are right on his heels as he races through the tall grass. He feels an impact on his lower leg and teeth penetrate his skin and muscle tissue. The sudden weight of the animal, bite, and sharp tug on his calf cause him to trip and he goes down feeling a bolt of pain shoot up his leg.

Rolling as he goes down hard, he kicks out at the four-legged one latched firmly onto his leg. The one who has hold of him is growling heavily and tugging sharply causing his leg to tear even more. He kicks out with his other leg, making contact with its head. With a loud yelp, the animal releases its grip and backs off a short distance.

The night runner rises quickly and begins to race for the fence once again. With each step on his injured leg, he feels a small amount of pain but it is mostly ignored. What he can't ignore is the fact that his leg won't support him as it should. The fence draws near when another impact hits him in the back. He immediately feels teeth sink into his rump. Another hard bump hits him on his already injured leg. Teeth sink deeply into both areas and he is knocked forward. He goes down again and rolls to face his attackers.

His ears are saturated with the sounds of growling and snarling which combine with his own deep, loud growls. Teeth-filled mouths fill his vision, snapping at him as he tries to fend them off. The one lets go of his rump but he feels the sharp tugging of the one clamped onto his leg. Another latches onto his arm and he feels the flesh tear. Still growling and fighting with everything he has, he sees one face loom close and feels teeth sink into the soft skin under his chin. Warm blood pours down the sides of his neck. The creature shakes its head sharply. He shrieks in pain but it's cut off abruptly as he feels the soft skin and cartilage tear free. Feeling white hot pain for only a split second, the night grows dim and fades into nothing. A different pack will feed well tonight.

* * * * * *

With the coming of dawn, we take care of refueling and rearming the Spooky and head back to the compound. The command group is waiting and we meet once I get cleaned up. Franks informs us that Leonard radioed before my arrival this morning indicating that he will be arriving the next morning. He said that he will try Olympia first but will have to wait for the tide in order to transit the narrow straits. Bannerman briefs that the supplies for the sub will be ready by the end of the day.

Wanting to be there when Leonard arrives and talk about his plans, I decide to take a night off from our evening flights. This will give the flight crews a night of rest as well. On one hand, I'm not eager to take a night off seeing as we seem to have the night runners on the run, but it's important to coordinate with Leonard. It's also important to rest the crews.

Lynn informs us that she sent Mullins with Charlie Team out to recon the campus buildings we destroyed last night. I'm very interested to see if we managed to take out a large number of night runners in their lair with the hope being that we eliminated a large portion of those we caught the night prior. While we wait for word, Bannerman brings us up to speed on the progress of our other projects.

"The inner wall will be complete either today or sometime tomorrow," he states. "We can then start on the towers and pouring the concrete in the containers that will serve as the foundations for the quarters."

"Starting today, we are going to use Roger, the pilot that arrived with Sam's group, to once again begin our search for others in the local area. We've just about completed the Tacoma area and will start up in the residential areas leading toward Seattle once we are finished there. Arranging for the pickup crews that far north will require one or two teams to be out for the entire day so we'll need to coordinate when we can do that," Frank states.

"We should be okay with regards to the teams once the supply runs are complete. Most of the projects we have are local and won't require any security," Lynn replies.

Mullins reports in that they arrived at what once used to be Saint Martin's College. The buildings are still smoldering piles of rubble and, from the two buildings they've searched so far, they haven't found a trace of night runner bodies within the piles or amongst the scattered debris. All indications so far point to the fact that we missed the large horde we witnessed emerging the previous night. We must have pushed the night runners out of the area, and that means there is still just as many of them out there somewhere. That does not give me warm, fuzzy feelings at all. I was so hoping we had made a big step in clearing the area out.

"Is there any way we can step up the training?" I ask Lynn, thinking about the numbers of night runners compared to our meager numbers.

Our numbers don't indicate our true fire power. We may have a few survivors gathered with us, but we only have a very limited number of trained personnel. Any increase in our teams will add to our ability to defend ourselves.

"Jack, you know we can't skimp on the training. We have to keep the concept of quality over quantity," Lynn states.

"Yeah, I understand that and wouldn't have it any other way. It's just that the number of night runners out there makes what we have here a very scary proposition," I reply.

"We can always increase the numbers we put through any class but that will draw away from resources in other areas. That will mean there are fewer to work on crews at any given time and we'll have to draw more from the existing teams for training," Lynn says. "We have another group graduating shortly."

"Will we be able to increase the number of teams with the graduates?" Drescoll asks.

"We have a few promising candidates and should be able to field another team," Lynn answers.

"What about putting those in the next training class that already have some degree of training and/or experience?" I ask.

"I've thought of that and have arranged for those in Miguel's group to begin. Do you have others in mind?" Lynn asks.

"What about putting Sergeant Prescott's group straight into phase two after testing them out to ensure they have the skills needed to graduate from phase one?" I ask Lynn.

"We can do that, but that will mean drawing from the other teams to assist in training," she answers. "Bannerman mentioned that we won't need as many security details so we may be able to swing it. My only concern with that is whether you are still planning to take two of the teams in search for the families. Has that been decided upon yet?"

"I think we should," Drescoll chimes in. "It seems we are pushing the night runners out of the area as planned. It seems the time is right if we're going to. Jack keeps mentioning our time is running out to get out there and search."

"I'm in agreement as well," Horace says.

"If I take two teams and we have the night watch to maintain, will that deplete us to a level where we won't be able to accomplish anything or put us at a drastically increased safety risk?" I ask, addressing the group.

"We have enough supplies to get us through the winter if our population stays where it's at. If our searches bring in greater numbers, well, we'll have to evaluate that at the time. I guess what I'm trying to say is that we won't need security details for supply runs," Bannerman says.

"And we'll have an extra team in about a week when the classes graduate. I plan to disperse them with the other teams and form the new team with our veterans," Lynn says. "I think we'll be okay if nothing out of the ordinary arises. And, if the soldiers with Sergeant Prescott go straight to phase two, we'll have two additional teams in just a few weeks after that. How long do you think you'll be gone, Jack?"

I notice Lynn's hesitation with that question. I know she isn't a fan of my heading out, but this may be the last time we are able to. Thankful for that, I am eager to be off and get it over with. It seems we are able to tread water for the time being with regards to our safety but that doesn't take into account any new adaptations the night runners may have made. The stress of not knowing is agonizing. I feel a measure of security, but at the same time, the numbers of them out there and their ability to adapt worries me.

"I'm not really sure to be honest. With the limitations and the few in number who are going, I'm guessing we'll be gone anywhere from ten days to two weeks. I'll start planning the route after I wake this afternoon," I answer.

"Shit, Jack! Two fucking weeks?! Really, that long?" Lynn asks.

"Well, we have ten left who have families within the parameters we set. We covered that for Gonzalez and McCafferty, so that is two less than the original twelve. When we first talked about it, I mentioned two days per search, and I don't see any way that can be shortened to be honest," I answer.

"Fuck it. Ten days it is, but I don't have to like it. You know the one reason, but the second is that we'll be two teams shy for an extended period of time," Lynn says. "I know it's important…and I'm all for it, but I'm not a fan of being out of communication for that long."

"I know and neither am I. So, it seems we are in agreement to do it and in a week after the next trainee graduation, right?" I ask. Nods from around the table indicate that everyone is in agreement.

"Okay, I'll start planning today. I'll take Red Team as they are the on the list along with a single C-130. I may swing down to Canon AFB on the way back to pick up a second Spooky so we have a spare on hand," I say.

"I'll see to reorganizing a team with the other six on the list. Who do you want to lead the second team?" Lynn asks.

I look over to Greg who rolls his eyes and then says, "Sure, I'll go. It was so much fun the last time. Besides, I can't very well miss the chance to see what fucktardity you come up with next."

"Come up with that all on your own, did you?" I ask.

"Yep. It's the only word that fits what processes through that extremely warped mind of yours," Greg counters.

"I couldn't agree more," Lynn says, smiling.

"You realize that the aircraft latrine needs to be cleaned daily and I'm currently in the market for volunteers, right?" I say.

"Oh, is that where you vomit out the ideas you come up with that don't actually get made into plans?" Greg says to the amusement of the group.

"I give up. I'm taking my ball and going home…taking my ball…going home," I reply. "Oh, and before I go, let me leave you with this…fuck off!"

I retire to Lynn's and my small partition trying to think of what a good comeback would have been but fail miserably. I'm a little disappointed at not hitting the large night runner lair while they were in it. However, my pillow is calling in soothing tones and it doesn't like to be ignored.

*   *   *   *   *   *

Observations in the Dark

Captain Leonard watches the shoreline as they make their way through the narrow strait. The shore rising sharply from the blue-gray waters is lost after a few feet by the low-lying clouds. The trees, along where the land and water meet, are indistinct. The black bow pushes slowly through the small waves making its way north. Leonard relishes the feel of the cool, moist air against his cheeks. It's not often he is able to run on the surface and it fills him with elation. The tangy smell of the sea completes the feeling of harmony.

"Are you heading directly to Olympia?" his XO asks.

"Plot a course to Whidbey Naval Air Station first. I want to take a look there. Then let's head over to the eastern side of the Sound and make our way down the seaboard," Leonard answers.

"Aye, aye, sir."

Emerging from the narrow strait into a wider one, Leonard looks to the east towards Seattle and the crowded eastern shoreline of the Puget Sound. Most of the view is lost by clouds drifting barely above the water. The *Santa Fe* turns to the northwest and parallels Whidbey Island. Although he now knows the chances of sighting any other vessels are small, he keeps a sharp lookout nonetheless. A few seals raise their heads above the surface as they make their way through the channel but nothing else appears.

They pass the town of Port Townsend off to the left and the waters open up into the Strait of Juan de Fuca. Angling north, the *Santa Fe* continues along the shores of Whidbey Island. Once, Leonard catches a large black fin break the surface a short distance away. The waters around are the home to several orca pods. *They are usually farther north away from the main shipping lanes, but the quiet of the waters must have brought them south*, he thinks, watching the dorsal fin sink back below the waters.

They eventually arrive off the naval air station and take a

position close in. Lifting his heavy binoculars, Leonard looks for any signs of life. The runways near the sandy shore come into clear focus. He spies several jet aircraft parked on the northwestern ramp, a couple of hangars, and other buildings, but doesn't detect any movement. It appears exactly like Bangor – completely abandoned.

"Let's move farther out and submerge for the night. Have the crews listen for ship traffic and monitor what we can of the base," Leonard tells the XO. "Wake me with any reports. I'll be in my cabin."

"Aye, aye, sir," the XO replies.

The night passes in silence. There's neither the sound of propellers in the waters nor sight of any movement onshore. The only thing they pick up on the acoustic gear are the calls from several orca pods that inhabit the waters. Leonard surfaces his boat with the coming dawn. The broken clouds overhead provide better visibility but also bring more of a chill to the morning. They backtrack toward Seattle and eventually pick up the buildings that line the eastern shores of the sound.

Cruising along slowly, Leonard and the others of the watch glass the shore. It's much the same as the bases. The mechanisms and buildings of humankind are there, just itching for people to meander through and into. The streets which once held a multitude of people on errands or browsing the shops remain empty. Dark windows stare back as if sad that the people that once looked in gazing at their wares have vanished.

Rounding a point, with Bainbridge Island to one side, the straits open to the actual port of Seattle. The skyline rises above the still waters. Ships ride at anchor waiting eternally for their turn at the busy docks. Their anchor lines stretch taut as all point toward the incoming tide. Off to the side, cruise ships sit berthed at their docks. Ferries which once carried commuters and visitors alike are nestled in their piers. The city and waterfront are like the other areas, looking like they should be teeming with people but what greets the onlookers seems more like a ghost town.

The cranes lining the main docks lie still with ships

berthed beneath their mammoth arms. The large ocean-going vessels sit quietly as if holding secrets within, as if they were witnesses to all that transpired but are unable to tell their story. The bridges spanning the waterways are empty of the cars that used to sit bumper to bumper during rush hours.

Pulling close, Leonard blasts out greetings through a handheld loudspeaker. His voice echoes off the waters and tall buildings lining the narrow streets, bouncing and fading into the inner city. There isn't any corresponding greeting or movement. Thinking of the warehouse, he wonders how many night runners lie within the dark, silent buildings. He thinks of putting Chief Krandle and his SEAL Team ashore but doesn't really see anything that can be gained. He thinks they'll just find more of what he is already seeing – an abandoned city. This is a new world he has found himself in and, as hard as it is to do, he needs to wrap his mind around it and begin to think differently.

The major with Captain Walker said it would take three days to gather his requested supplies so Leonard decides to sit off the shores of Seattle and watch for the rest of the day. He'll submerge at night and continue his observation.

On the bridge, he watches as the lowering sun is reflected off the thousands of windows that rise up the skyscrapers. It looks as if a giant mirror was placed in the middle of downtown. Glints reflect off the dome of the space needle stretching high into the air. Countless thousands and millions once stood on the railing of the landmark looking over the city. Now it stands as one more relic of the past. The streets between the mammoth buildings darken with shadows cast by the tall towers rising high toward the broken layer of clouds.

The sun sinks to the horizon creating an orange glow on the sides of the buildings. Leonard watches as the city seems to hold its breath as the glow changes to reflect the sunset behind him. As if pulled on a string, the colors vanish leaving behind the grays of a landscape moving from day into night. No lights twinkle from the condos along the waterfront. With a final hush, the grand city is cast into darkness. Leonard thinks about submerging, but hesitates, wanting to watch the city in transition for a moment longer.

The stillness is complete. The waves lapping along the hull the only sound. Then, as if a bubble burst, the silence is broken by the faint sound of screams resonating over the waters. Leonard brings night vision binoculars to his eyes and scans the shoreline. There is movement along the narrow streets rising away from the waterfront. People emerge from buildings and race in all directions, some disappearing farther into the city and vanishing over the hills. Others head toward him and the buildings built on piers stretching into the bay.

In his magnified view, he sees several of them press against railings lining the water, their noses lifted into the air and their mouths open wide. A myriad of shrieks bounce toward him, echoing off the tall buildings as his voice did earlier in the day. He catches a glimpse of what appears to be a glow emanating from the eyes of several of the figures along the railings. Pulling the binoculars from his eyes, he shakes his head and rubs his eyes before looking once again. He sees the same thing.

"Chief Krandle to the bridge," he calls on the intercom.

Leonard wants the chief to get a look and see if these are the same things he saw on his mission to the Philippines. A few minutes later, Krandle appears on the already crowded bridge.

"Take a look at that," Leonard says, handing Krandle the binoculars and pointing toward the city.

Chief Krandle takes the offered set and brings them to his eyes. Leonard watches as the chief stares long and hard. Krandle withdraws the binoculars and rubs his eyes in the same manner as Leonard did before looking once again.

"Are their eyes glowing?" Krandle asks, incredulously.

"That's what I thought I saw as well, chief. Are those the same things you saw in the Philippines?"

"I wouldn't swear to it, but they look very much alike. They have the same pale skin and those shrieks are definitely the same," Krandle answers with a shiver of remembrance.

Leonard thought much the same remembering the faint screams from the warehouse. He now knows he is looking at what Captain Walker called night runners. It still seems so alien but there is the proof right in front of him. The stories match what he sees. He doesn't need to go ashore and see them attack to obtain a hundred percent verification. As strange as it seems, humankind has turned into some new species leaving little alive in their wake. Watching the hundreds of night runners run through the streets, some he only catches a glimpse of as they transit cross streets, he wonders how many survivors can be left in the world. Certainly there can't be any here. Having seen enough, he clears the bridge.

"Prepare to submerge," he orders, dropping the last foot from the ladder to the deck. The control room crew responds and they are shortly diving under the chill waters in the bay that once served Seattle. Their black silhouette becomes smaller until the waves lap over the last vestige of the conning tower before it vanishes altogether below the surface.

"Keep a watch out on the shore and listen for any vessels. Wake me if anything changes," Leonard says and retires to his cabin.

The views on the monitors changes little during the night watch. Night runners come and go in the small section of the city that can be seen. The fascinated crew watch as, just before the first faint lighting changes occur in the east, the creatures roaming the city vanish within minutes of each other. It's almost as if a switch were thrown.

Leonard rises, receives a brief on the activities of the night, and surfaces the boat. He orders a heading toward Tacoma putting Seattle on his tail. The city has taken on the forlorn aura of a ghost town once again but, to him, the windows take on a menacing look knowing what lies in the darkened rooms behind them. The *Santa Fe* rounds the corner out of the bay and into the straits of the Tacoma Narrows. Seattle slides from view and Leonard glances back watching the Space Needle disappear behind a tree-clad hill.

They slide down the straits passing the forested islands of Bainbridge and Vashon. Looking through binoculars, all of the small towns lining the shore tell the same story – seemingly abandoned and left to the whims of Mother Nature. Putting in to the bay serving Tacoma, it looks much like Seattle, all of the mechanisms of civilization in place but no one around using them. The only evidence of a departed society Leonard spies through his magnified view is the tall grass growing in the yards of residences sitting on the hillsides and in the medians of several streets.

White specks dot the area as gulls circle the waters near shore. Large, black birds wheel over a spot in the distance. Several seals surface in the waters but that is the only movement. Leonard notes that the docks are only partially full of cargo ships allowing room for him to dock the sub if needed. He'll head down to Olympia to see if he can put in there. Having to wait for the morning tide in order to transit the narrow passages, they will remain parked off the shores of Tacoma and observe.

*   *   *   *   *   *

The Widening Rift

Waking in the afternoon, I want to just remain lying on my cot. However, there is only so much time one can spend on a cot without permanently realigning the back into a not favorable position. Walking downstairs of the mostly empty interior, I gather Robert and Craig to plan our little jaunt across the western part of what used to be the United States. I still think of it in those terms even with the collapse of any governing body because, well, it's just easier that way. The states are just drawn lines on pieces of paper, but in regards to planning, it's still much simpler to refer to them in that manner. A place has to have a name when referring to it and the old ones are just as good as any.

We settle at one of the larger tables and spread out flight navigation maps. I have the information on where we need to go for each of the soldiers. Now it's just a matter of planning the exact route to make the best of our time. It takes a few hours to plan out the route but the overall flight will take us in a clockwise circle around the entire western continent. Our first stop will be at Mountain Home AFB, Idaho and then off to Malmstrom AFB, Montana. Then it's off to Ellsworth AFB, South Dakota, McConnell AFB, Kansas, Petersen AFB, Colorado, Luke AFB, Arizona, Nellis AFB, Nevada, Vandenberg AFB, California, Travis AFB, California, and then McClellan AFB, California before returning home. I plan to drop by Canon AFB, New Mexico on the leg from Colorado to Arizona to pick up another AC-130 gunship and ammunition for it. *Why couldn't everyone who has family we are looking for have grown up as neighborhood friends?* I think, looking at the route drawn on our maps. It's a long series of flights that we'll be lucky to finish in a mere ten days.

Once again, I weigh the balance of continuing our nightly attacks to clear out the area versus searching for the families. I feel torn. We decided as a group to do this but the conflict remains. I owe it to the soldiers who risked their lives without question rescuing the kids and who continue to do so every day. But clearing out the local area is important to providing a higher measure of security for our group of survivors. Keeping the night runners at bay and reactive – on their heels – allows us not only protection but it's my feeling that it makes it harder for them to adapt. That is what worries me more than anything else. But the group has spoken, and we did promise we would do what we could to help. The coming of winter and the deterioration of weather it brings dictates that we are closing in on the 'now or never' time. And so, off we'll go. Plus, having another Spooky in the arsenal, even if for just a short time, can't hurt. With the addition of Roger, we'll also be able to conduct local searches while we're gone.

We meet in the evening and I outline our planned trek. The only thing I'm not sure of is whether to take Humvees or a Stryker. The Stryker will make for cramped quarters and limit the amount of people we can take back should we encounter any but it's armament and unexposed firepower will be a benefit should we need it. Taking one will also decrease the distance we can travel, but with the route we currently have planned, that really won't make much of a difference.

"What about taking two 130s? Like we did returning from Canon AFB? We could drop down to the Guard base in Portland and pick up another one," Robert suggests.

"That will make it decidedly more difficult to bring a Spooky back up with us," I answer.

"Oh, yeah, that it would," he responds. "My only problem is deciding whether to take Humvees or a Stryker."

"Will it make a difference with the flight?" Lynn asks.

"Only with regards to the range, plus it will take longer to get to altitude. We may not be able to climb as high with a full load of fuel but can after we burn some off. Takeoffs from high altitude airports can be a little sporty," I answer.

"You're the best to answer that one really. If you think it's safe enough, flyboy, then I'd say take the Stryker," Lynn says.

"I'll have to seriously think on that. We'll be taking off in

Colorado so I'll take a closer look at the data figuring in some worst case scenarios. I agree that the Stryker is a better choice, but turning the 130 into an all-terrain vehicle is not my ideal solution," I state.

"It's kinda hard to clear the mountains that way," Robert says.

"Yeah, kind of, but it does make landing a whole lot easier," I reply.

"Ugh. And with that, I'm going to bed. If I don't stop you two here, you'll go on all night," Lynn says. Robert and I merely smile knowing the truth of her statement.

We turn in for the night with the intention of waking early to meet Captain Leonard and his crew. Whether that will be in Olympia or Tacoma remains to be seen. Bannerman has crews ready for either scenario.

* * * * * *

Sandra runs down the empty streets with the moon casting its silver rays through a break in the clouds overhead. The rumbles and flashes of light of the night previous are not present and she feels a measure of relief with their absence. She still looks to the sky, watching for the streaks of light that mean death, and listens for the telltale droning that precedes the deadly explosions of fire.

The large pack she has brought with her thunder behind as they search for prey. Michael has turned her and her pack loose in the night after other packs reported good hunting grounds nearby. She returned to the lair last night loaded with the containers of food she and her pack raided from the many buildings they entered. The rays of the bright orb overhead causes her skin to tingle but that is ignored as she trots through the dark. Her breath comes out in puffs of white as her exhales condense in the chilled air.

She keeps looking north toward the large two-legged lair and feels herself drawn to it again. She passes the old lair which now lies in ruin with wisps of smoke rising in places through the rubble. A thought crosses her mind that Michael was right in moving the pack farther away. *This must be what the white flashes and the blasts were about last night*, she thinks as she keeps driving northward with her pack on her heels.

She pauses at the distinct dividing line between intact buildings and the debris of ruined structures. The wariness she felt several nights ago takes hold and she comes to a stop. The hundreds behind her halt with her and position themselves in the street and grassy strips along the side. She listens carefully for any signs of the droning in the sky but hears nothing except an occasional cricket chirping in the distance. Faint scurrying comes from the debris as the thousands of rodents inhabiting those places scamper about. Her pack will feed on them again tonight.

She sends her pack forward among the ruins to catch the quick, wily, small ones. Standing watch by the side, she will feed after the others have had their fill. She thinks of telling Michael about this abundant food supply, but she has held the information for two reasons. One, he will know for sure that she has ventured close to the two-legged lair again. He may anyway, but she doesn't want to make it overt. And two, she doesn't want this place swarming with other packs. Having them this close may alert the two-legged ones. Of course, Michael most likely wouldn't allow them to get this close, but she can't take that risk. She doesn't know how she will get into the lair, but she means to try. The pull of the two-legged one is strong and she is still intent on capturing the female she saw in his mind that one night.

She continues to watch her pack dash among the piles of rubble as they chase down the small prey. Pained squeals permeate the night air indicating the capture of food. Other squeals pervade the night as the rodents sees one of her pack and run farther into the protection of the wreckage. Her head comes up sharply as she feels something else in her mind. Coming to her abruptly, it's the thought images of another one and it is coming from the two-legged lair. It's not the feel of one of her kind but it's close. Nor does it feel like the brush she had from the two-legged one. She can follow this new one's thoughts and actions, though, and there is no doubt that he is within the lair.

For a moment, she is tempted to take her pack to the tall walls once again, but the memory of being tossed to the ground and losing one of her pack when the ground erupted under his feet causes her to hold back. Instead, she sends this new one an image. She waits patiently for a return message but receives nothing. Just as abruptly as this new one came to her mind, he vanishes. She looks into the distance hoping for him to come back and is disappointed when he remains silent. Shaking her head to clear her thoughts, she focuses on the area around her. With thoughts of how to get over the walls to capture the female and draw the two-legged one out, she lopes into the debris-scattered parking lots to feed.

* * * * * *

Alan finds himself downstairs once again. In his confused state, he has the overwhelming feeling of wanting to be outside. The feeling is so strong. It is a distinct need to be out in the dark which confuses him even further. His heart races thinking about the thrill of the hunt, his mouth waters thinking about the sweet taste of fresh blood. His teeth sinking into warm flesh and tearing it from bone. The eagerness as he chases down prey, closing in from behind and the excitement of him about to feed. A quickly fading image hangs in his mind of being called, the call being one to join the pack and hunt.

He shakes his head as the images fade from his mind and he becomes more conscious of his surroundings. His heart still pounds in his chest and there is a lingering feeling of excitement. With it is a fear that one has upon suddenly finding oneself in a different place.

What the fuck is that all about? What in the fuck is happening to me? he thinks as he turns from the door leading into the warehouse and makes his way back upstairs. Falling onto his cot, he wonders if he will experience the terror dreams or find himself waking downstairs again. With these thoughts, he falls into a dreamless sleep.

*   *   *   *   *   *

I rise early remembering that I woke at some point last night with a strange sensation. It felt as if something brushed my mind. It wasn't like a thought or anything similar; it was as if something literally brushed up against it. It didn't keep me up long, but the memory of it still lingers. Lynn stirs beside me and rolls over. Usually she is the first up and it's me rolling over to ignore the world and get more sleep. I grab my boots and exit as quietly as I can to let her sleep on. She's been keeping this whole thing together and needs her rest.

A few others are emerging from their little caves and do the usual morning stretching before trudging slowly to wherever their tired brains lead them. Some to eat, others to the showers. I head down to the small control room and ask if anything showed up on the monitors last night. I have just the ghost of a memory that what brushed my mind felt similar to a night runner. The woman monitoring the video feeds from the cameras looks through the logs.

"I didn't see anything and the logs don't indicate that anything was observed," she reports. I nod and thank her.

Walking out with the thought of taking a shower to clear the last of the cobwebs, I look up to see Lynn emerge from the cubicle. Upon seeing me, she gives a tired wave and makes her way down to me.

"Good morning, hon," I say, giving her a hug.

"Good morning, Jack. You're up early," she says, returning a quick hug.

"Yeah, I couldn't sleep," I state and tell her of the sensation I experienced.

"What do you think it means?" she asks, drawing away.

"I have no idea. This 'thing' seems to be more of a liability than an asset. It confuses me more than it lends any clarification. I just wish I knew more about it and understood it better."

"I'm sure you'll figure it out as time goes on, Jack. On another note, I was thinking…and if you're going to go on this search, you might as well start sooner rather than later. The ones in training will be finished in a number of days and are already trained enough to help should we need them. And the inner wall will be complete soon as well. We'll be fine here and you delaying your trip a few days just to wait for them isn't going to accomplish anything. The sooner you start, the quicker you'll be back," she says.

"You're probably right about that. Leonard is due to arrive today and I want to be there to see what his plans are. I also have to run the numbers with the Stryker on board but can do that today. Regardless of which we decide to take, we could be ready to leave tomorrow," I reply.

"I'm still not all that excited about you leaving, but I know you have to. The only plus is that this will hopefully be your last trip," she says.

"I know, and believe me, I'm not a big fan of leaving either. I don't like being away from you. Nor am I all that thrilled at giving the night runners a chance to recover. But it is only for a few days and I'll be back before you know it," I respond.

"I love you, Jack."

"I love you, too."

Coming out of the shower, there is a little more bustle inside from people getting ready to get on with the day and whatever assigned tasks they may have. Frank informs me that Leonard radioed in that he is sailing down the straits and should arrive in Olympia shortly. Bannerman is with the supply crews making sure they are ready while the teams gather for their morning formation and training. Close to two hundred and fifty people gathered under the roof makes for quite a din. It is definitely overcrowded, especially with everyone trying to get in a shower or grab something to eat.

Gathering Black and Red Team together, along with Bannerman, Frank, and the crews transporting the supplies, we head out for our rendezvous with Leonard. I'm hoping he can dock in Olympia as I'd rather not take the time to drive to Tacoma. I have a lot to do to get ready if we're going to leave in the morning on our little venture. If the numbers line up, I'd like to get the Stryker loaded today so we can be ready to leave first thing in the morning. The overcast and broken clouds of the previous days are absent and we are greeted with clear skies although a brisk breeze is blowing.

I am struck by how tall the grass in the median is. It and the tops of the fir trees bend with each gust that blows through. A red-tailed hawk swoops down from one of the trees and plummets into the tall reeds lining the Interstate. It appears moments later with something small grasped in its talons. One life ends so that another may continue.

Pieces of paper and a few leaves are pushed along the windswept streets of town as our convoy of vehicles makes its way through. Packed dirt, sand, and debris lie in the recessed doorways of the buildings. Windows, which once were the dreaded duty of employees to clean on a daily basis, are streaked with grime to the point that the displays sitting just inside are barely visible. The stenciled or decaled store signs on the doors and windows, along with a myriad of taped advertisements, are close to becoming unreadable. The city is quickly decaying.

Emerging from the city proper, we pass by the boarded up building that housed the once busy Saturday Market. *I guess all produce will be organically grown from here on out*, I think as we pass and drive down the crumbling street to the single dock that serves Olympia. Only one ship lies tied to the large pier jutting out into the waters of the south Puget Sound. The thick lines that keep the ship connected to the dock will eventually rot and the ship will then be at the mercy of the tides, either floating out into the large body of water or crashing into the boats docked in the marina. Those will also eventually become free and I have an image of boats piled up on the shores with the large cargo vessel leaning amongst them.

Driving onto the concrete dock itself, I see the sleek black outlines of the *Santa Fe* making its way toward us in the choppy waters. I exchange radio calls with Leonard and he informs us that there is enough room to dock and he will pull into shore here. We wait in on the pier with our pant legs and shirt sleeves flapping in the brisk wind.

The sub eventually nestles next to the pier and we toss heavy mooring lines to the waiting crew. Maneuvering a makeshift gangplank into position, Leonard and some of his crew meet us on the dock. Bannerman organizes our crew and soon supplies are being handed over and stowed below.

Leonard tells his story of the past three days and nights and I fill him in on ours. I begin to mention our plan to search for any surviving family members. He stops me and pulls me to the side.

"I'd rather not have my crew hear about your plans to look for families, captain. That will only spur them to want to look for theirs, and right now I need a tight crew. I would be interested in hearing what you find out, but please, before you exchange that information, make sure I am the only one listening," Leonard says once we are out of earshot of everyone else.

"I completely understand and share my own uneasiness about leaving. But we promised the soldiers we would try when we could and we don't have that long before our window closes. We only have a few months before the fuel goes bad and the weather will be closing in soon. I'll be sure to relay any information to you only," I reply.

"That would be much appreciated, captain. Speaking of communication, we should test the satellite comms," he says.

We break out the satellite phones Bannerman gathered from the base and, much to my surprise, we are able to make contact with them. This will also open up the ability to communicate with Lynn and the others while we are off on our little jaunt. I'm surprised I didn't think of that earlier as that was our main method of communication while out in the field. I guess I just assumed that, with the downfall of civilization, the satellites wouldn't be functional for long. That alleviates one big worry. I was always worried that something would happen to us while flying across the country and we wouldn't be able to let the others back here know. I had no doubt we could return as vehicles lie in abundance, but the time delay would cause worry at home.

"What are your plans?" I ask, watching another load of supplies make their way up the gangway.

"I think we'll head down the western seaboard and check out some of the smaller coastal towns and ports along the way. I'd like to take a look at San Francisco and LA with the eventual goal of checking out San Diego. I'll then evaluate whether to sail over to Hawaii at that point. If there are any naval assets still functioning, they'd be there, but after observing Bangor, Whidbey, and Seattle, I have my doubts as to whether we'll find anything," he replies.

"Okay. Keep in mind that we have aviation assets that can come assist if you need, although Hawaii would be a stretch," I say.

"I'll keep that in mind. And thanks for everything. I know we may not have hit it off well and, we still have a certain discussion coming, but thanks. I appreciate you digging into your stock and allowing us to resupply," Leonard responds.

"It's the least we could do. Just so you know, we tossed in enough weapons and ammo to arm your crew," I state.

"Thanks again," he says, reaching out his hand.

It takes time but the supplies are eventually handed over and stored. We shake hands all around and Leonard and his crew head on board. The gangway is removed and lines pulled back. The *Santa Fe* backs out of the docks, turns, and begins making its way across the waters, parting the waves. The figures observing from the bridge grow smaller. We watch as the black sub, far into the sound, turns north. It disappears around the point by Boston Harbor as it slowly makes its long trek to the open seas.

We head back and I spend most of the morning going over take off and flying data to include the weight of the Stryker. The Stryker is below the payload limitations for the 130 and the numbers look good. The only constraint will be our range which will be shortened to around one thousand miles. None of our legs come close to that distance so we should be okay. The only thing that sticks in my mind is if we find other survivors. With the Stryker on board and with the additional fuel we'll take along for it, we'll be restricted to eighty passengers. That puts the 130 right at its max parameters and I've never been enthusiastic about operating an aircraft right at its maximum weight limitations. Those are made up from engineers using new aircraft. Yes, there are the usual twenty percent margins thrown in…but still.

Gathering Red Team and some of the others that are going on the picnic with us, we head up to McChord to see if we can fit a Stryker in a 130 without knocking holes in the fuselage. After a few attempts and close calls, which involved yells, screams, and madly waving arms, we manage to get the behemoth parked snugly inside and tied down. Late in the afternoon, Roger returns from his search for local survivors. I'm notified that the pickup crews found eight additional survivors in the north Tacoma area. I'm surprised that we found any given the vast numbers of night runners we observed the other night. It's heartening news and lends hope that we'll be able to find even more. It's great to have an additional pilot that can help out with the searches.

We meet that evening and I lay out my planned trip once again, informing everyone of being able to take the Stryker along. Weather, and everything else permitting, the trip will take ten to eleven days. Picking up an additional gunship will be nice as we don't have any maintenance personnel who can conduct inspections on a 130. That would be a wonderful pickup but it's not that we can use aircraft for much longer anyway.

Bannerman notes that the inner wall should be finished with the coming day and then they'll start on the towers and apartment building foundations. He also mentions having crews begin to clean up the rubble created from our nightly poundings and starting to take down the trees. Counting our supplies, he tells us we should have more than enough to make it through the winter. There are literally tons of supplies in the one distribution center and if needed, there is another one some distance to the south.

"Any word on our ability to create bio fuels?" I ask.

"We've been stockpiling the used oils from the kitchen. As far as actually making it, well, that's a different story. I think I'll have to see if the libraries we've spared have any information. That will mean we'll have to go inside and search," Bannerman answers.

There is a moment of silence as we know what that means – another venture into a darkened building and possibly a night runner lair.

"Well, if we have to, then we have to," Horace comments. "I'll take my team in if we need to go."

"Let's visit that once we finish with the current training class. We'll have another team online then," Lynn responds.

"I have a potentially tricky topic to bring up. I was approached today by several individuals asking about religious services," Frank says.

I thought the group went silent thinking about heading into a darkened night runner lair, but Frank's comment brings an absolute dead quiet. I should have actually anticipated this, but my mind has been working in other directions lately. I am fully open to any religious preference and individual beliefs. It's the organization of it that worries me. It has the potential to tear a line of separation within our survivor group if there is any degree of fanaticism that goes along with it. Believe me, I am completely open and have my own beliefs, but they are my own and belong to me only. I want people to have their own set of beliefs, but it's the potential of developing the "I am right and you are wrong" division that worries me. Many wars have been started because of that mentality, and I'd rather not have a defined separation amongst us.

"Well, I don't know about anyone else, but I'm certainly not against it," I reply. The rest voice similar thoughts.

"Do we have anyone…I guess qualified, to lead services?

I mean, anyone can worship however they see fit. I mean, up to a point. I'm not all that big on gutting small animals and the like," I state.

"I'm not sure of that to be honest. I was just approached and asked whether we planned on having any," Frank replies.

"I suppose if we have a priest or minister, or the ones who asked know of any, we can definitely incorporate that. As long as everyone knows we still have work to do and can't really afford to be taking days off at this point," I say.

"I'll check around and see," Frank says.

"One thing, though, and this is my only worry about something like this, I don't want this to create a fracture within our group. Worship and praise as one likes, but I don't want it to develop into one's religious preferences being forced on others," I say.

"If I can interject here, and this may not sound right or come across in the right way, but, we also can't afford to have religion dictate or interfere with our leadership. Whether that is in our style of leadership or with the decisions we make. We make our decisions based on our best chances of survival at this point and that sometimes leads to hard or unpopular decisions," Drescoll states.

And, there's the elephant that just entered the room. We have an entity established by our leadership and allowing another entity to exist creates the potential for conflict. Of course, who am I to say people can't congregate together for religious preferences, just as long as that thought process is one of openness and tolerance for others. I may be getting way ahead of myself in my thinking, though. After all, it's only a few people that asked if there was a plan for having religious services. Ugh! I feel like just handing the reins over now and heading off for sunny beaches.

"While I agree with that, I also don't see anything wrong with having services for those who want it. If they find someone who wants to and can lead them, then by all means, let them. They'll just have to organize them around our already set schedules," I say.

"I'll let them know at one of our nightly training classes," Frank replies.

"And on another lovely note, I'm off to bed," Lynn says. "Coming, Jack."

My cat-like reflexes serve me well as I'm out of the chair before my mind or body even registers it. Lynn and I spend the night talking and, well… then talk further before falling asleep in each other's arms.

*   *   *   *   *   *

She is startled awake after having just dropped off into a deep sleep. The hunt was long and she is tired from running far into the night. It was a good hunt and her pack ate well, but her legs ache a little and she feels exhausted. She glances around to find what woke her out of her slumber and sniffs the air. She catches a scent of prey nearby.

Although her hunger has already been sated, her mouth begins to salivate and her stomach rumbles ever so slightly. It's both a sweet and musky scent at the same time. She knows this scent but hasn't smelled it in some time. It's the odor that emanates from the two-legged ones. Confused that it is coming from so close in the large lair, she turns her head sharply toward where the odor is coming. She sees a two-legged one, appearing much like her own kind dressed in torn and ragged clothing, standing off to one side looking around in a confused manner.

A low growl issues from her throat. The scent that comes to her nostrils evokes an overpowering rage and hunger – a thirst that can't be satisfied. She rises and, not able to control herself, emits a loud shriek. The two-legged one flinches, and takes off at a run toward one of the walls of the lair. Others around her wake in a flash and begin sniffing at the air. They pick up the smell that woke her and soon the room is filled with shrieks that echo off the concrete brick walls. Catching sight of the fleeing one, they chase after it. They are behind her though as she began pursuit as soon as the two-legged one began running.

The thrill of the chase fills her, heightened by the fact that it is a two-legged one she is after. Her elated shriek rises above the others. She can almost taste the sweet blood and fresh meat. The two-legged one ahead manages to find a door and stumbles through it. She has faced the two-legged ones before and managed to survive. His stumbling around in the dark confuses her as the ones she has encountered previously seemed able to see very well in the dark. This thought is lost in the rage, hunger, and anticipation she feels.

Racing through the closing door, she turns in a narrow hallway close on the heels of the two-legged one. She sees it crash into one of the side walls and falter. She is now right behind it. A few more steps and the feeding will commence. The chase and thrill fills her and she hungers for that first bite. Her mind registers the thuds of the others of her kind hitting the door as they enter the hall. She reaches out and catches hold of the shirt that is barely clinging to its body. Remembering another time when she brushed the shirt of another fleeing two-legged one, brushing but not catching hold, she clenches her hand on the shirt and doesn't let go. That one a while ago managed to get away and escape. This one will not.

The two-legged one screams as she jerks back and it loses its balance, falling to the soft flooring below. She immediately falls upon it, biting and tearing at the tender skin. Blood flows from the wounds she creates, its sweet smell permeating the air. The two-legged one is screaming beneath her, heightening the thrill of the feeding. She shrieks loudly with pleasure and leans over, sinking her teeth into the soft neck. Twisting her head violently, warm blood spurts out from the wound coating her with its stickiness. The one below her goes limp and the spraying blood slows to a trickle.

Shrieking once again, she lowers her head to feed as the rest of the body is covered with other pack members. They claw at the body seeking to get their fill. The clothing is shredded away exposing the delicious meat underneath. Mouths and hands attack and soon a sickly sweet smell pervades the air as the insides are laid bare. She goes for the tender parts of the face, tearing strips of flesh from the cheeks. Her exhaustion is forgotten as she and the others feed until only a few strips of flesh, tendon, and hair remain on the bloody bones.

* * * * * *

Lacing up my boots early in the morning, I feel exhaustion creep through me. Lynn and I stayed up late enjoying each other's company, not wanting the evening to end as that meant being the beginning of days on end apart. However, as time does, the night passes without any input from either of us. I throw more items into my bag as Lynn tiredly ties her boots. She looks up with eyes reddened from lack of sleep and exhaustion. No words need to be spoken, dawn is upon us and it's time for me to be on my way.

We grab a bite to eat together and watch as the others who are going with us emerge from their cubicles one at a time. Robert, dressed in a flight suit with an M-4 draped over his shoulder and packed duffle bag on the ground beside him, leans against the upper railing with his arm around Michelle. Bri exits with a huge yawn and stretch that belies her diminutive stature, nods at Robert and Michelle, reaches back inside for her carbine and pack before heading downstairs. The others of Red Team and the reorganized Echo Team gather around one of the tables on the first floor.

"Well, hon, I guess it's about that time," I say to Lynn.

"I know. I hate that you have to leave, Jack. I don't like this one bit," she replies.

"I don't either. One of these days, it will come about that we don't have to do this. This just, well, sucks," I state.

"Yes it does and I'm so looking forward to that time. We might as well get this over with. You know, the Band-Aid approach. I'll walk you down and see you off, again."

We walk downstairs hand in hand. Tired 'good mornings' make their way around and we gather our gear. The light of the early morning fills the parking lots without a cloud in the sky. The brisk breeze that was prevalent yesterday has passed by leaving a calm morning. The morning still has a chill to it that speaks of a new season approaching. I turn and wrap Lynn in my arms holding her tight. I notice Robert and Michelle enacting the same scene a short distance away.

"I love you, Lynn," I whisper into her ear.

"I love you, too, Jack. So much," she returns.

We stay that way a moment later exchanging a long kiss before she finally says, "Now get out of here. I have a busy morning."

I know it's her way of dealing with the pain of separation and, to be honest, without her saying something like that, I wouldn't depart. We release from our hug and I grab my bag. Our hands are locked together and then slowly drift apart with our fingers trailing. *Fuck! This really sucks*, I think as our hands part. With a heavy heart, I turn toward the parked Humvees where the others have finished loading their gear. Robert catches up and, together, we walk to a Humvee and throw our things in.

The drive is like many of the others we've had. My head doesn't clear much from its tiredness as we proceed through the base. I reach out with my mind and don't feel the presence of any night runners in the area. Wondering if the ability has receded, I reach out farther but still come up empty. I'll have to test it out if we receive visitors during the night on any of our stops. I was able to detect faint presences the other night when flying above the hordes of them emptying into the night. I just don't know. As we pull onto the ramp and the 130s parked there come into view, the tired feeling leaves and I focus on what's ahead of us.

We load our supplies and fuel on board. Robert has questions about the seating arrangements for the flight and I let him know I'll be flying the first leg due to the increased weight on board. Later, I'll let him get some stick time in to get a feel for the heaviness. He begins to load the flight data into the computer. There isn't much room in the bag with the metal monster tied down but we manage. I double check the tie downs. It really wouldn't do to have it shift on takeoff or in flight. On the list of bad things to happen, that would come close to topping the list. Twenty-six tons of metal shifting around in the cargo does some funny things to flight characteristics. Like turning it from having flight characteristics into that of having falling characteristics. A C-130 does not make a good parachute.

We are soon started up and, with an increase in power, the 130 reluctantly begins to move. It takes more runway than usual, but we are airborne and slowly claw our way to altitude. I look across the Puget Sound thinking I may catch a glimpse of the *Santa Fe* but there is nothing to be seen plowing the waterways. Turning toward the morning sun, we set a course to the southeast and our first stop at Mountain Home AFB where one of the soldiers has a wife and two kids. They apparently chose to reside in their hometown while he deployed to the Middle East.

It's only about an hour and a half flight to the base so we may be able to launch our search of the town of Mountain Home upon our arrival depending on what we see. I plan to fly over the town to scout it out before landing. The snow-capped peak of Mount Rainier is off to our left and we pass directly over the crater of Mount St. Helens. The warm crater has wisps of steam rising from the dome in the middle. The forested hills of the Cascade Mountains give way to the brown fields of Eastern Washington and we are soon over the Blue Mountains of Northeastern Oregon.

We pick up Interstate 84 on the other side of the mountains and I begin a slow descent. We will basically follow the highway to Mountain Home. Boise passes off to the left and looks much like the last time we passed by. Mountain Home soon appears on our nose as we edge down closer to the ground. Mountains rise on either side of the brown valley that the Interstate cuts through. Some areas are agricultural with the once green circle pattern of irrigation systems now overgrown and brown. Some others have cattle still roaming about in the fields. Only a few natural ponds exist in this dry, arid land and it's only around these that the black dots of cattle still thrive.

Leveling off about two thousand feet above the terrain, with a few bumps from the winds blowing off the mountains and still warm land, I put the town of Mountain Home off to my side. The town itself is nestled between two major roads with the interstate branching off to the eastern side. Off in the distance, I see the runways of Mountain Home AFB – our destination.

Slowing, I circle over the city and see that the town is mostly residential. While the trees that line the residential streets are still green, the golf course, baseball and football fields, parks, and yards have turned the same brown as the outlying fields. Other than a few cars parked in some of the parking lots serving some stores, the streets and lots are clear. Cars sit in driveways and the town appears normal with the exception of the lack of movement. It's like most other towns we've encountered and I have a feeling that every town we fly over will be the same. It doesn't bode well for the soldier in back who I imagine is glued to the window looking out.

"I don't see anything here. Anyone else see anything?" I ask on the intercom. Craig has risen from his seat at the nav station to look.

"I don't see anything," Craig answers.

"Nothing here," Robert replies.

"Okay, take note of the streets and layout and let's head over to the base. We'll do a flyby there and practice a few touch and go's so you can get the feel for the extra weight," I say.

I swing us to the southwest toward the small base and line us up with the single, long runway serving the base. Putting runway 30 on our nose, I lower to just a couple hundred feet. I want to do a flyby to check wind direction. The turbulence picks up this close to the ground and we pass a few parked F-15s on the hot ramps. I see a few others parked on the main ramp farther down. The main section of the base is similar to the town, a few green trees with the rest overgrown and brown.

Our low approach shows a moderate wind out of the

northeast so our first approach was a good one. I bring the aircraft up and around wanting to do the first touch and go with Robert following on the control stick to get the feel of the heavier response. We circle around and set up. The wheels settle to the runway with a slight jostle and, after resetting the flaps to their takeoff setting, apply power and are soon airborne again. I hand the aircraft over to Robert and monitor his approach. The heavy weight, only slightly diminished with our fuel burn, causes the nose to drop more than usual when he decreases the power. Making the adjustment, he sets it in with more of an arrival.

Setting the flaps for him, I catch a quick glimpse of movement off to the side out Robert's window. Of course, with the aircraft moving down the runway, everything outside appears to be moving. I do a double-take and see a blue Air Force pickup truck speed on the tarmac to our right. Others pull onto the ramp behind it.

"I have the aircraft," I call out, taking control. I lift off and turn, low to the ground, to the southwest and away from the ramp.

"What? What did I do wrong?" Robert asks, looking at the instruments and then over to me.

"Nothing. We have company on the ramp," I say, climbing away from that base. I see Robert turn to look back out his window, but we are headed directly away and I doubt there's much he can see.

"Craig, would you go get Greg and have him come up here, please," I say.

I climb to five thousand feet and circle a distance away. I tell Greg, Craig, and Robert that I spotted four vehicles on the ramp during out last landing.

"I'm not sure of who they are, or their intentions. We weren't on the ground long enough to see what they may be up to," I say.

"Could they be Air Force or military personnel?" Greg asks.

"I have no idea. If they do have a presence here still, they may not like us just showing up. Although, if that is the case, they won't just shoot at us. They'll most likely let us land and then take us in to interrogate us. If it isn't military, then all bets are off as to what they'll do," I answer.

"Well, what do you want to do? Should we just bypass this and head to our next stop?" Greg says.

"I don't know. If there are survivors here, and it's apparent there are, I'm thinking we should at least drop in and say hi," I reply.

"And if they shoot at us on approach or while landing?" Robert asks.

"That wouldn't be a good thing," Craig chimes in.

"We'll do a flyover at this altitude and see how they respond. This will keep us out of small arms fire range and allow us to have a look," I say.

"Alright, let's check it out then," Greg says.

I turn back ready to dive the aircraft and beat cheeks the best this 'ol bird can do if I see tracers or smoke trails heading our way. The 'Herc" can take a lot of damage, but I'm not all that keen on testing just how much. I call on the emergency frequencies with no response.

Flying across the runway and base, I look to the ramp below. Five blue pickup trucks are parked in close to the middle of the ramp with tiny figures of people standing around. No tracers or smoke trails reach out toward us. Passing the base, I descend and come back, crossing from a different angle. Several people look upward shielding their eyes with their hands. A couple of them stand off to the side with weapons in their hands, but they aren't pointed in our direction.

"Well, we're still flying," I say, heading the aircraft back to the southwest. "What do you think?"

"They weren't firing or pointing weapons at us. It did appear they were dressed in civilian clothing although those weapons were either AR-style carbines or actual M-4s," Greg responds.

"Well, let's see what happens then, shall we," I say. Greg heads into the cargo compartment to brief the teams.

I do a combat overhead landing and drop it in, stopping on the runway after only a couple of thousand feet with the engines revved and ready to go. My feet get tired of standing on the brakes watching for a response. Robert looks through a pair of binoculars and reports that the people, who he counts at fourteen, gather together in a group with a six of them heading behind the cover of the vehicles. I do not like their actions of folding into cover, but I'm sure our actions aren't making them all that comfortable either. I ask about their clothing and Robert confirms they are dressed in a variety of civilian clothing. The others continue standing and looking in our direction.

"Okay, someone has to break this stalemate," I say, releasing the brakes and bringing the power back. Greg pokes his head back up in the cockpit.

"I'm taxiing in but parking down the ramp away from them. I want Red Team to be ready to go outside with me. Greg, you and Echo Team get the Stryker ready to go, but only take the tie downs off. If we're attacked, drop the Stryker out and return fire. I'm not overly thrilled with inviting fire toward the aircraft, but if others appear and we find ourselves in a precarious position, fold back in and we're leaving. Robert, I'm leaving the engines running so hop in the left seat and get us ready to go in a hurry," I brief.

"You mean in more of a precarious situation than the one we're in?" Greg asks, only half joking.

"Yes, Greg, in one worse than we already are," I answer.

"Touchy, touchy. Okay, you got it, Jack."

I leave the seat and Robert takes over with Craig folding into the co-pilot seat. Heading down into the cargo area, I see Echo Team releasing and stowing the tie downs from the Stryker. I don my vest and check my gear, meeting Red Team assembled by the rear ramp. Gonzalez looks at me and nods toward Bri by her side.

"You keep her close beside you," I say to which she nods again and smiles at Bri.

I hear Robert comment over the radio that two cars are driving our way. I drop the ramp and, with Red Team close behind, head down it and take station near the rear of the aircraft. The roar of the engines increases in the open air and wind whips to the rear behind the giant, rotation props. Through the blurring propellers, I see the two approaching vehicles. The whine of the Stryker's diesel sounds just above the roar of the 130 engines.

"How many in each vehicle?" I say into the radio.

"I count five all told in the cabs with no one in the beds," Robert responds.

"Okay. Thanks. Keep an eye out among the hangars and surrounding area for more that arrive or that we missed," I say.

"Okay, Dad," he replies.

I watch as the trucks pull up short of the nose of the aircraft and five people emerge to stand by the front of their vehicles. No fire has been exchanged which is heartening. I nod to Red Team to follow and head out with the gale force winds trying to blow me into the surrounding mountains. I walk with the others to the small group telling Greg to be ready to head out with the Stryker.

"I have to say it's nice seeing you folks. We thought we were the only ones left. I'm Jason," one of the men shouts above the engines as we draw close.

"Jack. Jack Walker," I say, shaking his outstretched hand. I turn and give Robert the hand across the throat cutoff signal.

The roar winds down as Robert cuts the engines. I radio Greg letting him know the cavalry isn't needed. His disappointed sigh and, "Dammit. And here I dressed in this silver armor for nothing," in response says it all.

"Are you what remains of the military? Is there a larger force either incoming or based elsewhere? The military folks here say they haven't been able to raise anyone for months," Jason says as the props slow to a stop.

I'm not really sure what to tell him and feel I've been a little free with our story to strangers to this point. Everything here seems well enough and Jason appears to be above board but my experiences of late have made me jaded. I don't like it but there it is.

"Before answering, I'd like to hear your story here," I answer.

Jason tilts his head as if re-evaluating us. "Eh, what the hell," he eventually says and proceeds to tell us the story of those here.

He tells of the sickness and the attacks at night. With some help from the few remaining military people on base, he and some others gathered the rest of the people from town and moved here. They cleaned out the base and set up shop. All in all, it sounds like what we have set up back home. With the exception that we are facing a much larger population of night runners. The isolation of the base has protected them to some extent.

"So, how do you keep the night runners out?" I ask.

"Night runners? What are those?" he says and I describe them.

"Oh, we call them changelings. They don't bother us much out here," he says. "We cleared out the base and we're rather isolated with the town being over ten miles away. We patrol and take down the occasional one who manages to meander out this way. We also take a cow up to the northwest part of town every couple of days, chain it up, and essentially feed them so they don't take a mind to wander down here," he states.

I think over that idea. It's a good one but won't really apply to our situation as there is no way we could feed thirty thousand night runners. Jason goes on to describe setting up cattle pens on base and using the hangars as greenhouses. They took most of the roofs off and lined them with clear, plastic sheeting.

"I'm just curious, doesn't feeding the changelings, as you call them, run up your stock of cattle?" I ask.

"Nah, there are thousands of cattle in the valley. We knocked down most of the fencing and they congregate around the natural watering holes. They're also far enough out that the changelings can't get to them," Jason replies. It really seems like they have a pretty good setup going.

"Any problems with marauders or bandits?"

"None so far. I imagine there might be some like that up in the Boise area, but we're truly pretty isolated out here," he answers.

"No one is so isolated that satellites can't find you," a man behind Jason says. I notice Jason roll his eyes without the man seeing.

"You know, Captain Walker I take it, this wasn't any accident. This whole thing was planned," the man continues.

"Harold, knock it off. Jack, this is Harold, our resident conspiracy theory nut," Jason says.

"Seriously, Jason. I hacked their systems before this went down and I'm telling you, this was planned and those bastards are still around," Harold says.

"Yeah, and like I keep sayin', why haven't they shown up," Jason responds.

"Because they aren't interested in us…yet," Harold says.

"Seriously?! You can't plan something like this. It's too easy to get out of control," I state.

"And that's why we haven't seen them. They're recovering, but they'll be here. I can assure you of that," Harold says.

"And where are they then?" I ask. I'm intrigued, but really just primarily amused.

"I don't know that. I was just getting there when I was discovered in the system and booted. Then I blew outta town. I was passing through when the shit hit the fan. But I do know that it was at a high level. The Pentagon, the CDC, USAMRIID, the World Health Organization, high levels of government, some who looked like corporate bigwigs. Everyone, man. I saw a list before being slammed outta there," Harold answers.

"I'm pretty sure we'd have seen something by now, Harold," Jason states.

"Captain, let me ask you this then. You must have flown around some. You wouldn't just drop in here as a first look. Have you noticed the satellites still operating? Your GPS systems still functioning? I mean, you'd expect those satellites to decay pretty rapidly, wouldn't you?" Harold asks.

I think to my surprise that we were able to use the satellite phones. Honestly, I haven't tried the GPS systems thinking they wouldn't be accurate for long. I also think about the cell phones operating as long as they did but chalked that up to good old Northwest environmental folks and the transition to solar power. Still, this conversation is more amusing than holding any degree of truth. There will be conspiracy theorists in any group, and I'm surprised one hasn't cropped up in our survivor group.

"I guess that depends on the automated systems and the fuel they had onboard. If there was anyone left like that, we'd have seen something of them," I respond.

"Wait and see, captain, wait and see."

"Harold, that's enough. I listen to you and let you amuse yourself with your ramblings, but I won't have you spouting that nonsense to our guests, so knock it off," Jason says.

"So…what does bring you out to our neck of the woods, Jack?" Jason continues.

I tell our story and end with, "So, to answer your question, we are out searching for any surviving family members."

"I take it one of yours possibly has family located here? I know who we have. If you want to give me the name of who you're looking for, I can let you know if they're here or possibly what happened to them," Jason states. I give him the name of the soldier noting Jason's eyes widen a touch. He turns to one of the men with him and whispers. The man leaves with one of the trucks.

"If you want to bring him out, I think we may have a welcome surprise for him," Jason says. I'm hoping this means good news and feel elated.

The soldier joins us and the truck returns a short time later. A young brunette woman steps out from the passenger side with a young boy.

"Jeeeeeeenny!" the soldier shouts and takes off at a run. They join in a tight hug with the boy joining in. We all look on at the joyful reunion. I'm glad to see a moment of pure joy in this harsh land.

"I'm sad to say that his daughter…well…didn't make it," Jason whispers.

It's another moment of ultimate joy tempered with that of extreme sorrow. I see the soldier sink to his knees and bury his face in his hands. His wife kneels next to him with her arm around his shoulders shaking with his sobs. I know exactly how he feels. It's not something that time heals. You learn to deal with it, but that hole will remain forever.

We talk for a few moments and I extend an invitation for his group to join us if they would like. It's mostly to fill the uncomfortable moments as the sad scene continues a short distance away. I tell Jason it would take us a couple of trips to gather all of them as we are loaded down at the moment. I notice Harold listening with interest. Jason says he will have to talk with the group but gives an indication that not many will want to leave. They have a sense of security where they're at and are well supplied. I can understand not wanting to leave a place of security for an unknown. He extends an invitation to spend the night with the promise of an answer in the morning.

The soldier asks if he can be given leave to go with his family. I nod and let him know that we are spending the night. I let Jason know that we are used to spending the night in the aircraft but he tells us there are plenty of homes that have been cleaned up and are available. I feel a little anxious about being in an unsecured place like that. He offers to give us a tour of the place and makes vehicles available as long as we don't leave the base. I talk it over with our group with the census coming to, "It sure would be nice to sleep in a real bed."

It seems they are secure here and, from what I can judge by meeting others in the little town they've created, it seems okay. I meet with those that were assigned to the base and provide security. They report they have had little problems with the changelings and seeing they are "feeding" them today, they don't anticipate any difficulties. Still anxious but understanding the others wanting to sleep on a comfortable bed, I let them stay. I'll remain with the aircraft along with Robert and Bri. I tell the team members that if anything happens, they are to make for the aircraft. I also arrange for us to maintain radio contact. And, with that, we dine with the others here and adjourn to our sleeping quarters.

I radio Lynn on the sat phone before turning in. Oranges, reds, and purples paint the sky behind the mountains rising in the west, bathing the cockpit with the last of the day's rays. We secure the aircraft and make a final radio call to the teams.

"I hope you are enjoying that cot, Jack. Don't think about me sinking into this pillow top mattress," Greg says.

"I hope you sleep well. Don't lose any sleep thinking I might just take off on you in the middle of the night," I respond.

"You wouldn't do that. You'd miss me too much," Greg replies.

"Yeah, I would. And by that, I mean no, I wouldn't. That popping sound you'd hear would be a bottle of bubbly opening and me celebrating."

I set the radio by my side making sure the volume is up and turn off the aircraft battery. The kids and I lay in our bunks talking for a few hours before we drift off.

* * * * * *

The moon hangs bright and crisp in the velvet black sky. The pinpoints of light that share the night sky are lost from view directly around it from its brilliant glow. The sharpness above goes with the brisk evening below. The moon and stars remain suspended over the earth, witnesses to all that transpire below, but not caring. They have their thing to do and those below have theirs. They wheel about the sky as they've done for time immemorial. Those below are relatively new to the universe and therefore merit little of their attention. Their trials and glories are short-lived by comparison.

All of that is lost on her as she deals with her own struggles. She is separated from her pack. Those that survived the quick but brutal fight with a large pack of four-legged ones fled. The others that were members of her pack lie on the darkened street where they fell, bathed in the silver glow of the tingly, bright light hovering in the night sky above. She is at least thankful that the four-legged ones fled as well or she wouldn't be around to have these thoughts.

She and her pack were out hunting when they found themselves tracked and then beset upon. The night hunt had already been a long one, the fight short, and now the time of darkness is drawing to an end. She is badly injured and crawling across the hard pavement as she has been doing for some time. Realizing that time is not on her side, tired and in pain, she reaches out to struggle another couple of inches.

Pain flares inside at the movement, but she must make it to shelter before the bright, burning light rises, signaling the end of her time outside. She has felt the agony of it for a fleeting second before and has no desire to experience that again. It's like a hand on the burner that is quickly withdrawn but the memory of it lasts forever.

She slowly raises her head to see she is close to the side of the hard path. Ahead is high grass with an abandoned two-legged lair beyond. That is her goal, her salvation, shelter from an excruciating, painful end. With a grunt to mask the pain that shoots through her body, she pushes up and over the small rise at the edge of the street. She then collapses again waiting for the pain to subside. Behind her, a dark smear along the pavement marks her path. It doesn't look far but, to her, it seems like she has been crawling for an eternity. She looks at the distance she's traveled and eyes the shelter ahead. A measure of despair and fear, the feelings different to an extent to what we'd know as feelings, enters as the distance looks impossible.

With the pain reaching a tolerable level once again, she stretches her arms forward, lifts up slightly, and pulls herself forward a little more. That's the way it's been for hours – reach, rise, pull, collapse, wait…reach, rise… Her senses tell her she doesn't have long, which pushes her to greater endeavors – reach, rise, pull, collapse, wait. The pain she is feeling now is nothing to what she'll feel if she doesn't reach the lair.

Her mind reaches out, but the only packs she senses are far away with many already heading back to the lair. She'll get no help there. Reach, rise, pull, collapse, wait. The white hot pain encompasses her entire body, flooding her mind with the shooting agony. Reach, rise, pull, collapse, wait. She makes it to the edge of the grass and, with another effort, enters it. The safety of the lair draws closer.

It's a race against time. Distance is her enemy and willpower her only tool. She wants to just lie down and give up. The desire to live won't let her. She has no idea how she'll enter the lair just a short distance away but will deal with that when she gets there. First things first, she has to make it there. One thing at a time. Reach, rise, pull, collapse, wait. She knows she is badly injured and not even sure her body will make it through the night. That worry will be dealt with later. She does feel her life force ebbing from her with each effort. Each exertion tires her even more and she feels her energy being sapped. Reach, rise, pull, collapse, wait.

Her surroundings are lost from view in the tall grass. The world has collapsed down to the foot she can see around her. The next few inches of progress require her entire focus. Off into the distance, she can barely hear the shrieks from the returning packs. A few howls of the four-legged ones drift on the night air. A hissing scream issues from nearby as two feral animals meet and fight for territory. Reach, rise, pull, collapse, wait.

Her senses tell her that the sky toward the high rises of land is lightening. She has made it far, but her crawling isn't the only thing that has been moving. Time has followed her every effort. She feels a trickle of blood escape from her lips, hanging down from her mouth in a long string. Pain grips her insides as the throws up a mixture of liquid and the remains of the little food in her, hitting the ground with a splash. Reach, rise, pull, collapse, wait.

She can't see anything but the very top of the shelter ahead appearing to loom over the top of the reeds. She's close and a small amount of hope enters. Along with that measure, another tearing pain grips her and she slowly folds into a ball attempting to ward off the agony. With a small part of her mind that is still hers through the pain, she tries to will the hurt to go away. She needs to keep moving. Her panting breath is the only sound as the misery begins to ebb. On her side, she makes out the blackness of the night sky lighten, becoming the dark blue of the impending day. Her heart races with fear.

Uncoiling, she pulls herself another foot. She wishes her legs would work so she could push off and not have to rely totally on her arms, but she lost the feeling in those long ago. The stalks of grass surrounding her become more defined as the light increases. Panic enters her mind and she reaches out again, the dread of what is coming overpowering the pain to an extent. More of the shelter appears. She's close and her mind begins to have thoughts of how to enter. Hope increases. Reach, rise, pull, collapse, wait…closer by another few inches.

A flare of golden light strikes the top of the lair and then the grass, slowly traversing down the stalks. She shrieks with fear and despair. Reach, rise, pull, collapse, wait. The light from the bright, burning ball inches slowly downward.

Reach, rise, pull, collapse, wait…

Reach, rise, pull, collapse, wait.

The light is halfway down the blades. She sees the entrance ahead through the grass. She is almost there. Just a few more efforts. Reach, rise, pull, collapse, wait. Her forward progress is matched by the march of the light downward. It's just above her position in the grass. With a shriek she reaches forward. The light falls upon her.

The moon continues to sail across the sky in the dawning light of the day, uncaring to the troubles below.

* * * * * *

Feeling drawn by both the two-legged one occupying her thoughts and the other strange one she felt, Sandra leads her pack north again. There are plenty of the small furry creatures to feed her large pack so she's not worried about them eating. She's intrigued and not sure which intrigues her more, the one who brushed her mind so long ago or the one who felt like her own kind but didn't respond to her call. The intrigue with that one stems from his being inside the two-legged lair yet not feeding on them, or responding to her call. She also wonders why the two-legged ones allow him in their midst.

Watching over her pack once again as they scurry among the ruins to feast, she reaches out. She knows this will allow Michael to know where she is but she'll deal with that later. She rubs her stomach subconsciously in a protective nature. The young one inside of her has started to show lately. Soon, she won't be able to hunt with her pack and they will have to bring her food. That time will be short and then she'll have to hunt for him or her.

Her protective nature, however, is overcome by her intrigue and infatuation with this two-legged one and that confuses her. It feels alien as she knows she should normally be concentrating on her young one. She feels torn but can't help what she is doing. She senses the other strange one. He is still inside the lair and she wonders if he is being held captive by the two-legged ones. She can't imagine being inside without wanting to feed…needing to feed…the rage would be too intense not to attack.

She sends the mental image for him to join but receives no response which puzzles her even more. She sends other images in order to establish some sort of contact, but there aren't any return messages indicating he heard. She calls once again for him to join her, to hunt with her and her pack. Nothing. She searches for the two-legged one but doesn't sense him. With a shriek of frustration, she stops searching and joins her pack to feed.

* * * * * *

Alan wakes in a cold sweat. He looks around feeling terror mixed with eagerness and a strange thrill. His heart is racing as he becomes aware of his surroundings. Fearing he is downstairs again, the few objects in his cubicle become clearer in the dim light of the interior. *At least I'm not waking somewhere downstairs tonight*, he thinks, rubbing his face.

The dream – more of a nightmare but a thrilling one – fades slowly, and he tries the catch the quickly disappearing remains. He feels more than sees that there was a call. For some reason, that call seems familiar, but he associates that with the other nightmares he's had since arriving at this compound. He feels welcomed by the people here and has a sense of safety, but there is a strange pull to be outside. It is a deep-seated feeling of needing to be out that he can't place. He feels drawn.

Images swirl in his head that both terrify and exhilarate him, arousing him in an odd way. They are pictures of him running through the night. Instead of the terror he used to feel in dreams like this, he feels a sense of delight. Perhaps that's because he wasn't being chased but rather doing the chasing. The visions he has in his head are of hunting and rending flesh. This repulses him, but he can't shake the stimulating feeling they present. This frightens him more than anything else.

The images vanish completely as dreams are wont to do. Alan rubs his face again and stretches. A giant yawn escapes and he settles back into his sweat-soaked sheets. His eyes close and he is soon asleep again. He doesn't realize it yet, but a seed has been planted.

*   *   *   *   *   *

Michael runs through a vacant field. He feels grass brushing against the remains of his pants as he races under the bright white light shining overhead. The chill of the evening he felt at the start of the hunt is gone. It is replaced by the heat of exertion and of the chase. He and his large pack are in pursuit of one of the larger four-legged ones. This one has large horns rising above its head and is fleet. These are hard to catch, but the sweet meat is well worth the effort.

It's been a while since he's actually chased down prey and he relishes in the excitement. His nose picks up the musky scent, they are slowly but surely closing in. This spurs him to greater efforts. He sent part of his pack around to the sides in an attempt to corner the animal and he keeps them directed with images.

He caught this scent earlier and the chase has led them through parts of the burned out relics of old two-legged lairs and across open fields like the one he is in. Some fences appeared out of nowhere, but he hurdled those with ease, the solid thumps behind telling him his pack was still behind him.

He still hasn't sighted the prey but this doesn't surprise him as there is a wall of trees a short distance ahead. Leaping over another fence, he plunges into the dense brush lining the entrance to the wooded area. Michael keeps one ear peeled for any sound from the intruder from the sky. It hasn't shown up for a couple of nights but that doesn't mean it isn't out there somewhere…waiting. He still doesn't know what it is other than it is deadly and to be avoided at all costs.

His breath is coming hard as he races amongst the trees, darting to the side to avoid crashing into them. Low hanging branches scratch his face at times but he doesn't register it as he knows he is getting closer. He can almost taste the sweet meat and feel the blood run down his chin as he tears into the flesh. His eagerness and hunger increase with the thought.

He breaks into a small open area enclosed by a border of trees. There, on the other side of the clearing, the animal struggles. His massive antlers are caught in the branches. Michael watches for a moment as the animal labors to break free. Breathing hard, with his exhalations causing puffs of white mist to appear, Michael launches forward. The large animal is still dangerous but the pack soon swarms over it and it is brought to the ground in a spray of blood from its neck.

He dives in with the rest of the pack. The eagerness of the chase is replaced by a deep-seated hunger. The smell of blood is thick in the air, spurring his excitement even further. He tears into a tender part ripping the flesh and chews on it with enthusiasm. Swallowing the enjoyable morsel, he lowers his head for another piece. Before he is able to sink his blood-stained teeth into the cooling body, he senses something he was worried about all night. He brings his head up sharply sensing Sandra far off into the night. She has taken her pack north by the two-legged lair again. With a growl of anger, he leans down to rip another piece of flesh off, his enthusiasm cooled.

Michael returns to the lair as the sky threatens to lighten over the mountains. Many of the packs preceded him and are finding places to rest. All of them ate well tonight and their small stockpile of alternate food grew. The only damper was Sandra's insistence on traveling by the two-legged one's lair. That will bring harm to the pack as a whole, and he can't allow for that to happen. The last thing they need is to stir up trouble from them. He waits by the entrance for her to arrive with her pack. Even though he felt a few of the pack members vanish from his thoughts this evening, he somehow knows she will return. She has become quite effective at concealing herself and her pack and he is surprised he sensed her this evening.

She appears just before the sky begins to change color. He stops her and draws her off to the side as her pack continues inside. It takes a while for them all to enter the narrow doorway but they eventually all pass inside.

"You went up to the two-legged lair again when I specifically told you not to," he verbally says.

"There's food to be had up that way," Sandra replies, sending an image of the rodents in abundance. She has chosen to share this information with him hoping it will suffice for a reason to be up there and now knowing he won't venture that way, even for food.

"I don't care about that. You know why I don't want any of us up there. You are endangering the pack by being near the two-legged ones," Michael states.

"You are endangering us all by scurrying away and leaving them to roam at will," she counters.

"I can't have you endangering the pack by going near their lair. You will stay here and only go out to gather the alternate food," Michael says. "They are dangerous and will be dealt with, but we need to hunt and survive until then. We can't fight them in their own lair. I'll think of a way, but until we do, you are to stay away."

"I'll find a way in and deal with them," Sandra says, thinking of the strange one in their lair.

She doesn't want to tell Michael about him just yet, feeling he won't use the information to find a way in employing him. Not knowing how to use what she knows just yet, she does have a semblance of a plan circulating in her mind. If Michael finds out about it, he'll definitely make her stay and ruin her chances of getting in and taking the female.

"No, you won't. If I have to, I'll make you stay in the lair. You have your own young one to think of," Michael says.

"That's who I'm thinking of. We can't run forever and they'll eventually find us. If they do, they'll destroy this lair like they did the last. We were lucky we weren't all in it. That is not protecting the pack. That is providing a slaughterhouse and easy pickings for them. We have more than enough to overwhelm them," she replies.

"How are you going to get over the walls? How are you going to get into their lair? You've seen it. We can't do that right now but we'll find a way when we're more secure and stronger. We'll draw more packs together," Michael growls.

"Every night sees the two-legged ones stronger. Our chances won't get any easier."

"We're staying away for the time being and that's that."

Sandra growls her disapproval but nods. She'll wait for her chance and scout out another lair for her pack. She can't very well bring the female back to this lair, the pack will tear her apart and Sandra needs her alive. Plus, Sandra knows she won't survive if she does, Michael will kill her. She also has no intention of staying away from the two-legged lair. She'll figure out how to get in and then find a lair of her own. For now though, she'll watch and wait.

Michael heads to find a place to rest from an exhausting night of hunting. He settles in knowing Sandra is keeping something from him. She is planning something and he'll have to keep a close watch on her. He closes his eyes with his thoughts drifting back to the chase. The thrill of the hunt returns and, with those images drifting through his mind, he falls into a deep slumber.

* * * * * *

We wake the next morning, peel back the window blackout covers, and the gray of the pre-dawn light enters in the open windows. My back is sore from sleeping on the cots and I wish now that I had taken up the offer of a comfortable bed.

I radio Greg to check in, "Rise and shine, pretty boy."

"Seriously?! Yours is the voice I hear first thing in the morning?" he answers.

"Sexy, isn't it?" I reply.

"No, Jack, it's the exact opposite."

"Ah, come on, you know you like it."

"If you knew what I was dreaming, then you'd know just how wrong that is," he replies.

"And, now this conversation comes to an end. There is nothing I want to know less than what you were dreaming. As a matter of fact, the mere fact of you mentioning it makes me want to pour bleach on my brain," I say.

"Okay, fine, I'm up, but I'm bringing this mattress with me."

"There is no way that mattress is making its way on this aircraft. Especially with you mentioning dreaming on it. I'm pretty sure it will need to be burned, and I'm not sure even then that there is a fire hot enough to take care of it," I say. "Now get your sorry ass up, round up everyone, and meet me on the ramp."

"You are such a buzz kill, Jack. We'll be there shortly. Greg, out."

A short time later, with the sun sitting fully over the eastern mountains, Greg and the teams show up with Jason and a few others.

"I've talked it over with the others and, with the exception of a few, I think we'll stay here. Thank you for your offer, though. However, Harold here wants to go with you and, between you and me, you're welcome to him. He's been nothing but a pain with his conspiracy theories," Jason says.

I see Harold by one of the trucks with a couple of stuffed bags at his feet. I do not really want him, but I can't think of a valid reason for turning him down. I call him over and let him know that I won't have any dissension spread among the group and he is to keep the conspiracy crap to himself. He looks down and then, with some obvious reluctance, agrees.

"Why do you want to come with us anyway?" I ask.

He shrugs and says, "I'll say just this one thing and then, as you say, keep the crap to myself. Make no mistake, I'm sure that those that started this are still around, and they'll be coming soon. It seems you and your group is better prepared to handle whatever comes. And now, like I promised, I'll keep quiet."

"Okay, fair enough. Stow your gear onboard and find a place," I say.

He grabs his bags and disappears inside with four others who decided to come along. The soldier, with one arm around his wife and another holding his son close, approaches.

"Sir, if it's okay with you, I'd like to stay here with my family. Or what's left of them," he says with his eyes red and a tear welling up.

"Of course," I say. "I'm glad you found them and am sorry for your loss. Truly. I know what you are going through. Stay with my blessings. We'll miss you, but I completely understand."

"Thank you, sir. It's been a pleasure serving with you," he replies, saluting and then reaching out with his hand. I return his shake and he walks over to say goodbye to his comrades.

"Well, we'll fuel up, if you don't mind us stealing some of your gas, and be on our way," I tell Jason. I leave him with one of the spare satellite phones I brought just in case we met with others and needed to stay in contact. "We'll be able to communicate this way. Keep in touch and let us know if you need anything. Keep in mind that we may not be able to respond quickly by flying in a few months, but we'll do what we can."

"That's much appreciated. Thanks," Jason says, accepting the phone and charging unit.

Robert and Craig grab one of the fuel trucks at the end of the ramp and we are soon refueled. With our next stop at Malmstrom AFB, Montana input into the computer, we say our farewells and, taxiing to the end of the runway, Robert takes off into the clear blue sky heading to the northeast.

The flight will be a short one of just under four hundred miles putting us there in about an hour. We slide over the Salmon River Mountains clawing for altitude. The brown patchwork of the valley quickly changes to forested hills and mountains with deep canyons between major off-shooting ridge lines. The blue sky is completely devoid of contrails that I was used to seeing on any point of the compass when flying during the day. We have the sky to ourselves. It's too bad we have to share the earth with the night runners.

As we traverse over the tall peaks and deep valleys of the Rocky Mountains, I'm not sure which is really worse – the night runners or the bands of marauders that we've come into contact with. The night runners are relentless and dangerous, yes, but the humans running around have knowledge of weapons and a modicum of tactics. Given one or the other, I'm not sure which I'd pick. With the bandits, at least I can factor in a semblance of understanding of their behavior and capabilities. I don't seem to be able to do that with night runners as yet, and I don't like surprises.

The mountains give way to the plains of Montana and Robert begins a descent into the base which lies just east of the Great Falls. The Missouri River winds its way through the town before continuing on its way across the plains. I have him fly over the city as we look for any movement that would indicate survivors still existed in the large city. The sprawling urban area looks much the same as Mountain Home – much of the greenery has changed to match the surrounding brown fields. Some green still exists near the great waterway, but for the most part, without irrigation, the green fields and yards have been transformed.

Robert flies over the airfield at about five thousand feet above the ground. I want a good look at the base before we just merrily set it in like last time. Jason caught me by surprise showing up like he did when we were doing touch and go's. Like I said, I hate surprises. Complacency had set in and that can be a killer. Seeing so many towns abandoned, I just assumed that Mountain Home would be the same. I have to keep the A-game going all of the time. We're just lucky they didn't start shooting at us when we were the most vulnerable. We can't figure everything, but that was a no-brainer.

We fly over the airfield a few times and do a few low approaches. Nothing appears on the bare ramps. There are only a couple of helicopters sitting on the large pad. This used to be a base for missile crews and the helicopters were for flying the crews to their stations. If some form of military was still around and here, they will not take too kindly to our just setting down. Our radio calls go unanswered. To all appearances, the base is abandoned. We'll park at one of the run-up areas just off the runway far away from any building and hangars. I tell Greg to get ready to exfil the Stryker in a hurry. Robert sets it down on the long runway with a slight thump as he still isn't used to the extra weight. He'll get it though.

We pull off at the end and park just beyond the runway but at a distance from the ramp. Leaving the engines running, I glass the surrounding area with a pair of binoculars. I see nothing but tall brown grass growing in patches by the edges of the taxiways and ramp. The rest is dry, dusty fields. Nothing moves except an occasional dust devil rising in the air from a breeze moving through the area. Robert sends out additional unanswered radio calls and we eventually shutdown. The rear ramp is lowered and the Stryker untied and driven out. It too shuts down and quiet settles over the area. Even the birds and other wildlife that might be around are silent.

"Well, how do you want to handle this?" Greg asks as we gather around the Stryker.

"We can't all go. I figure we'll leave three of your team with Craig and the others. It might be a little cramped but we'll take the rest of your team along with Red Team. The town is about fifteen miles to the southeast along that highway," I say, pointing to a two-lane road just on the other side of the perimeter fence. "I don't like leaving so few, but I don't see that we really have a choice."

I would really like to take the full teams. The Stryker won't carry all of us but we can always pull a vehicle from the depot next to the ramp. I don't want to leave the ones we picked up in Mountain Home unguarded though. I don't really know them and someone full of conspiracy shit may do anything if spooked. The 130 is our only way out of here. Well, quickly, that is. It's a helluva drive to the next base with any aircraft and I'm not about to quick-learn one of the Huey helicopters parked on the ramp. The last "first" helicopter lessons weren't pretty. Plus, with the 130 being our only quick departure plan, I do not want to leave it completely unguarded. We'll only be a short distance away and can respond quickly if called. I wish we had brought another team, but I also didn't want to leave the compound short-handed. We'll make do with what we have, which always seems too few.

"Is all of Red Team going?" Robert asks, standing just behind me.

"Yes, you are going," I reply.

"And…ahem…me?" Bri asks.

With a heavy sigh, I respond, "Yes, you can go, but you stay right with Gonzalez."

"I will, Dad," Bri says.

"Gonzalez?" I say, questioning with a raised eyebrow.

"No worries, sir. The princess warrior and I will be just fine."

"I'm not shitting here, Bri. None of this 'I think I'll climb on top of the aircraft and shoot night runners' shit," I state.

I'm not very happy about taking them along, but I'm even less happy with leaving them in this world unprepared and inexperienced. I would keep Bri by my side, but I know I'd be far too protective and not allow her to gain any experience.

"Okay, Dad. I promise no climbing on the aircraft," Bri replies.

"I mean it, Bri," I state.

"Okay, Dad, sheesh…sense of humor much?" Bri responds with a smile.

Seeing her smile melts my heart; but I'm also reminded of another smile that I miss so much. I just want to duct tape Bri in foam padding and set her in a room. Maybe even a padded room. It's much the same thought I had when I thought about her dating. However, I know that has the same odds of happening as keeping her from dating has. And that is less than zero. However, I never thought of arming her if she dated. Seeing her now with her M-4 slung over her shoulder, perhaps I should have. That would have kept the hormone-induced fifteen-year-old boys at a distance. Hmmmm…food for thought.

"No, sense of humor nil. Now get your gear together and ready to saddle up," I say.

Loaded up, we drive through a chain link fence surrounding the airfield, across a narrow ditch, and up onto the highway. Dry, barren fields line the road, with the occasional farm house and outlying buildings here and there, as we make our way to the southeast. Some fields have tall grass growing, but for the most part they are dry and barren. We pause at the entrance to each farm house looking for anyone around but come up empty, just like the road we are traveling. We are headed for the small town of Belt where one of the soldiers has parents.

Dust has blown across a lot of the road masking it completely in some places. The earth is slowly taking back its own, and I wonder how long the roads will be distinguishable. I imagine the dusty places with little rain will be the first to disappear as the blown sands and dirt shift. The rainy part of the country will keep this at bay for a while but they will eventually crack with moss and plants retaking them. Over time, the outskirts of the cities will fall into ruin and vanish in a similar manner. Small towns, like the one we are heading to, will be the first to go.

Reaching Belt Creek Road, we make a left. The road parallels a narrow creek lined with small trees and dense bushes. A little farther, we pass under a railroad trestle and, although faded, it is spray painted with the usual graffiti. On the other side, the town begins abruptly with a few residential houses stretching off to both sides of the road. One larger white building has "Harvest Moon Brewing Co" on its side. *I've had that in the past*, I think, watching the building slide by. *How cool would that be to live next to the brewing company?*

The road curves ahead and the soldier tells me that it turns into the tiny downtown area with a small number of shops lining the street. He goes on to say that his parents live on the east side, on the other side of a stream that runs through town. The only way to get there is by going through downtown and taking a bridge across. I halt the Stryker before the turn and lower the ramp to disembark. I want to find out if we can see or hear anything prior to jumping into the middle of the town.

Standing on the cracked pavement with high grass and trees surrounding the few houses along the street, I hear the swish of a breeze as it blows through the grass and tree limbs. The late morning sun shining down belies the chill in the air. The larger stream lies just a short distance to the side and burbles as it makes its way along its tree-lined path. Over the top of these close sounds, I hear what sounds like a shout. Yes, it's definitely a shout.

"Did you hear that?" I ask those around me.

"I don't hear shit. Are your spidey senses tingling, sir?" Gonzalez replies.

"No, listen. I swear I hear something," I say. I understand I can hear better than the others, but it seems so loud that I'm sure they must be able to hear it as well.

I hear a muttered, "…super powers…"

Turning to Greg, I tell him, "Shut the Stryker down. I think I hear something and want complete quiet."

"What?" he says, incredulously.

"Shhh…just do it," I say.

The hum of the Stryker vanishes and I strain to hear anything carried on the breeze. There, it's faint but I definitely hear shouting from around the corner. I can't distinguish what is said, but it's definitely a human shout. I tell the others.

"Red Team, on me. Greg, you stay here with the others. We're going to creep to the corner and see what we can," I say.

With Red Team following, I step into the tall reeds of grass in one of the yards. It isn't quite as tall as me so I creep through at a crouch. The small field of grass stretches all of the way to the corner and seemingly beyond. I cross a narrow walkway leading to a foot bridge spanning the stream and continue. Looking to my rear, I see Robert spaced behind me with the shadows of the others in trail. I part the grass ahead slowly not wanting to make a trail or to let anyone ahead know we are coming by any obvious grass movement. Slow, step by step, I make my way to where I can see down the street into the heart of the very small town. I halt and the others crouch facing to the sides.

Grabbing a few stalks of grass to stick in my boonie hat and top of my vest, I rise slowly to a point where I am able to see just above the top of the grass. I bring the binoculars up ensuring I shield the front lenses with my hands. Not too far away is what looks like a pub with the entrance to a parking lot adjacent to it. A couple of other storefronts line both sides of the road. In the open lot, a couple of pickup trucks are parked with several people behind the beds and hoods aiming hunting rifles and assault weapons toward a store across the street. I count eight, but from shadows that appear and the shouts, it appears there are more out of sight from us in the lot itself.

From all appearances, it seems the ones outside have a group trapped in the store. I see a couple of barrels sticking out from windows facing the street. There is shouting from both sides, but I still can't make out individual words. In most situations, there are the good guys and the bad guys. Sometimes, though, it's good guys versus good guys and sometimes bad against bad. It's hard to tell which is which just rolling up in the middle of something. One thing I do know, there are survivors here. It does seem like the small towns may have a higher survival rate but that hasn't really shown itself to be an exact trend as yet.

"Henderson, Denton, to the front," I say over the radio. The two snake by the side of the others to me.

"I want you two here with your M-110s covering. Keep low and out of sight, but watch and keep me informed of what is happening. Although you can't see in the store, be ready to engage either force," I say.

"Hooah, sir," Henderson replies.

"Seriously! You too?" I whisper.

"Can't help it, sir. It's just a reflex," he says.

"Well, tame that reflex," I counter.

"Hooah, sir," he says with a smile.

"Red Team, we're backtracking to the footpath. Follow it to the stream. We'll move along the water's edge behind the buildings and come up from behind to see what is going on. Slow and quiet is the word. McCafferty, you have the lead," I whisper in my throat mic.

"Hooah, sir, heading out," McCafferty responds.

"Fuck me," I whisper to myself and hear Robert chuckle quietly.

I inform Greg of our plan, telling him to stay with the Stryker and be ready to respond. "Leave the Stryker shut down, but be ready to move."

"I'd give you a hooah, Jack, knowing you like it so much. But I'll refrain…this time. Call if you need, I'll just be lounging here with my beer," he replies. I can sense the smiles emanating from Red Team ahead as we slowly backtrack to the narrow path.

McCafferty leads us down the concrete path a short distance to the stream where we gather. The stream is shallow for the most part and, while it doesn't have an overly strong current, it's not a slow one either. We'll have to take the rocky bottom carefully in order not to make noise or sprain an ankle. The bank is rocky and steep which will mean we'll have to traverse in the water itself. My choice would be along the bank but the embankment won't allow that. I'm worried about being in the water and exposed to anyone on the other side but the trees droop over the edge in most areas so we'll have a measure of concealment.

I lead us down the short but sheer embankment and into the stream. The steepness continues into the water putting me at knee depth right at the edge. The bottom flattens out quickly though so we'll be able to stay close to the shoreline to our left. It's the larger rocks that will have to be negotiated carefully. The stream runs over a few rocks sticking above the surface and the gurgle of the water rushing over and around them blocks any other sounds. We'll have to rely on our eyes as we approach the two groups ahead.

Robert is behind me focusing on the immediate bank and to the left front. I wave for him to increase his spacing a touch. Behind him, Gonzalez looks for her footing before stepping and is focused on the far bank. I notice her check on Bri following at times. Gonzalez points to the near shoreline. Bri nods and focuses her attention and M-4 there. McCafferty is bringing up the rear keeping her attention behind and to the sides. I have the immediate front and keep an eye to the left and right in front of us as well.

We make our way slowly down the waterway. The current is going with us and helping with our steps and noise. Going upstream is always harder, slower, and noisier if care isn't taken. The trees on the far shore shield any view of buildings across the way. However, it also shields anyone who happens to be lying within those trees. The odds are against anyone being there but if that's where people are gathering water, well, any look in our direction will give us away. I'm especially wary of the footpath behind us as that's where anyone would venture to do just that, get water. I radio McCafferty to keep a lookout there.

A bridge crosses the stream a short distance ahead and that's where I focus most of my attention. Obviously, anyone transiting the area will take that bridge, and if I see anyone, I will signal quickly and we'll edge into the trees hanging over the water. Just short of the bridge is my eventual goal as that is where the parking lot with one of the groups is. I haven't heard anything from Henderson or Denton so I assume everything is the same as when I left. Trees also line the waterway to the back of the lot so we'll have cover as we approach. As I near, I can hear some shouting above the babbling stream but I still can't make out individual words.

We reach a point behind the parking lot and, with care, climb out of the water making sure to minimize any sound of water running off our pant legs. We are on line as we climb the short distance to the ground above. Near the top, we crouch and then crawl the last couple of feet. At the top, we lie on the embankment and peek just above the crest of the hill. There are low-lying branches just overhead so we have concealment and cover alike. Ahead, twelve men are lined behind pickup trucks at the front of the lot and farther into it, all facing the store front across the street.

The shouted words become immediately clear. The group outside in front of us is threatening the ones inside.

"Like I told you, you came into our territory and tried to take our things. For that, you'll pay. Now, I said you can make that easy. Throw down your guns and step outside. We'll make it quick and leave your women alone. But if you make it hard, we'll make it hard on them. I think you get my drift with that, assholes," shouts a burly man in the rear, dressed in a red, plaid shirt and jeans. A chuckle rises from some of the others at his comment about making it "hard" on them.

Yeah, heard that one before, and it's pretty easy to tell the good guys from the bad guys now. If there's one thing that gets me riled, it's shit like that. Of course, there's no telling if the people inside are good guys as yet, but the ones to our immediate front aren't the likable sort and I place them immediately in the bad guy column.

"Look, we didn't know and we were just out looking for supplies. If we'd have known, we wouldn't have come into town. Just let us go and we'll be on our way. If not, we'll pick you apart from in here," a reply from the store shouts out.

The burly man laughs, "There's not enough of you to do that. You should have seen the signs posted. Save your women. Last warning."

I look at Robert lying a few feet away questioning about the signs the guy mentioned. I sure didn't see any, so I don't know how anyone else would have. He shrugs a response back. Oh well, they should have made it clearer. I'm not about to stand for this bullying bullshit. I've seen it way too much and it's getting rather tiring.

"Try us if you think you have the balls. You'll have to come in and get us," the man inside the store shouts in return.

I like the guy in the store. Good guy or bad, I like his attitude. Of course, they aren't in a good position to be boastful or egg the other group on. They're surrounded and I'm guessing there isn't a back door or they would have used it.

"Henderson, Jack here," I say.

"Go ahead, sir," Henderson replies.

"Can you see the back of the building? Is there anyone posted outside?"

"Standby, sir."

A few seconds pass. "I have a clear view of the rear for a ways back and I don't see anyone there," he says.

"Okay. We're in position behind the group out front. I'm initiating verbal contact with them. Standby," I state.

"Roger that, sir, we're standing by," Henderson responds.

"We're here and ready when you need us, Jack," Greg says.

"Greg, start 'er up and bring it to the corner," I say.

"Be there in just a sec," he replies.

"This is Captain Walker. You are covered on all sides. Everyone slowly lay your weapons on the ground. That goes for everyone inside and out," I shout.

The men behind the trucks, especially the large man and those around him, turn quickly toward the sound of my voice. They look side to side searching for where we are. The bushes and tree limbs are hiding us well. I see panic and bewilderment form on many of the faces. Some, including their apparent leader, bring their guns up as if they'll just fire randomly and fight their way out.

"Don't even fucking think about it. You'll be dead before the bullet leaves the barrel," I state.

Heads swivel to the sound of my voice, but I can tell they are still having a hard time locating my exact position. Some are still turning their heads and the big man's is twisting from me to the store front. He knows he is surrounded now regardless of where we might be. Losing face is not his exact favorite thing to do and he knows his bullying is what keeps him the leader of this group. At least, that's what he thinks. And it may well be the case.

"Lay your weapons on the fucking ground... Now!" I shout. "Those who do will make it through the next few minutes still breathing. Those who don't will see what awaits them in the next world. I'm not fucking kidding around here! Now, anyone want to be a hero?"

I see several have located me hidden underneath the branches. Or at least they have located where my voice is coming from. I also notice that the barrels of the weapons that were protruding from the store windows have vanished. That's either a good thing or bad, but I'm taking it as a good sign. We are in a decent position regardless of what happens next.

The whine of the Stryker approaching barely penetrates the babbling of the stream directly behind me. Several begin to lay their weapons to the ground at my gentle request. They look toward the sound coming their way. The mammoth turning the corner hastens the actions of some and their weapons clatter to the ground. A few begin to stand back up at the sound of the approaching Stryker. I have no idea what they think they can do against it armed as they are. It's most likely an instinctive reaction.

"I would highly recommend you don't do what's going through your mind," I shout. "Fire on us and you lose your free pass."

All of the men gathered look stricken with a few turning

toward the beefy man asking what they should do. The men who were lowering their weapons freeze in their position. The leader is in a tough spot and he knows it. He doesn't want to sacrifice himself and is looking for a way to save face – something that he can say 'it's not worth it' or something to that effect. Well, I do not really want to give him that chance. If he's allowed to do that, he'll just return and make for more trouble. We still have the search for the soldier's family and I don't want to be lingering around with these assholes trying to think of a way to get back at us.

"Greg, a warning burst down the middle of the street if you please," I say on the radio.

"I aim to please," I hear his reply.

"That's the lamest thing I've ever heard…ever!" I state.

His reply is lost as the .50 cal opens up with a quick burst. The chunk…chunk…chunk… of the heavy caliber fills the air. The large rounds impact the street just in front of the trucks and create sparks where they hit. The thick whine of the bullets ricochets down the street. They impact a building farther down the road with substantial thumps. If my voice, the realization that they were surrounded, or the sight of the Stryker didn't create a stir, the sound of the heavy gun firing and hitting so close sure spurs greater action. The weapons the men were holding now fall from loosened grips with a multitude of clatters.

Various forms of, "Fuck this! I'm outta here," sound out as the group takes to their feet in a hurry. I've never seen such a big man run so fast in all my life. I'm pretty sure land-speed records are reached as they all take off down the street with him passing the lot of them in the process. They are soon lost from my view but I can hear their footsteps pounding on the pavement for a short while. I turn to look at the bridge expecting to see them cross, but it remains empty. I'm guessing they ran farther to the north, a guess that is verified by Greg as well as Henderson. There still remain the people inside the store and the need to ascertain their inclination.

"Okay, those of you inside, it's your turn," I shout.

"Who are you?" a male voice asks.

"I'm Captain Jack Walker. I want you to lay down your weapons and come out single file showing your hands," I respond.

"How do we know you aren't like the others and just trying to lure us out?" the voice says.

"I guess my word is all I have. That and a .50 cal Stryker parked up the road," I state.

"Works for me. We're coming out."

I watch as three men and two women emerge from inside with their hands raised. I don't notice any weapons immediately visible. They spread in a line near the front.

"Is that everyone?" I ask.

"This is it," one of the men answers.

"Okay. If we go in and find anyone, and we will go in, they'll be treated as hostile. That means..." I say, leaving the statement hanging.

The small group in front of us looks at each other. I see the man doing the talking emit a sigh and his shoulders sag slightly. "Fred, Jim, come on out," he says, looking over his shoulder. Two additional men exit the store.

"That's it?" I say.

"Yeah, that's everyone," the man replies.

"You're sure this time."

"Yeah, I'm sure. This is all of us."

"Greg, Henderson, and Denton, keep us covered. We're moving to the group. Keep an eye out for the ones who fled," I say over the radio. Greg and the others respond positively.

We leave our cover and approach the group cautiously. Gonzalez and McCafferty frisk each of the people as Robert, Bri, and I cover them. No additional weapons are found with the exception of a few knives and survival tools.

"Okay, and you are?" I ask.

"I'm Carl and this is..." he says, introducing the rest of his small group.

The group seems okay and we have them covered regardless. I have Greg move the Stryker past us to the main intersection of town just a block away. He'll keep watch in that direction with Henderson and Denton providing cover behind us. I'm still not sure how fast the other antagonistic group will recover and respond, or if they even will, but the leader will want to save face somehow. I'm guessing they will return to whatever hideout they happen to have if they want to rearm themselves. Sitting out in the open like this isn't giving me warm, fuzzy feelings so I want to make this quick.

"So, Carl, what's your story?" I ask. I can tell he is hesitant about revealing anything but looking around at a dozen well-armed soldiers who happen to have a Stryker as a pet and the fact that we haven't harmed him or his group seems to loosen him up.

"We have a place not too far away up in the hills. We are fairly self-sufficient and prepared to some extent for this. Occasionally, though, we come down into these small towns to scavenge for supplies. Great Falls was overrun almost immediately, so we avoid that place like the plague, pun intended," Carl says. I give Carl and his group a quick rundown of our story, including the reason we are here.

"Sorry to give you bad news, captain, but no one has been around here in some time. I'm not sure where those other folks came from, but they're new here," Carl says.

"Are there others in your place? You are welcome to come along with us if you'd like," I say, explaining what that would entail.

"We have two others watching the place and we'd have to talk it over amongst ourselves," Carl replies. "If you wouldn't mind if we talked in private for a moment, we'll let you know."

"That's fine, but make it quick. There are still those others around and I'm not interested in finding out what they have for an encore," I state.

Carl and his group gather together in a circle and I hear their murmurings. I can actually hear their conversation but I tune it out to give them a semblance of privacy.

"Hang tight everyone. We're having a little pow-wow here," I radio.

Carl and his group finish their conversation and accept our invitation. "Supplies are running low in the area anyway," he states. "We will need to gather our gear, though. Is it okay if we retrieve our guns?"

"Yeah, that's fine. You'll have to be quick about gathering your gear. We're going to search some more here to make sure there isn't family still around. You can meet us at Malmstrom AFB. Do you know where that is?" I ask.

"Yeah, captain, I know where that is," Carl answers.

"Call me Jack. Okay, we have a C-130 parked there by the runway. Do you know what one looks like?"

"I've ridden in one way too many times not to know one intimately," he responds.

"Fun rides eh? Okay, it's the only one there so make your way there, but be there before dark as we'll be sealed up by then," I state.

"You won't find us out and about after dark. We'll be there. The others seem to have left us a couple of vehicles here. Perhaps they won't mind if we borrow them," Carl replies.

"They don't look like they're being used to me. Now, if you don't mind, I'd rather get off these open streets. See you soon."

With that, Carl and his group retrieve their weapons, load up into the vehicles they brought along with a couple of the pickup trucks, and drive down the road we entered on, disappearing around the corner. I have Red Team pick up the weapons dropped by the other group and pile them into the Stryker.

I get with the soldier whose family lives, or lived, here to get directions. Although Carl seemed familiar with the area and what happened to it, it wouldn't do to come this far and not check for ourselves. I owe that much to the soldier and hope we find his parents alive and well.

Henderson and Denton join us and we load into the Stryker. We turn toward the short bridge and, not seeing any signs indicating weight limitations, proceed across following the soldier's directions. The town is very small and there are only a couple of crossing streets. We take the first and only left. An alley appears half way down the street and the soldier directs us down it. I do not want to have the Stryker in such cramped quarters as the others are certainly about. Being such a small town, they can easily track our progress and position by the heavy whine of the diesel engine. We park and disembark. I send Greg with the soldier and his team up the alley and to the house in question. I have Henderson and Denton tag along with them in case Greg needs them for entry. I cast out and sense a few night runners in the area but none nearby. It's almost a relief to feel them. It would be nice if I actually figured out how this stupid thing works.

I send Gonzalez and McCafferty to opposite ends of the street we are on to keep a watch down the streets. They trot off and each finds a position by the corner of a house. The sun has risen overhead and the houses and trees along the street cast very little shadow. Although there is still a chill in the air, it is warming up. One squirrel, perched high in a tree on the corner of the block, squawks madly at our intrusion into its domain. It's apparently not happy with our being here and is letting the world know.

I take a moment to bask in the rays of the sun shining down on my shoulder. I try casting my thoughts out farther. I sense just a couple of others but find it easier to reach out now for some reason. I cast out farther and farther. I know there are only empty plains around and don't expect much but am seeing what my limits and capabilities are. I keep going feeling a pressure in my head as I concentrate. I notice the harder I concentrate, the more limited it becomes. I try relaxing and just visualizing. By relaxing, it seems easier to expand and I sense a small group of night runners farther to our southeast. I don't know if it's just the area we're in or whether it's the night runners themselves that seem to limit this back home. For whatever reason, it's just easier now. The distant night runners are harder to pinpoint and I can only sense them being in a general direction. The squirrel chirping in the branches above enters my consciousness and I pull back.

Greg informs me of their entry and subsequent search. The house is empty and I turn to watch the team members walk into the alleyway and make their way back. The soldier has his head down with others patting him on the shoulders consoling him. I was hopeful that we would be successful with the partial success we've had so far. I guess every ending can't be the happy one and I feel for him. I'm sure he was feeling hopeful after seeing some of the other team members find some of their family alive. I stroll over and give him my condolences as well.

"What about those folks we ran into that fled, sir. They might know something," he says, hopeful.

"I wouldn't know where to look for them and am not sure I want to run into them again," I reply.

Seeing his head and shoulders sag tugs at my heart. I'd like for all of the soldiers to find their families, especially after they risked all to help rescue my kids.

"They might be holed up at the school, sir. That's where I'd go," he says.

Once again, that torn feeling surfaces. I'm not all that eager to run into those folks again, especially close to wherever they call home. They have the advantage of knowing the area better and will definitely hear us coming. Surprise – gone…knowledge – gone…advantage – marauders. However, we are here and I feel we should make every effort to find out what happened. He didn't question going into an armed compound at night with night runners all around to get my kids. I just don't want to sacrifice the many for one. If smoke trails appear, we're outta there. I pull the others aside and ask them their thoughts. After all, it's their ass. To a person, they not only agree that we should go, but are quite adamant about it. So, we board the Stryker and set off to see the wizard.

We backtrack to the center of town. The school is only a block up and on the left so it's not like the large man and his merry band of followers had to trek far. I'm sure they were gasping for air upon arriving, though. And maybe a few wet spots located just below the belt. I know I almost wet mine when the .50 cal went off and struck the street in front of us.

That's about as close to being on the receiving end that I want to get. The soldier shows us a side path to an open lot by the school so we don't become trapped on the narrow street in front of it.

We edge around one of the houses and flatten the tall grass growing in the yard. The single-story light-colored school building appears with the gym on our side. I immediately spot, through the mounted camera, two men perched on the roof with weapons aimed our way. We halt and I open the top hatch. With a mega phone in hand, I call out saying that we aren't looking to harm anyone but looking for some people and give them the names. There isn't any response to my call except the men on the roof shifting positions.

"I'm going to need a response," I say, asking again.

A shot rings out and I hear the ping of a bullet striking the armor close to the hatch. The ricocheting round pings off into the distance, quickly fading. *Really?! How stupid can you get? I think. Why is it that people think firing on an armored vehicle is a good thing?*

"A simple yes or no would have sufficed. Now, let's try this again, are they there or do you know their whereabouts?" I ask. Again there isn't any response. At least they don't try firing on us again.

"Do you really want this .50 cal to start chewing your place to ribbons?" I state.

Finally, a voice calls out. It sounds very much like the man shouting in front of the store. "No, we just arrived a few days ago and there was no one here. Now, get lost!"

I think about opening up anyway but merely close the hatch and have the Stryker reverse out of there. I look at the soldier sitting amongst the others with tears streaming down his face. The others around him console him again. I ask if there was any other place they would go and he just shakes his head. With a very melancholy feel within the interior, we trace our route back to the 130. Parking the Stryker off to the side, we set up a small perimeter with each team taking turns on watch. We settle in with the sun passing its zenith and into the afternoon.

I make contact with the base. The delay seems a little long and the connection sporadic but I'm able to convey our location and update them. MREs are opened and we eat our meals in small groups. The fact of not being able to locate the soldier's family casts a pall over us and our day. Shoveling the food in our mouths without really tasting it, we sit and wait for Carl's group to show up.

The shadows lengthen as the sun settles into the later afternoon. There's not really much to do so Craig and Robert load our next flight data into the computer. Our next stop will be Ellsworth AFB, South Dakota – a flight of close to four hundred miles to the southeast. The base sits a few miles to the northeast of Rapid City with our eventual destination being Sturgis. I wonder if there will be an abundance of Harleys in the area. We'll leave in the early morning and begin our search right after landing if all goes well. These one-day-per-location trips will cut our total time away from home down considerably. My only concern is continuing to use the 130 without maintenance. Well, that's not my only worry but it is a major one.

I hear vehicles approaching in the distance and rise. I get a few strange looks as I stare off into the distance down the highway. Eventually, I catch the glint of the sun reflecting off a windshield and then see trucks approaching. The pickups pass through the hole in the fence we made earlier and park by the Stryker. Carl and his group offload their equipment piled in the beds and, with some help, load it into the aircraft. We then begin loading the Stryker in. There are fewer arm wavings and shouts of dismay spelling impending doom this time. We tie the behemoth down and, with the sun beginning to settle behind the Rocky Mountains, seal the aircraft. With the last of the rays coming in the windows, we put the blackout window seals in place and settle in for the night.

All Bets Are Off

Shrieks enter faintly through the metal fuselage. It's been a while since I've heard the sound of night runners out hunting. I heard them in the warehouse when the sailors entered, but hearing them outside prowling in the night raises my heartbeat. Well, hearing them anytime does that. That happens every time I hear that awful scream and it's not something I'll ever become comfortable with. We've been through too much not to have that sound elevate every sense. Lying in my bag, feeling the chilled air against my cheeks, parked in the middle of nowhere far away from home, I know the night runners will always be a part of this world. I'm only looking to clear them out of our little patch of woods.

Some shrieks grow louder and soon the first slam is felt against the fuselage. Although they have never been able to come close to breaching the 130 before, I am a little anxious thinking about their tremendous ability to adapt although I don't know how they can adapt enough to get into a rugged aircraft like the 130. Even if they could manage to manipulate the door or ramp entries, we've chained them shut. However, I don't want to assume anything with regards to the night runners so we keep a watch posted.

I notice Carl and his group sitting up and shifting in their bags nervously. I tell them we have been out a number of times and haven't been breached yet. I see by their eyes this doesn't put them completely at ease. I can't imagine it's too easy feeling trapped like this and sitting in the dark for the first time. For me, the slams against the aircraft seem heavier and the accompanying shrieks louder. This is most likely because it's been absent, for the most part, since we established our compound and it's been a while since we were out in the 130.

Not being able to sleep with the awful racket outside, I decide to experiment more and reach out with my mind. I sense only a few night runners just outside of the aircraft. They show up in my mind clear as can be. Reaching farther out, I sense others in and around the base. I relax rather than force the sensing and cast out even farther. I pick up a tremendous number of echoes from the direction of Great Falls. The city is filled with a multitude. I shut down the images from them and just concentrate on sensing them.

At first, this is hard to do as I haven't really thought about the two being different. The "noise" from all of the images I pick up is overpowering. Shunting that aspect to the side allows me to actually continue. The vast amount of images I had from reaching out threatened to overwhelm my mind and I was on the verge of having to shut them out altogether. I find I can limit the images by focusing on certain ones or shut the images out completely. *Interesting*, I think, playing with this.

The sense I have of them never leaves, yet it doesn't create "noise" in my head. The images and sensing of the night runners is, in fact, two different parts of the same thing. I notice that the sensing of them comes and goes to an extent. The whole of the host doesn't leave, but more that some seem to vanish and reappear. This seems to be with those farther away.

This confuses me though. The city is miles away and I was only a mile above the horde we saw emerging from the buildings just a few nights ago. Here, I seem to be able to sense them clearly but wasn't able to get but just a glimmer then. I wonder if it's the area, the relaxation of the mind, or something completely different. Maybe it's just an ability – if it can be called that – which comes and goes.

Although I can't shut out the sensing completely, I can compartmentalize them in a way and concentrate on a select group or area. I push farther although that becomes more difficult. It's farther than I was able to go earlier today and maybe it's with practice that this develops. Perhaps there is a limitation to the distance. That would make the most sense. I mean, I can't imagine pushing out to cover the globe. At the far edges, the senses are dulled to the point that I can sense something there but not define the exact location or see images from them. It's more like I know something is out in a general direction.

At the limit, I feel a strange sensation. It's similar but not like a night runner. That has a different sense than the one I barely feel. And it's not like a host but seems like it is coming from an individual. It somehow feels familiar. I can't even begin to describe the impression. It feels like a night runner in some ways but completely different in most others. I feel whatever it is brush against my mind. A series of images form, "Who the fuck are you? Get out of my head!"

The strange sensation vanishes from my mind.

* * * * * *

The attacks against the aircraft continue, tailing off after a period of time as the group of night runners outside run off to find better hunting grounds. No others show up to replace them. Our distance away from the buildings must be keeping us from being smelled out or there is an abundance of food in the area. Although we keep a watch posted, the rest of our night is one of relative peace.

I pull Greg aside in the morning telling him of my feeling that there may be a few other survivors in the area and my desire to search for them. The sensation I felt last night is still with me and I want to investigate what it was. With the early morning light streaming in the now open windows, it feels to me that the strange one I felt last night wasn't a night runner and that leaves only one other option – it was a survivor.

There is a part of me that wonders if I didn't imagine the whole thing. However, we are ahead of the schedule we set and we can afford to take a day to investigate. It will also give us a day to rejuvenate to a degree. Greg is in agreement that, if there is a chance of finding someone else, even if it's just one, then we should take a look. We brief the others, unload the Stryker, and head over to the vehicle lot by the ramp. There, the Stryker is refueled and we locate a fuel truck to refuel the 130. I attempt to radio base and Leonard with the sat phone but am unsuccessful raising either one. Worry sets in, but the fact that I can't raise either leads me to believe there is something wrong with the phone or satellite itself.

Downing a quick breakfast, we load up into the Stryker leaving three to guard the aircraft and watch over the others we have with us. I reach out in an attempt to find the other one I felt. I feel night runners holed up in groups in various areas. The sense of them is diminished to a large degree, and I don't feel them as clearly as I did during the night, nor do I feel them in the numbers I did. Perhaps their sleeping causes the ability to fade or it's one of those times when the ability is weaker. I do, however, vaguely sense the other one.

It still feels different than the other sensations I have of the night runners. I can't put my finger on exactly what that variation is, only that it is distinctly different. The other contrast is that the sense is much clearer. It's far enough away that I only have a general direction but feel that, if I were to get close, I would be able to pinpoint the location like I can with the closer night runners.

The direction I sense is to the west-northwest. I don't know the area well, but flying over the city on our arrival gave me a basic layout. The highway we traveled down yesterday heads through the heart of the city in the other direction. I'm all in favor of avoiding going through such a crowded area. Not crowded in terms of people but rather in terms of buildings. Running into a group of marauders or someone trying to defend their area is not how I want to start my day. Instead, we'll try to circumnavigate the city and get closer in order to better ascertain where this sensation is coming from.

Heading out to the highway, we take the first large road to the north that runs between the base and the city. The sun is above the plains to the east but still low enough to cast long shadows. A few birds skirt low over the street as we travel along. To the west, a few residences lie near with flat brown fields lining the rest of the road. The windows glare briefly from the sun striking their surface as we pass. We could be on the start of an early morning family outing. The exception is that we are packing M-4s instead of picnic baskets and our ride is not the family sedan.

The road curves to the west and we are soon passing through abandoned industrial complexes. Many of the industrial yards are filled with piles of scrap metal, stacks of forged steel beams waiting for shipments that will now never occur, and tractor trailers parked in rows. A few places house storage tanks. We pass through this lonely area and soon come to the river. The road proceeds along its banks passing a dam spanning the river's width. With no one to regulate the flow of water, it flows over the top of the dam. I look on with interest. Dams aren't meant to hold that amount of water for any great length of time and I imagine it will only be a matter of time before the dam gives way.

There is a large dam, actually several large dams, across the Columbia River back home and I imagine it now looks the same with the similar span. The Hanford Nuclear Storage Facility lies just downstream from one of the smaller dams on the upper Columbia River. I wonder how it will be affected when the dam breaks. For that matter, I wonder just how long that facility will last before spilling its contents into the Columbia River and how that will affect us. That's just one more worry to pile on the list. Frank is keeping measurements of the radiation in the area, but a large spill of this nature could cause us a lot of problems. The south winds during the winter months in our area will bring any radiation in the Columbia in our direction.

These thoughts occupy my mind as we leave the dam behind. We are closer to the sense of the other one and I can now locate the source. It's almost directly north from us across the river. I see several bridges ahead spanning the waterway and we cautiously cross reminded of the barricade Sam threw across the Tacoma Narrows. We haven't sighted a soul, and the only movement has been from birds wheeling through the clear morning sky and a couple of dog packs.

I keep trying to raise the others on the sat phone without success. It's not like we haven't been out of contact before but now that we have that capability, I expect it and am a little concerned that we can't. I still have the sense of the other one but without a return statement like last night. We cross the river without incident and continue to navigate streets drawing closer with each turn. I'm hesitant about this as I don't know exactly what I'm sensing other than it's different and there is more clarity about it.

We are out of the town and passing through a golf course. The greens can no longer be named that and the once pristine fairways are now fields of brown grass. Turning around what once looked like it was an open field driving range, we enter a lot with a single pickup truck parked close to the pro shop. I have the Stryker halt at the edge of the lot and see a man walk around the corner of the shop carrying a golf club in his hand. *Surely he can't be thinking of attacking a Stryker with a golf club,* I think, watching him come to a stop. *It's just as stupid as shooting at one with a handgun I guess.*

The man looks startled at our appearance but continues to stand by the pro shop entrance watching us with a hand shielding his eyes. The .50 cal isn't pointed directly at him, but its aim point is certainly in his vicinity. I look around through the magnified optics searching for others. I can't imagine one person being alone in this world and we've always come across a group of individuals regardless of how big the group is. I see no one in the area and the sense I have in my mind is coming directly from the man in front. I have the ramp lowered and walk out with the rest of the teams flowing out and taking up a perimeter.

I look to see that the middle-aged man hasn't moved. His medium-length brown hair hangs limply and in disarray. The dirt-stained jeans have holes in the knees and tattered hems cover sullied white sneakers. His plain gray sweat shirt is a little cleaner but shows stains of various natures. He stares at us with interest. I walk up to him making sure to keep clear of the club he is holding in his hand.

"Are you the one who was in my head last night?" he asks, eyeing me up and down.

"I do believe I was. And you are?" I say, unbelieving that what I sensed is actually another person.

The sense of him still feels something like a night runner and then the light dawns bright in my mind. He is like me – this is what I must feel like to him. He is much the same as me with regards to being able to sense others.

"I'm Ken. And you would be?"

"Jack, Jack Walker," I answer, shouldering my M-4 and holding out my hand. "Did you get bitten by the night creatures and survive?"

"Yes, I did," he replies. I nod at the verification of my thought.

I tell him my belief about what happened and is happening with regards to our ability to sense each other. I send a simple thought image to him which he returns. That further verifies the concept of what surviving a bite brings. I never thought for a moment that there would be others similar to me. This has interesting implications. We finish conversing about our remarkable connection. His shoulders relax.

"I thought I was going crazy and thought sensing you last night was part of my insanity. With you standing right here, it's obviously real. These others that I see nightly are driving me crazy, though. I can't get them to shut up and luckily, I've been able to keep them out. They are here every night," Ken says.

"I thought I had lost it when I first came to and found these images running through my head," I respond.

"I was pretty sure my mind had turned and, to be perfectly honest, I was about ready to pack it in," he says. "I can't take any more nights of this shit, but having you arrive and knowing I'm not going insane helps. I've actually heard a couple of others like us some nights. I haven't felt them in a few nights though."

"Well, Ken, you are more than welcome to join up with us," I offer, explaining our situation.

"I was going to hit a few more balls and maybe play a round or two…but what the hell. Give me a second to get some of my things and I'll be ready," he replies, accepting the offer.

With Ken's small pack loaded up, he tells of where he last sensed the others. Loading up once again, we head toward the nearest one picking up a woman hiding out in a storage facility. She seemed a little shell-shocked but mostly relieved to find someone else alive and joins with us willingly. I'm curious as to why I could sense Ken but not the woman named Linda.

"I had to shut all of them out before I went insane. The ability to do that came about accidentally," Linda comments.

The third is strangely back in the abandoned industrial complex we passed earlier. We pull up to a small, cinderblock warehouse located toward the rear of all of the other foundries, manufacturing plants, and warehouses. As we disembark and spread out, a man about my age opens one of the heavily sealed doors and emerges.

"Get out of here. You aren't real," he shouts, waving a couple of long knives about.

"We're plenty real," I reply.

"No, you are in my head and I'm imagining you," he says.

"Do you think the night runners are pretend?" I ask.

"Who? What the hell are you talking about?" I go on to describe who and what I mean.

"Oh, them. No, they're real alright," he states.

"How is it we are figments of your imagination then?" I ask.

"Because I'm the last one alive and my mind is fucking with me. This is what happens when you are the last one left," he answers.

"So, why are you talking with me if we're merely something you made up?"

"Because, it's what the mind does when there's nothing left," he replies.

"So, if I shoot you, say, in the leg, you won't feel it or bleed, right?" I say. He hesitates pondering that question.

"See, that hesitation means you believe that we're real. At least a part of you does," I state.

"Now you're just trying to fuck with me."

"That would mean you're fucking with yourself," I respond.

"Aaaaaaah…get the hell away from me and leave me alone," he loudly says.

"Dude, just for a moment, wrap your mind around that we're real. Have you ever seen a vehicle like this?" I ask, waving at the Stryker. "I mean anywhere…TV, books, movies?"

"No. I can't say that I have," he answers.

"Then how can you imagine something you've never seen or imagined before? You have to base imagination on experience."

"No, that's not true," he says, but I see that he is perhaps contemplating the situation differently.

"Okay. If you're imagining something you made up, wouldn't it change each time you looked at it? In some small way?" I ask. He rubs his chin, coming close to shaving his eyebrows with one of the long knives.

"Perhaps," he responds.

"Well, has it changed?

"No, but I wouldn't know if it had if this is all imaginary," the man states.

"You know, we could go back to shooting you in the leg," I say.

"Don't even think about it," he says, taking a step back.

"What do you say you come with us and see just how imaginary we are? I mean, what do you have to lose?"

"I could wake from this and find myself stuck out at night with those nasty creatures about to come out," he replies.

"I tell you what. Why don't you try coming with us. If you find that you are still imagining all of this shit before dark settles, we'll bring you back," I offer.

He hesitates another moment and then responds, "Okay. I'll try that, but you better bring me back long before the sun sets."

"You know, I could still shorten this and just shoot you," I state, chuckling.

"I'd really rather you didn't," he responds.

"I'm Jack," I say, offering my hand.

"Randy. Just so you know, I still don't think you're real,"

he states, returning my shake.

Randy gathers some gear and comes with us and, by nightfall, begins to believe we are real.

As the sun begins to set behind the hills in the west, I try calling base but don't get a response from the satellite phone. I try Captain Leonard with silence my only answer. I keep trying until night falls before giving up. Maybe the satellite finally decayed enough to quit working. Who knows? For whatever reason, we are out of communication for the time being.

*   *   *   *   *   *

Unconscious to the world, Alan throws off the bedding. His only drive is the need to be outside…the need to hunt. He makes his way down the unmoving escalator. He sees, but not with the eyes of the waking world. The seed that was planted has taken hold and he knows only that he wants to feed. He wants the freedom of the open air and it fills him with the intensity of it. The vast room is mostly empty, but he smells the others inside. He has an urge to turn back and rampage through them but the pull of the outside is stronger.

Remembering the call of the one the other night, it motivates him to join in the hunt. He misses the chase…the taste of the sweet blood pouring from prey…the succulent taste of flesh in his teeth. He is only vaguely aware of where he is but knows the way out. That is the driving factor, the need to lose himself in the night.

Making his way downstairs and into the warehouse facility with the docking bays, he removes the clamps locking the doors down. Lifting the doors enough to crouch through, Alan hops down and drops to the ground. The feel of the night air is refreshing and almost fills the urge he has deep inside, but the freedom isn't complete and he knows prey lies outside of the high walls surrounding the place where he finds himself.

He lifts his nose to the night air and smells prey in abundance. Some of that prey lies on the other side of the mostly high wall that surrounds the interior of this lair and he wants to be completely outside. The need to be completely out holds him and he begins trotting toward the big portal that will let him be free.

The cool night air flowing across his cheeks feels good as does the sweet smell of the tall grass brushing against his pant legs. The urge to find the pack leader he heard the night before is strong. The bright stars and silvery moon accompany him as he jogs through the open field. The walls in the distance slowly grow taller as he draws near. He senses others like him a short distance away, and he only needs to get through the heavy portals to be with them.

He sends an image to them which isn't returned. This perplexes him as he remembers them always answering his calls. He can feel them and hear them, but they don't seem to be talking with him. That doesn't matter much as he approaches the large gate. He'll be with them shortly.

It takes some doing but he eventually manages to lift the heavy bar holding the portals closed. The heavy metal bar falls to the ground with a loud clang. Alan pulls on the gigantic door and it slowly swings open a few inches. Eagerly wanting to be out of this lair, he pulls harder. With the hinges emitting a mighty, metallic grind, the steel door inches open. It's enough to squeeze through and Alan finds himself standing on the very spot he squatted down on upon his arrival. This memory is lost as all he knows is he is free. He wants the thrill of the chase and relishes in his ability to do so.

* * * * * *

Watkins, standing on the upper balcony, watches Alan walk downstairs and vanish beneath the overhang. He has observed him and others wander the facility on many of the nights he has kept watch so thinks nothing of it. It's not uncommon for people inside to become restless and meander the interior trying to work off whatever is causing their sleeplessness. He'll investigate if Alan doesn't appear before long. Keeping the man in his mind, he turns back to watch the interior. His mind wanders to the times before the world changed.

*   *   *   *   *   *

Sandra heads to the same area close to the two-legged lair where she has been on many nights. She knows Michael won't be pleased, especially when he finds out she and her pack didn't gather the alternate food as he ordered. Going against his explicit order and endangering her very place within the pack, she feels close to a solution to getting inside. She wants to see if she can sense this other one and get him to answer her. Wanting information about the inside, she opens up just enough to see if she can sense the strange one that has somehow become enmeshed in the lair.

She still isn't sure how he came to be inside or why the two-legged ones tolerate that one being in there with them. As confused as she is about the situation, she is not against using it and seeks to establish some form of communication with the one. She sensed him and sent messages but hasn't received any indication that he even heard her. His thoughts and movements were easily seen and she understood all of them. She knows that Michael will know of her coming to the two-legged place and she will have to find another lair before the night is over. She knows of several possibilities and will have to reserve some of the evening to search for one that will accommodate them.

She has kept her ear to the skies listening for that unforgettable droning sound but the night remains quiet. On occasion, the shriek of one pack or another finding prey drifts through the evening air. With her keeping watch once again, her pack rushes forward into the reduced-to-rubble ruins to forage.

Sandra immediately senses the strange one just a short distance away. She locates his exact position and follows as he makes his way through the inside of the lair. His thoughts don't give her a picture of what the inside looks like but she does see his desire to be outside. The hesitation the one had about staying in and feeding on the two-legged ones gives her no small amount of worry. Not understanding how he is controlling himself with two-legged prey so close, she is relieved when she feels his thoughts change and he moves on.

She squats on the boundary line where the intact structures meet the ruined ones. The bright white light in the night sky casts rays through a small tree above her, creating dancing shadows as a very light breeze blows through the area. Her focus though is on what is transpiring only a short distance away and her curiosity is peaked as to what this strange one will do. Knowing he wants outside, she wonders if he'll be able to scale the tall walls from inside.

Sandra sends a message asking the one to answer and tilts her head as if this will enable her to better receive his response. Although she can still see the images emanating from him, she doesn't get a reply. She tries once again receiving the same silence. Frustrated, she shifts minutely and continues to watch.

Standing excitedly as she sees the one open a door that leads inside, she stops herself after taking a few steps in the direction of the two-legged lair. The door is open and their den is vulnerable. She looks to the sky to gauge how much time is left of the darkness. They haven't been out long and most of the night remains. *If we can just get over the walls, we can enter*, she thinks, feeling an eagerness rise within. *I'll watch to see if he can get over the walls. Perhaps he'll show us a weakness and a way in.*

Sandra becomes even more interested as she observes in her mind the one's departure from the building and into the night. He isn't making directly for the walls as she thought he would. He is running under the starlit skies for the far side of the walled lair. She senses his objective is a large door leading through the walls. Literally quivering with excitement, she calls to her pack telling them to forget what they're doing and come to her. They all rise from gathering the furred rodents and look in her direction in a questioning manner. Hesitating for only a moment, the large pack drops what they are doing and quickly surrounds her.

Sandra leads them in a fast run in a wide, looping circle around the walls toward the metal gates she remembers seeing on her one circle around the lair. *This must be where the one inside is heading.* The one inside is jogging slowly toward the gate and the pack settles in the woods a short distance from the large portals. Keeping the pack out of sight of the walls, she edges forward, stopping just as she senses the strange one struggling with something heavy that is keeping the doors shut.

Her heart is racing with anticipation as she witnesses one of the large doors move. It opens only an inch or two. She maintains a watch on the gate and soon it swings open farther. The one emerges from the opening. Sandra can barely contain her excitement. The way into the two-legged compound is open. Now's her chance.

She sends a quick image of the female to her pack with the instructions that she is to be taken alive. Kill any who stand in their way but the capture of that is their goal. *"Getting the female is a priority over feeding. Grab her and go. We'll leave immediately when we get her. No stopping to feed,"* Sandra sends.

With that, the pack launches forward out of the woods toward and then through the gate.

* * * * * *

"Sergeant Watkins!" Watkins hears his name shouted from downstairs.

He leans over the railing and sees one of the people manning the night watch in the control room standing at the entrance. The person waves frantically upon seeing him. Bounding down the stairs, he enters the control room. Looking at the monitors lining one of the walls, he immediately understands the urgency of the shout. Hundreds if not thousands of night runners fill three of the screens. Most are still emerging from the woods on the far side of the road leading to the entrance but they are speeding toward the gate.

The sight causes his heart to leap in his chest and adrenaline floods his system. What makes him catch his breath is the camera showing the front gate slightly open with one person standing just outside. The way into the compound is open and a horde of night runners are on their way.

"Wake everyone!" Watkins says to one of the operators and turns in a flash. His last sight of the monitors before bolting from the room is of the first of the night runners beginning to pour through the gate.

* * * * * *

With the alarm given, the teams emerge from their cubicles. Their sleepiness wears off quickly as they slip on their vests and gather their gear. Forming into their teams, they begin to take their prearranged positions established in case they ever experience a breach of the walls and sanctuary. The interior turns from the quiet of peaceful slumbering into a madhouse of shouts, tromping boots, magazines being loaded, and weapons locked and loaded.

Those not on any of the teams emerge with panic-stricken looks but shuffle off to the upstairs dining room and surrounding area giving the soldiers the freedom to move and shoot at will. They lie on the hard, chilled linoleum floor with hearts racing and eyes wide with fear. They've all practiced this numerous times but now it is for real. Practice may make it easier to move into position and know where to go, but it doesn't help with the sheer terror of actually having to do it.

Watkins stands next to Lynn and Drescoll telling what he witnessed on the monitors. "There are thousands of them on the way," he reports.

Lynn knows they won't be able to get updates from the control room as the outside cameras were moved to provide coverage along the length of the walls and haven't been replaced. There just weren't enough cameras on base to provide coverage for the walls and the building. They had planned to locate more from the naval bases farther north but higher priorities overrode those plans.

Lynn and Drescoll stand near the upstairs railing

arranging the last of their gear on their vests and checking their weapons. The teams are all just coming into their positions along the upper railings as the first loud shriek sounds downstairs, filling the vast interior with its echo.

*   *   *   *   *   *

Sandra watches as her pack streams by her. She is running along with them but allows many of them to pass. She knows the two-legged ones are dangerous and she will lose many in her pack, but they are numerous. Among the eagerness and excitement she feels, she relishes in the fact that she was right and Michael wrong. A part of her sees this as an opportunity to take them down once and for all, but she has a specific quarry in mind. It overrides any other thoughts.

They will vacate after they capture the female. Deep down, she knows the wrongness of this with regards to the overall pack. An opportunity like this won't appear again. She thinks of keeping up the attack once she has the female and eliminate them all. The thought of feasting on all of the two-legged ones she smells brings about an overpowering, salivating hunger. The odor of them also induces rage. She'll have to control her pack tightly if she is to accomplish what she wants tonight. If the two-legged one is inside, she will capture him as well. She doesn't sense him but will direct the pack to him if she senses or spots him. If that opportunity arises, she will kill the female once the two-legged one is captured. She'll have to play this night as it comes.

She rushes past the strange one by the gate. He stands as if embracing the pack. She senses some of her pack turn on this one. He feels the same as them but carries the scent of one of the two-legged. Sandra hears his cries of pain but doesn't care and runs on. He's fulfilled his purpose.

*   *   *   *   *   *

His heart is beating fast...he is free. The night air

somehow seems cleaner, fresher. Alan is so eager for the hunt he is almost salivating. He wants that sweet taste and to feel flesh in his mouth once again – sweet, raw meat. And to be with a pack once again; to be safe and secure both in knowledge and numbers.

He senses a large pack waiting in the nearby trees across the hard path and watches as they emerge. He sends a call but doesn't receive any response from them. The leading ones race past him as if he isn't there and continue through the opening behind him. Alan smells them for the first time. They have a different scent than he remembers. It's the odor of unwashed, musky bodies and not the familiar aroma. He stands confused as they flow by him, looking left and right for any sign of recognition. The strong female he sensed the other nights runs by him with only a cursory glance.

Fear begins to surface and he's not sure why the others aren't acting like he is one of their own. He senses their eagerness to be inside and feed but that shouldn't cause them to completely ignore him. Among the picture images he is receiving is something about a particular female inside, but that is quickly shunted away as his alarm grows.

The others of his kind continue to stream by. The night is filled with their screams of hunger and excitement. Turning to the front, Alan is shaken by a transformed one directly in front of him snarling and coming right at him. The image fills his vision and he begins to raise an arm to fend the one off. He quickly realizes there is more than one coming at him. His heart rate kicks up another notch as he recognizes the hunger in their eyes. The one directly in front slams into him. Alan feels himself knocked backwards and begins to fall. His vision of the transformed ones flowing around him turns into one of small, bright lights above against a velvet sky. He impacts the ground on his back and his head rocks back hitting the hard pavement below. Stunned, he is only vaguely aware of growling bodies on him.

He is brought back to full consciousness by a loud scream of pain and realizes it is own. Coming out of his foggy state, he is aware that he was walking in his sleep again, only, this time he is not merely downstairs but surrounded by snarling faces. He feels agony beyond compare. A fleeting memory surfaces of waking in the crowded room of what he has become to know as night runners. This feels the same only, instead of the night runners chasing him through the building, they are on him, tearing into his flesh. Another thought intrudes through the pain, that maybe this is just another one of his nightmares. However, he has never felt pain in them before and it was usually him doing the biting and rending of flesh.

He screams as he feels another set of teeth sink into him and tear a chunk of flesh off. The white-hot agony races through his body like electricity and his flailing to remove the night runners from him weaken. All thoughts he had flee, and his mind is now only filled only with the redness of sheer agony. With his eyes squeezed close and teeth clenched hard, he arches his back as another strip of flesh is torn free. Suffering beyond belief envelopes his mind and body. His mouth is closed so tight that only a whimper escapes but the agony is too much. His back falls back to the ground limply. Darkness invades and his last breath escapes in a puff of white mist.

* * * * * *

Inside the once impassable walls and rushing through the tall grass, Sandra sees her goal. It rises above her surrounded by the hard ground the two-legged ones seem to favor. Her desire builds with each step through the field. She is trying to sense the two-legged one inside but is coming up empty. With the grass stalks brushing against her as she races through the open air, she directs her pack to the back where she saw the strange one exit hoping the door will still be open.

It will take some time to get her entire pack through the smaller opening but she is relying on her numbers to overwhelm the two-legged ones inside. She'll wait for a moment outside until they break in and through. It wouldn't do for her to be taken down in the first moments. She knows she will lose a few tonight, but it will be worth it. Her pack means a lot to her, as does her young one, but this urge she has is overpowering, she needs for it to happen.

The building looms large but not as large as the ones where Michael has the large pack. She sees the first of her pack race around the corner and disappears down its length. They are close to being inside and she feels her heart pounding with anticipation. Being open, she feels Michael intrude on her thoughts and she immediately shuts back down. The last thing she needs right now is him interfering with her plans. He may send others to her and, although that would be helpful, it would also mean that the female or the other two-legged one that has held her thoughts for so long would be killed and eaten. That, she can't allow.

Sandra turns the first corner leading to the back trailing a large contingent of her pack. She senses the leading ones as they turn the far corner at the rear and sees the entrance inside still partially open. They throw a door that slides up and down farther open and enter. Feeling almost lightheaded with the excitement of them entering, she knows she is so close.

She turns the last corner and sees her pack as they crowd the portal, pushing to get inside. Sensing their craving and rage that the smell of the two-legged ones brings, she sends a sharp reminder that they are not to feed and their goal is to find and capture the female. Sandra stops by the side of the door through which her pack is flowing, watching them struggle to get in. More of her pack arrives and crowds the entrance further. They are streaming inside so she doesn't feel the need to slow them. It's the onslaught of numbers that will make her attack successful. Her mouth waters with the thought. The first shriek echoes from inside.

*　*　*　*　*　*

Startled by a shriek sounding out inside the building, Lynn feels the jolt of additional adrenaline pour into her system. She expected to hear the pounding of night runners against the solid steel security doors. The sound of one actually inside stuns her and dread fills her mind. One inside means more on its heels.

That thought is verified as the first shriek is quickly multiplied by others. The once silent interior is swiftly filled with the screams of night runners emerging into the interior downstairs. She knows they are coming from the warehouse. Watkins' report of thousands of them fills her with a dread she hasn't ever known. Lynn takes a deep breath, knowing that if she lets fear take hold, they are all doomed.

"They're downstairs coming from the warehouse. All teams reorient to cover the entrance. Cover the stairs and escalator. No one makes it up," she shouts into the radio.

Lynn watches as some teams change their position and soon the shouts of the team members join the din of the night runner screams. The leading edge of the horde of night runners arrive and are brought down by a volley of gunfire. The muted sounds of the gunshots are lost in the vast noise filling the interior. The only evidence that rounds are streaking out to their targets are the night runners falling to the ground. Others push from behind and leap over the fallen bodies of their comrades.

Lynn sets herself up with Black Team by the large set of stairs leading upward. There are only two ways up and she has directed some of the teams to cover those chokepoints. The others she has set up to thin the mass of night runners pouring in downstairs. She knows their relentless nature, so they must keep them from getting upstairs. Some screams from the others crouched by the dining room and kitchen areas add to the massive volume of noise filling the sanctuary.

Night runner dead and injured pile up under the balcony, brought down by the substantial amount of gunfire pouring into their midst. Still others behind them come and they slowly advance regardless of the amount of rounds streaking into their midst. Soft flesh and hard bones are torn apart by the forceful impact of rounds slamming into them. Some of the injured attempt to crawl away but are trampled by the ones pushing from behind.

Slowly, the mass of night runners forge ahead in the face of the volume of fire. Magazines clatter to the ground as the soldiers reload. Night runners appear in all quadrants under the balcony as they spread out in the lower interior. Hundreds lie on the ground but are lost in the racing horde. Still they come. A fleeting thought occurs to Lynn wondering if they have enough ammo. The screams emanating from the other survivors force that thought from her mind and spurs her on.

* * * * * *

Sandra feels many of her pack vanish from her mind. The crowd around her stretches far beyond the corner of the building and she senses they have gained some ground. Still, she feels deeply the loss of so many. This must be done, but she wishes it wasn't at such a great loss. She'll need a host left after this to capture the two-legged one and to deal with Michael if he tries anything. Not that there's much she can do as his pack is so much greater than hers, but she won't give up her prize willingly.

Looking to the stars twinkling in the sky, she knows they have enough time left in the evening, but they will still have to be quick. She has to yet find a lair for her dwindling pack. Turning back to the door, she clears a space and enters.

Coming into the actual interior from the large room just inside the door, the full din of noise assaults her ears. It's so loud she wants to cover her ears to diminish the almost painful volume of it. Her pack crowds the downstairs under the upper level. They are brought down as soon as they enter and she senses rather than sees a growing pile of bodies. Shrieks from her pack resound in the large, open space; shrieks of hunger, rage, and pain. She edges around the sides under the overhang, looking upstairs over the heads of her pack. Seeing some two-legged ones as they rain death upon her pack, she searches for one of them in particular.

She continues around the perimeter searching upward. The stink of the two-leggeds' guns fills her nose as does the iron smell of blood as it pours from the wrecked bodies of her pack. She is anxious, and dread surfaces that she won't be able to find the female. If she doesn't, she'll take the secondary goal of killing all of the two-legged ones. A hint of their aroma ascends above the other odors and she feels rage begin to build. The anger is both an inherent one from the sight and smell of the two-legged ones and from the damage they are doing to her pack.

Keeping the rage under control but feeling it just below the surface, she edges farther around. Her eyes widen and her heart leaps. There! Above by the stairs on the far side. Sandra sees the female she saw through the two-legged one's mind so many nights ago. A mixture of emotions filters in. She doesn't have many, but those she does have mix – hunger, anticipation, rage, and a feeling that would be most associated with glee. She directs her pack to that single set of stairs and shows them an image of the female and her position. The pack responds with a louder chorus of shrieks.

*   *   *   *   *   *

Lynn sets her small crosshair on yet another target. The room is filled with the acrid stench of bodies torn asunder and gunpowder. The upper balcony has a haze from the smoke ejected with their rounds. They are keeping the night runners at bay for the moment. Hundreds have fallen yet there is still a multitude pushing from behind. They haven't reached the escalator as yet, but they are attempting to scale the elevator. She and Black Team have been holding the wide, wooden stairs clear, and the bodies lying at the foot of the stairs attest to their ability to do so. The bottom four steps are lost from sight under the carnage they are continuing to inflict on the horde attempting to gain the upper levels.

Lynn flinches as the shrieks screaming from below actually grow louder. She didn't think that was at all possible but it grows to the point where the very walls shake. The floor beneath her boots trembles from the pounding of night runners below. She watches as the night runners shift direction as a single mass. They are heading under the balcony and her way.

Some still try to get to the escalator and scale the elevator, but the majority of them seem to be coming her way. The shift is so quick and sudden, it takes her by surprise. She directs her fire into the horde starting to scale the stairs. There's no time to make a radio call redirecting the other team's fire, but she hopes they will realize the change in flow and respond. Her teams and others direct fire into those attempting to climb the stairs. Night runners are packed on them and race upward. As fierce as the fire is that is directed into them, it isn't enough to keep them from rapidly advancing upward. Lynn has the sense that they've failed but continues to target night runner after night runner with her fire.

The sheer volume of rounds leaving her barrel heats it. Exchanging an empty mag for a full one, she pours more fire into the mass of night runners closing in. Lynn thinks about pulling back and establishing another line past the escalator and is about to issue the command when a surge pushes the night runners up and over the teams protecting the stairs.

The suddenness of the surge surprises Lynn. The leading night runners that make their way through their fire slam into her. She is hit and goes down with her head hitting the hard linoleum floor. Stunned, she watches as her gun clatters to the ground beside her and is kicked away by a swarm of feet that are suddenly there. Rolling to her side, she reaches for it, but it remains just out of her grasp. She pushes upward knowing she must fight. If they don't fight them off, all will be lost. She is hit hard in the head again and slumps to the floor.

She feels the coolness of the linoleum on her cheek. Feet race by her limited vision. Fear envelopes her. Another hit to the head stuns her. She must rise. She is scared, not really for her own life as she's seen the face of death many times. She is afraid for the others and the sense of her own failure. Her vision hovers on the edge. *This is the end. Please make this quick and painless,* she thinks as her breath stirs dust on the hard floor. *Jack, please forgive me for failing. I love you!* Her peripheral vision of the small amount of floor and feet she can see draws inward. A tear leaks to the ground, dropping to mix with the dust under her head. She is at least thankful she doesn't feel any pain. Her vision fades.

# # #